Patterns *of* Illusion

Books by James Hoggard

PROSE

Trotter Ross
Elevator Man
Riding the Wind and Other Tales
Patterns of Illusion

POETRY

Eyesigns
The Shaper Poems
Two Gulls, One Hawk
Breaking an Indelicate Statue
Medea in Taos
Rain in a Sunlit Sky

TRANSLATION

The Art of Dying, poems by Oscar Hahn
Love Breaks, poems by Oscar Hahn
A Chronicle of My Worst Years, poems by Tino Villanueva
Alone Against the Sea: Poems from Cuba, by Raúl Mesa
Splintered Silences, poems by Greta de León
Stolen Verses & Other Poems, by Oscar Hahn

Patterns of Illusion

stories and a novella

by

James Hoggard

San Antonio, Texas
2002

Patterns of Illusion: Stories and a Novella
© 2002 by James Hoggard

Cover illustration: "One in the Hand"
© 2000 by David Horton

ISBN: 0-930324-80-3

First Printing

Wings Press
627 E. Guenther
San Antonio, Texas 78210
(210) 271-7805

www.wingspress.com

Cataloguing-in-Publication Data
Hoggard, James, 1941 -
Patterns of Illusion: Stories and a Novella / James Hoggard

Contents: Mesquite – The Leaning Tower Of Babel – Wild Onion
Leaves – Woman Of The Region – Night And The Blood Washed
Away – A Gift from the Scorched Moon – No Accounting Shall Be
Asked – Turning The Deer Free – A Bit Of A Bitch – The
Scapegoat – The Way The World Is – Waiting For Rain – The
Last Campout – The Circus – Four Letters: Brother Bill To His
Cousin,   Papa Writes Pound, Heidegger To Mama From College,
Hammer's Home – Patterns Of Illusion

    235 p.; 14 cm.
ISBN 0-930324-80-3 (non acidic paper)
1.United States – Social life and customs – 20th century –
fiction. 2. Texas – fiction. I. Title.
PS3558.O34752 P377 2002
813—dc21

for Lynn again

and for Bryan Woolley

CONTENTS

Patterns *of* Illusion

Mesquite

"That's how it happened, awful though it is," Ben Wayne said. Jesse Pickett was listening to him, sitting in his lawn chair. Ben Wayne now was leaning on the picket fence separating their yards and telling his neighbor how his son had left his wife, "and they hadn't been married but a month. We didn't even know about it till Cilla, that was his wife – still is till the divorce comes through – no, we hadn't heard a word till she called up Wilma and told her, then hung up and next thing we knew she was back in Kiowa where she come from. That's been two weeks ago and we still hadn't heard a word from O.L. I aint gonna go look for him either, not after him running off from his wife – even though I reckon he had his reasons. Hell, Jesse, this caught me off guard as much as his getting married. One day he come in the house and said this is Cilla his wife then they left just as quick as they come and he got a job at the filling station."

Pickett looked under the unruly dagger limbs of the mesquite tree at Ben Wayne and spat tobacco. Even though he had a brass cuspidor, his wife had made him chew outside. She had died a year ago, but out of habit and maybe a ghost of respect, Pickett never chewed inside the house. He had been listening to Ben Wayne for nearly an hour now, and three times he had heard the whole story of Ben's son O.L. running off from his wife. He was bearing the fourth telling now.

Pickett ran the hardware store in Rhineland. Wayne sold cars at Funston's Ford Motor Co. They had lived in the same two houses more than thirty years, and most evenings after supper they would sit in their own backyards and talk to each other, though Pickett would mostly listen. In the thirty years they probably hadn't been in each other's backyards more than ten times. Finally, after staring at Ben Wayne for several minutes, Pickett asked him how the wife was taking O.L.'s shenanigans.

"You know her, Jesse. She says her life's not involved so there's no reason for her to lose sleep over it. She's funny that way. Probably why she'll outlive me, and Ora Mae – why she died before her time, because she was always bothering about everybody else's business, kin or no kin."

Pickett told Ben Wayne he was probably right, and Wayne started in about his son, saying, "He wasn't raised to do something like that, breaching the promise he made to that girl before God and the town, even though it wasn't this town he made the promise in. I can't understand it, Jesse, why he'd run off like that and not say anything. She seemed like a nice enough girl to me."

"Yes, but you weren't her husband."

"No. Reckon I'm not."

Pickett was lighting his pipe now, and Ben Wayne saw his friend wasn't going to be any more talkative than he had been in thirty years, so he sat down in his wooden lawn chair whose limegreen paint was flecking and pulled a half-smoked cigar from his shirt pocket and stuck the still damp, chewed end in his mouth. He lit it and blew puffs toward Pickett, but the wind brought it swirling back in his face. Both men smoked without speaking or paying attention to one another. After awhile Ben Wayne brushed the ashes off on the sole of his shoe and uncrossed his legs and recrossed them the other way.

Suddenly a gaunt woman with gray hair frizzing out of a tight bun stuck her head out the back door of Wayne's house. She stood looking at her husband. As if sensing someone behind him, he turned around. "It's O.L.," she said. "He's gotten in trouble in Kiowa. Hurry up, too, it's a long distance call and we're the ones paying for it."

Almost before she had said "O.L." Ben Wayne was running into the house. Though not fat, he was much heavier than his wife, who was three-fourths of an inch shorter than he was. Twenty-two years ago they had measured naked in the bathroom. He had had to talk Wilma into that but she finally agreed, telling him that this was the last "for this kind of foolishness." O.L. was born nine months later. He was the only child they had.

"O.L.'s in trouble, huh?" Pickett said to Wilma, without a great show of curiosity.

"That's what he said," she replied. "I didn't dispute his word."

"Hope it's not anything serious."

"I don't know whether it is or not, he didn't tell me." She then turned and re-entered the house as Pickett beat his pipe bowl against the butt of his palm.

Although O.L. had always been hot-tempered, he was also given to long periods of silence, like his mother. Over six feet and lean, he had made All-District end his last two years in high school and had received a football scholarship to a state university outside Fort Worth. He was put on probation the first semester for fighting in the dormitory. He also got a high school girl in Fort Worth pregnant but talked his way out of that problem by convincing a few friends that they should admit to having had relations with her also. He believed that they had. His midsemester grade reports averaged out a little better than a C, but he flunked almost all his finals and finished the semester with a C and four D's. He quit going to classes during spring training that year, and after cursing an assistant coach one day at practice he was kicked off the team and left school altogether. He and a friend, who was also flunking out, decided to find work in Kiowa. They worked construction jobs at the Air Force base there the first six months, then the other boy decided to go back to his home where he could live with his parents until January when he was going to try to get back in school. A few weeks later O.L. got a job as a lineman's helper for the electric company. That lasted until Christmas, when he decided it was too cold to hang around poles.

During Christmas with his parents in Rhineland he decided he wouldn't do anything for awhile. He had $650 in the bank. His father tried to convince him he should get a job. He said sometime he would. Then Christmas night the mother found her son yelling at her husband in the living room, telling him, "It's my money and I made it myself and by God you don't have any right to tell me whether I ought to make any more or not!"

"I'm just trying to help you, Son."

For a few moments the mother listened in the doorway, then stiffly, her lips pursed, her nostrils pinched, she told her son, "You're not going to live here and not work."

The room hushed. The father nodded his weak agreement without looking directly at the son. O.L. stared at his mother, then said, "All right, I'll go back to Kiowa." She told him what he did there was his business, so he left. The father did not protest but added that he hoped he would learn to control his temper and find what he wanted. O.L. answered that he wasn't looking for anything. The next morning he caught the bus for Kiowa and didn't return to Rhineland for a year and a half. He saw his parents twice during that time. They had gone to Kiowa to shop both times. The visits were short and to all three meaningless.

When O.L. did come back to Rhineland he brought Cilla with him. They rented a house and O.L. got a job at a filling station on the highway. When the mother found out Cilla's maiden name was Pérez, she refused to have anything to do with the daughter-in-law. Ben Wayne said it didn't make any difference to him if her name was Mobutu, "She seems like a nice girl to me." Ben Wayne then tried to make Cilla as comfortable as possible. He took her out to eat during his lunch hour twice a week, but as it turned out he had only three weeks to make reparation for his wife's icicled shoulder. And when O.L. left his wife, the father was taken aback, embarrassed. He could tell the girl cared a lot for his son and O.L. himself had seemed to have a better disposition since his marriage. What really hurt Ben Wayne, however, was that his daughter-in-law had called Wilma to tell her that O.L. had left and she was leaving, too. He could never understand why the girl had not called him, since it was he who had been kind to her.

Wilma refused to go with her husband to see their son, who was in jail on an assault and battery charge. The night before, O.L. had beaten up one of Cilla's brothers in a bar in Kiowa. The way O.L. told it to his father, the brother had begun cursing him in the bar where they had met by accident, and he was afraid the brother might try to pull a knife, "So I cold-cocked him because, hell, Dad, you can't tell what them Mexicans'll do."

The father found out from a detective in Kiowa's police station that Cilla's brother was O.L.'s age, had never been in trouble, "but is now, healthwise. You ought to see his face. Christ! You ought to do something about your son. He's gonna get shot if he keeps up this hellin'. We've had him in here before. For gettin' drunk and fightin' and sometimes fightin' without being drunk. Goddamn, friend, you got a mean son."

Ben Wayne had never thought of his son that way before. O.L. had always been rough on the football field, but never dirty, just rough enough to make his father proud and even awed, especially when friends would say, "Godamighty, Ben, that son of yours is the toughest thing this town's seen since before Prohibition. Hell, you're gonna be a rich man. He keeps up like this he'll be All-America easy and then get one of those big contracts. Sheee! He'll be able to buy this town before he's twenty-five." But the son had not made All-America; he hadn't even played on the varsity at college, and now it looked to Ben Wayne as if he would just be another hothead drifting from cleaning up bars with fists to holding up filling stations and liquor stores until he got shot or put in the penitentiary.

O.L. was calmly picking his huge fingernails when the jailer let

Ben Wayne in to see his son. When the son glanced up at his father, he turned toward the wall and began filing his nails on it. The father sat down on the end of the cot.

"What's the trouble, son?"

O.L. told him about his fear of Charlie Pérez's knife, but Ben Wayne had a hard time believing his son had ever been afraid of anything. "Was Cilla's brother mad about what you did to his sister, leaving her?"

O.L. told him that was what the fight was about. "Cilla and I were together at the bar. She'd snuck out of her house so we could go out, said her father said he'd kill me if he ever saw me. We were just in there drinking and her brother come up and began cussing me. Cilla started crying and I told her to shut up. Then the brother came at me and I hit him. Hope I busted his jaw," O.L. said. "If they hadn't pulled me off I'd have knocked his head down between his legs, the sorry sonofabitch. . . . And the hell of it is, Cilla and me was having a good time."

The father asked how could you have a good time with someone you ran away from, "unless y'all had gotten back together."

"Naw. We were just having a good time. Weren't even talking about getting back together – at least on any kind of permanent basis. We were just swinging together that night, having a few beers, listening to the juke box, not even talking much. And then that sonofabitchin brother of hers come in raisin' hell and ruined the whole goddamn night. He's lucky he didn't get hisself kilt."

The father looked nervous, not out of fear but out of ignorance of his son's way of life: fighting and raising hell while he had money enough; then when he didn't, working until he had enough to raise hell once again. He had tried to teach his son, he thought, the value of money and work, but the lesson had never taken. Even as far back as his junior year in high school O.L. had said he thought money was to be used, spent for what you wanted to buy, not made like a carrot hung in front of a mule's eyes to keep you going wherever it was the person driving you wanted to take you. The father had mentioned about the virtue of sacrifice, but the son had told him he understood well enough about sacrifice: "That's what you do when you run out of money." The father had added that sacrifice was a godly virtue, that other people were involved in your life besides yourself. It was then that O.L. had laughed outright at his father, who from then on quit giving advice and prayed to himself that his son would make All-America and become rich from playing professional football. Because if he doesn't, he told himself, he's going to get in trouble.

In a few minutes the father found out why O.L. had left his wife. She had begun giving advice, had tried to get O.L. to get a better job, go to Kiowa if necessary, said she had seen in the paper classified ads about training programs which prepared you to run drive-in stores and make $100 a week. He had told Cilla he would think about it and she told him no he wouldn't and he had answered that if she knew so well what he would do that she was wasting her time bothering him. She had started crying and he had yelled that he didn't like to see people cry, that if she wanted to go back to Kiowa and get another husband she could, but that he was tired of her getting all snot-nosed and red-eyed over something that wasn't any of her business in the first place.

"What do you mean, Son, wasn't any of her business? She's your wife."

"Yeah, but I aint her mule."

"I failed, Son. I failed. Should've taught you more common decency when you were little. Shouldn't have been so careful to pull the thorns off the mesquite sticks when I switched you. I shoulda bloodied your bottom steada just raising welts."

O.L. cursed.

His face flushing, Ben Wayne left, and on the way out he told the jailer he hoped he could drive some sense into his son. The jailer acted as if Ben Wayne were speaking a foreign language. He eyed the father, then the son slouching on the cot, and picked tobacco off his tongue as he punched the button to open the heavy steel door to let Wayne out.

When he returned to Rhineland, Ben Wayne told his wife what had happened, but she wasn't interested. He then told Jesse Pickett what had happened. The friend listened and tamped ashes in his pipe with his stained middle finger. "You know, though, Jess, I don't have the slightest idea in hell why he called us."

The Waynes didn't hear any more about their son until a year later when they received a Christmas card from him. O.L. was with the Marines in San Diego. Over supper that night Ben Wayne told his wife he hoped the military would teach his son some discipline. "It might and it might not," Wilma said and cleared the table.

About two weeks later Ben Wayne and Pickett were talking to each other across the fence when Pickett asked what Wayne had heard from his son and Wayne said, "Nothing."

"I'll tell you, Ben, I wouldn't worry about it. You can't make him over, not this late. Mark it up to experience and get on with your own business, that's all you can do. I remember when Ora Mae died, I was all choked up and . . ."

"I guess you're right. O.L.'s the same as dead as far as we're concerned, that's what Wilma says. It just don't seem right, though, not to be able to do anything. I shirked my duty somewhere. How'd you make your kids turn out right?"

"I didn't. Ora Mae done that. I was always too busy, except to take them hunting once or twice. She's the one deserves the credit. I guess that's why they don't write me more than they do. Last I heard one was in New York and the other in Nebraska. I'll hear from them at Christmas and on my birthday, but I reckon they're busy, too."

With his thumb and index finger he probed his two shirt pockets then asked Ben Wayne, "Got a match?"

Wayne gave him a book of paper matches, told him to keep it. Pickett lit his pipe with one and gave the others back.

They were both sitting in their lawnchairs now and smoking. Saying something about the need for rain, Ben pulled a handful of mesquite beans off the tree between them. He began splitting the covers and dropped the beans on the ground. A few of the pellets spilled into his palm. He pinched at them with his fingernails, but they didn't break. He slumped in the chair and, straightening his legs, pulled his knife from his trouser pocket. He dug the point into several beans, but when he tried splitting one, the blade slid off the bean and dug into his thumb.

"Good thing I lost my whetstone," he said. "A sharp knife would've opened the skin good." Pickett agreed that it probably would have. "You know, Jess, a mesquite tree aint good for nothing 'cept switches. A jackrabbit's all that can get shade out of them. And you can't eat the beans, unless you're a Hereford or Angus. And mesquite's about all we got around here. You can't kill one without a bunch of expensive chemicals and then you got to bulldoze them down. They ain't good for a damn thing except switches, and I guess in my case they weren't much good for that either."

"I always used a belt."

"I probably would have too except I've always worn galluses."

Pickett beat his pipe on his palm, then tried blowing through it. His cheeks ballooned red but no air passed. He dropped his pipe in the grass and pulled a plug of chewing tobacco from his shirt pocket. He then reached in his trouser pockets and fumbled around but brought out nothing. "If you've still got your knife out, how about throwing it over?"

Ben Wayne did so, but the knife hit a limb of the mesquite tree and fell to the ground on his side of the fence. As he got up to retrieve it, he said, "See there. Goddamn mesquite always causing trouble." He flipped the knife to his friend.

Pickett cut off a quid of tobacco, put it in his mouth, then cleaned the blade by spitting on it and rubbing his fingers over the stain. He threw the knife back to his friend. Ben Wayne smiled, suddenly remembering that years ago Pickett used to bite off his quids but his wife had made him start cutting them off; and even now, after his wife was dead, Pickett still cut off his tobacco chaws out of habitual respect to his wife's sense of etiquette. Also Pickett would only spit no more than twice an hour, but his wife had nothing to do with that. He had chewed long enough that he didn't have to spit much, although when he wanted to he could spit farther than any man in town. Years ago when they still had spitting contests on Saturday afternoons, Pickett most always won. Even as a young man he could beat the old-timers.

"Listen, Ben, I was just thinking. You hadn't read me any of your poems in I don't know how long. Must be a year now. You still fiddle with them?"

"Naw, not much. The last one I wrote was about these mesquite trees around here, but it wasn't much good so I threw it away, or lost it."

Pickett sucked the lump in his cheek. "If you ever do another one, let me hear it."

"All right. You're the only one who'll listen to them anyway. Wilma never did like them, said she was always busy and didn't see any sense in writing about something when you could always go out and see it if you've forgotten what it looked like."

"Well, women are practical like that. You never heard of a woman poet that had any kind of a name, have you?"

"Nope. Just that one in the *Dallas Times Herald* and she's not much good. I don't call her stuff poems, I call them sermons, and besides you can't ever see what she's talking about because she's always fiddling around with pious thoughts that you can get in church. When I write, I always write about what you can touch. Hell with the thinkin' and advisin' – you can always get that."

Wayne's cigar had gone out, so both were chewing now. It was almost dark, and both men were slapping mosquitoes. Every now and then a lightning bug would poke its light at the approaching blackness, then disappear. A breeze needled through the mesquite limbs onto Ben Wayne's face and sticky neck which he wiped with a handkerchief. He slapped his bare arms. Pickett did the same. Then without speaking both men went into their own houses.

The next night Ben Wayne was in his lawnchair before Pickett came out. A piece of paper was sticking from his shirt pocket. Pickett came out, sat down, packed his pipe, and fired it. Ben Wayne said he had something he wanted to read to him. Pickett nodded that he would listen; his pipe wheezed as he sucked it.

"It's a letter I wrote to O.L. I expect the Marines will forward it to him if he's still with them. I did some thinking about what we were talking about last night, about how O.L. turned out and where I failed with him. I guess the mesquite, though, gave me the idea. Anyway it's short so here it is."

The way he always did before reading one of his compositions, Ben Wayne coughed, then readjusted himself in his chair. And as usual Pickett didn't say anything to encourage his friend to read. He just waited silently for him to begin.

"Dear O.L.," Ben Wayne read, "I ran across a quotation today. It seemed to fit. Being that you're like your mother and not much on letter writing I probably won't know if you get this or not. I'm used to that so don't worry. Here's the quote: 'Life is strange in that the dead can, through memory and love, be alive to the living. But yet how much stranger it is that the living can be dead to each other.' Dad. P.S.: I was sorry to hear you'd passed away."

He put the letter back in his shirt pocket.

Pickett tamped his ashes and eyed his friend, who relit his cigar.

"Do you want me to read it again?"

"No, I got it the first time. It's good, Ben," he said thoughtfully. "Probably the best poem you ever wrote."

"It's not a poem. It's a letter I'm sending O.L."

"It's still the best one you ever wrote."

Ben did not argue. They went back to smoking and not talking, and when the mosquitoes got bad they went inside.

Three months later the Marine Corps sent notice that O.L. had been promoted to corporal, but O.L. did not write. One day when Ben was in Kiowa, he saw Cilla down the street. She was with a tall, lean man who reminded Ben of his son. When the couple stopped at a street corner, the man turned around and Ben saw that it wasn't his son. The situation made him feel strange and took his breath for a moment. Cilla turned around, too, and saw Ben. She smiled and, tilting her head, acknowledged his presence, then crossed the street, holding hands now with the man she was with.

During the next years there were no Christmas cards from O.L. And since Wilma never mentioned her son, the father didn't either. Ben and Pickett kept up their ritual in their backyards, but O.L. never came into the conversation. Ben never mentioned that he had seen Cilla, and before too many years he was not certain that he had. This didn't change the evenings Ben and Pickett spent together in their backyards, though, because their women had never played much part in their conversation. When the funeral home checked the list of Wilma's survivors with Ben, he told them he was the only relative she had.

One day a postcard from O.L. came in the mail. It said: *Dear M & D, As you can see from the postmark I'm in Brazil. I married a Rio de Janierian. You won't get a chance to dislike her, Mother. We're not coming home. I work in a hotel. Bartender. Tell Coach Reasor, if he's still there that I've settled for making All-Brazil. Adios. Your wildhaired corpse of a son, O.L.*

Ben fingered the postcard, turned it over and examined the picture of the beach and the city's shoreline. He went into the closet of his son's old bedroom and pulled from the shelf a scrapbook which contained yellowed newspaper clippings of his son's high school football career.

He laid the postcard on top of the clippings and replaced the book on the shelf. He went into the kitchen to fix himself a sandwich for supper. He opened the refrigerator and tore some strips of withered lettuce off the head which would last yet another week. He slopped peanut butter on a piece of bread and laid the lettuce on top of that. He opened a bottle of beer and took it and the sandwich on a plate into the breakfast room where he had eaten two meals a day for more than thirty years. He started to sit down but shot back up. Quickly he headed for his son's old bedroom and took down the scrapbook. He removed the postcard and turned the scrapbook over and inserted the card in the back with his old poems and a handful of mesquite beans he had put with them several years before. He looked at the top poem but could not remember writing it. He turned it over and saw a date. Almost ten years ago. The beans had been there nine.

He closed the book and laid it back on the shelf. As he closed the door, he noticed a daddylonglegs spider crawling onto the scrapbook. The spider stopped. Ben Wayne watched it. It did not move.

The man's eyes were red now and he pulled the door back slowly. He leaped and his hand came down on the spider, crushing it. The spider did not stick to his hand. It lay dead on his son's scrapbook which also contained the man's poems and some mesquite beans. He left the spider lying there and closed the door, went back into the breakfast room, and finished his sandwich and beer.

Pickett was already in his yard when Ben Wayne went outside. When Ben started to sit down in his rickety lawn chair he noticed some mesquite beans had fallen on it. He brushed them off and sat down. He unwrapped a cigar but found he had no matches. Pickett pitched him some over the fence. Ben Wayne used one then sailed the book of matches back to his friend. They didn't say anything that evening.

When Ben went to bed that night, he lifted the bedspread from the side and flopped it over on the other side so that just one half of the bed was uncovered. That was enough because he only used half of the bed anyway. Before he fell asleep, he absent-mindedly told himself that he had all he needed, which is better, he said, "than needing all I have."

The Leaning Tower of Babel

Impossible – it's impossible to do anything about it. It? Not it so much as them. They come in swarms, except on seldomtimes when, tendril-haired, one solos out of the group and works its way to where we, mildly deranged, keep grubbing for goodness while struggling with embarrassingly minor specifics: mending clothes, repainting strafed walls, gluing furniture, buying retirement, washing windows, sucking dirt out of carpets with machines. Major things: breathing and eating; chattering in circles; observing then forgetting how they alter our psyches, loosen the grip of our skin on meated bone.

One's here now. I wish I could accurately say that there's something eccentric about its appearance, but I can't. They resemble us but, more than we, maintain firm roundness. The one here is the lumpier of the two. It tries hardest to harass us and often succeeds. Sleeping has gotten more and more difficult. So has the maintenance of coherence. It's easy to write a sentence, to write two or several sentences, but it's hard to create the flesh they should refer to. The appreciation and drive are there, but something is missing. The thing has been whipping us silly, and we often become hysterical, stuffy with ancestral fears of conspiracy. Our voices assume weird volumes berserk with screeching and terribly artificial laughter. Actually the thing doesn't resemble us that much after all. Its complexion is greenish, though sometimes it turns strawberrily creamy, and its wing-busy appendages are soiled brown. The eyes sparkle, but not with personality. They flicker because tiny strobe lights are wired into two hollowed recesses of the skull. They seem actually to see. They have already removed my wrinkles: replaced them with hives. They scream and laugh like banshees. Flawless, their skin steams at the pores, and the power they exude creates a constant warning whistle that heralds a swamplike stink.

I must get rid of them. They distress my equilibrium. Their fingers flick at me. They demand feasts of colored slushy ice. They seem to have no function beyond disturbance. They rarely mention God. In that, at least, they're like us, but the parallel does not comfort me. Their attitudes toward authority are inconsistent. I haven't yet learned how to approach them.

Sometimes they act as if they love me, but many times they attack us, make me afraid that blood will spurt from my ears. A number of mornings I've found stains by my head, but our sheets are blue satin and I can't tell what color the unknown liquid is.

The one that was here has disappeared. I do not want to know where it's gone. Briefly free, I'll try to understand our odd arrangement of power. According to appearances, the only advantage we have over them is our productivity, artistic and industrial. They don't seem to mind. We stir ourselves with fiction and technology, painting and music, timedreams of dollars fragmenting us; and out of our torment have come volumes – mountains! of work. Our agonies have given us the sublime, have enabled us to laugh and weep, express outrage and be outrageous; and the stuff that comes from us is (has been), according to documents, worth the suffering we endure(d) to produce it. They pay little attention. They do, however, notice our more primitive efforts. They laugh at our table manners, refuse to be tamed enough to imitate them. They wolf down the food off their unbreakable trays but leave half-chewed hunks for ghosts, other pests we don't want to invade our home. Gone, they laugh. We laugh, too. They return, smiling as if welcomely baited. Full of secrets, they flee screaming away. For a moment we, at least I, wish them harm.

I don't understand them. Their anarchy harasses me. My digestive system is undependable, and my endocrine system has lost moderation. I seem to be doomed to attack my mate or cringe away, not from her but from too-well-foreseen interruptions. I have forgotten what her skin feels like. I have memorized, however, the many textures of her clothes, buttons, zippers.

It's difficult to sustain anything, and I feel awkward when I try to emulate them. Sloth makes me impatient. Their deposits and barreling amplitude encage me. Horrible to say, they seem unmanageably healthy. Wild, they climb over everything. They rearrange us and our home.

The sounds of scraping are constant. I exaggerate. They've excised my sense of perspective. Their tendrils crawl with toads and bright-colored insects. Scraps of crayoned paper stick to them.

If I could only re-create their flesh. If I could do that I might be able to control them, but because they're celibate their energies are anarchic. Worse, they know magic. When they go quiet they force me to feel soft about them and guilty for being imprudent in my waking rages against them. Many times they do not seem to hear. Off and on they go deaf. I never can. I snarl at them and spray sputum in my anger. They rebuke me with razzberries: sounds which, frankly, are nasty.

Sometimes, though, I feel basically calm, in spite of the fact that they're spoiling the pleasurable usefulness of our loins. At least mine are going to ruin. I'm not sure about my mate's. She spends tremendous periods alone in the bathroom. Demented, I've often listened at the door, but I've never heard anything rewarding. My left ear burns, but not from curiosity – from one of the creatures having put a match to it when I was lunatic enough to think I could nap.

I feel weak, as if something is preparing me for possession. I would like that, to be transformed. It would free me from the itch for flesh. I could then be content with my abstractions. But the feeling of imminent possession is going, draining from me like infant's slobber. It's gone. They laugh. Taking the Lord's name in vain, I curse them.

This is all so unsatisfying. One tells me food makes muscles and earwax. They laugh again. I join them, but soon they dissemble all my joy. They mess on themselves, and the bigger one threatens to pee on me. I've gotten bloated. I need a kind of nourishment I'm not getting.

I wish I could spray myself clean from the inside out. They become sublimely quiet, and I remember I've been told before that I helped bring all this on myself and that there will surely come a time when I'll miss their plundering ways. I don't hoot at that opinion. In fact, it sounds quite reasonable to me. It means that I'm doomed to misery forever.

What is more important now, though, is for me to protect myself. They're shooting fluorescent darts which have black suction cups on them. One, through some miracle of force, has stuck on my forehead. I'm not going to remove it. That pleases them. I've become a unicorn. To celebrate, they spill and hurl trash, knock askew pictures on the walls, attack me with pencils, drumsticks, typewriter ribbon, tom-toms, and wet balls which, I realize, have become tadpoles and birds' eggs.

Scrambling over my incompetently dodging, battered body, they, screaming in wondrous delirium, bury me beneath the unreasonableness of their momentary love that I, as crazy as they, am unable to reject.

Wild Onion Leaves

Yes, we did 'cause we did," Corby said, "and I got a bumblebee in my body!"

"A what?" his father asked, on the king-size bed with him.

"I did because I did."

Sitting in a low-backed rocker, nursing her infant daughter, the boy's mother listened, loving the bewildering tumble of his chatter. The father, grimacing, tugged at his already loosened tie. He lay back then brought his knees up, but that position was also uncomfortable, so he turned, crooking his legs. Two days ago he had had a vasectomy, and it was hard to find a position free from the pinches of stitches. Smiling futilely at his wife, he kicked his shoes onto the carpet and, after tugging his trousers away from his hips, he listened to his daughter's loud sucking.

Corby glared at his sister then crawled to the edge of the bed. Stretching to reach over his mother's extended legs, he rubbed his two-week-old sister's downy scalp. His mother pulled a wrinkled candy wrapper from a cuff of his lederhosen and laid it on the chest of drawers, antiqued scorched yellow and speckled brown. Corby folded back down on the bed with his still-fidgeting father, who noticed his wife had missed the stringy wild-onion leaves in his son's other cuff. Corby had pulled them before going to church.

Watching her son stare at the hem of her emerald green velours robe, she said, "Now tell me again. Where'd you go?"

Corby's enormous brown eyes went brilliantly alive and, sitting on his leathered rump, he sang, "We went to the big woom!"

"What'd you see?" his father asked, knowing Corby's Sunday-school teacher had taken the pack of three-year-olds to the sanctuary.

"The big woom," he said bluntly. "And we did 'cause we did."

His mother asked him who was in the big room.

"Jesus – and she was dead and a big biter-bug ate off her feet."

"What biter-bug?" his mother asked.

"A great big biter-bug, 'cause it did, it ate off her feet!"

His father asked him what else was in the big room.

"No thing!"

Fussing, the baby finally found the nipple she had lost. Her desperate sucking was like snorting.

Mad knocking then on the front door. It didn't stop.

"I'll get it," Corby said, jumping off the bed, and his father rumpled his hair as he went by. Corby jerked away. "Don't! Leave my hair alone!"

"I'm sorry, little Oedipus, I'm sorry," his father said.

"I'm not Eh-pus – I'm Corby!" The mad knocking kept up. "All right!" Corby yelled. "Shut up!" he snapped at the knocker. "You'll wake up my baby!" But just as he passed through the bedroom doorway he whirled around and told his parents, "Yes, he did! The biter-bug ate off her feet!" Disappearing, he yelled, "I'm coming, Gonkhead – I'm coming!"

Both parents, Gene and Jeanne, knew the knocker was Lindal. They both disliked him, but had decided it best to tolerate him because Corby was unmanageably decent when it came to defending underdogs.

According to his parents' standards, however, everyone was an underdog because there was no such thing as a successful stand against chaos. Six months ago, working on a graduate paper in Humanities, Jeanne had found the key term for this: "entropy: the tendency of all systems, including the universe, to proceed toward maximum chaos." After reading about entropy in the library, researching the relevance of dynamism to contemporary art, she had gone home and in front of her confused husband cried over a plate of broccoli, garlic toast and London broil, sources of energy that that night seemed too absurd to ingest. Gene didn't tell her then, but a large fragment of him considered her reaction foolish. As advertising manager for a television station, he worked daily in what she called entropy. Besides, for almost as long as he could remember he had never been able to make sense of God or any other system, political or personal. He went to church for two reasons: it felt good to stir his body around on Sunday morning and church was cheaper than golf.

He looked at Jeanne. He felt warm toward her but suddenly laughed. Their lives were going nowhere. They were not saving for any grand project. All they were headed toward were graves or cremation ovens. He wanted to take a nap, but Lindal was causing trouble.

Corby told him, "Go home! I don't want you in my house!"

Lindal sassily fussed back, telling Corby he didn't have to obey him, but Corby kept yelling, "Go home! Get out of my pwopaty!"

Gene winced, resisting the impulse to chase Lindal out of the house because he knew what Corby would do: turn against his father, defend his friend. He gritted his teeth and glanced at Jeanne. She didn't seem at all upset. She rocked and nursed the baby. Gene knew that he had been wrong. He was not resigned to chaos and his wife had the higher level of tolerance. He wanted to make himself small so that, without being a bully, he could go in and maul the noisy sissy who was agitating his son.

Smiling, Jeanne said, "I love you."

Lindal was crying furiously now. Soothed by the terrible sound, Gene could now doze off. He knew what had happened. His son had found the .410, had fashioned a silencer out of Lincoln Logs and dishtowels and had shot Lindal, who had gone delirious. Soon the fuss would be over, and there would be no evidence left of the incident because one of Corby's giant biter-bugs would come, devour the corpse and disappear.

Finally Jeanne asked him to settle the war in the den, "and don't make it worse than it already is."

"You don't ask much, do you?"

"You want *me* to calm them down?"

"Yes."

"Then hold the baby."

"Never mind," Gene said, getting up.

"What's wrong?" Jeanne asked. "You don't want to hold your daughter?"

"Sure I want to hold her, but I'm afraid to."

"Why?"

"I might forget who she is and throw her at the monster in there – let her gum him to death."

"You won't either," Jeanne said. "I don't want her to get pyorrhea."

The baby had dropped off to sleep. Jean's naked, large-nippled breast was pressed up, staring at him over the infant's ear. Pulling her brassiere flap over her breast, she said, "I think you've both had enough."

"Hardly."

"At least you get to look. I don't get anything."

"Hold on," he said. "You're supposed to be bovine – saintly and chaste."

"Nonsense. They didn't stitch up my thinker." She fingered her dark hair off her cheek and smoothed it behind her ear.

He sat up, wrapped his arms around his knees. He watched her wiggle her toes. "That exercise you're doing," he said, "is good for circulation."

"Mama!" Corby cried. "I'm going up to Lindal's."

"Okay," Gene replied. "Shut the door, though."

Corby stormed into the room. "I wasn't talking to you! I was talking to my mama!"

Jeanne rolled her eyes ceilingward. "Fine," Gene said.

Corby squinted meanly at his father and doubled his arms in front of his suspender-bibbed chest. "I got a bigger muscle'n you – I'll gonk your guts out."

"No, you won't."

"Yes, I will 'cause I will."

"Corby," Jeanne said patiently, "don't talk like that."

"I will if I will. I got a bigger muscle."

"No, you don't either," Gene said, clenching his fists and flexing his biceps. "See? That's called thunder."

Corby jutted out his chin.

For devilment Gene asked him, "You want to kiss me goodbye?"

"No!"

"I didn't think so."

"No! 'Cause a big biter-bug and poison snake is going to come bite you."

"I'll crush them with my feet."

"I'll gonk your head."

"I'll make you laugh."

"You won't! I got a bigger one!" he said, thrusting up his fist.

"Don't laugh, now," Gene said, frowning. "Don't laugh. Be mean. Come on now – be mean – ferocious, Corby. You can do it. Be hateful."

Corby tried not to laugh but he couldn't help it.

"Corby! Quit that laughing. . . . I told you, now stop it!"

Corby kept laughing and, trying to fight it off, rushed the bed and bounced off the mattress. Then he picked up one of his father's shoes and threatened to throw it, but Gene, crossing his eyes, bared his teeth at his son. Corby made the face back and, dropping the shoe, ran out of the room, hollering for Lindal to hurry up. "Let's go to your house!"

As the outside door slammed shut Jeanne laid the baby in the McGregor-plaid baby carrier beside the bed. The baby sighed, groaned, and bringing her knees up under her stomach she rubbed her cheek on the pillow-cased mattress and then was still.

After zipping up her robe, Jeanne crawled onto the bed beside her husband. "You going to leave your suit on?" she asked.

"Any reason not to?"

"It'll get rumpled."

"How awful!" he said.

Putting her arm across his chest, she snuggled against him. He kissed her hair and then whispered, "What's for lunch?"

"Whatever you go out and get."

"You're abusive."

"I know."

"You don't feel guilty?"

"No," she said. "Just totally unburdened, now that everyone's quiet."

He squeezed her thigh. She kissed his jaw. They rolled against each other, and his fingers rumpled through her long hair, his thumb massaging the back of her ear. She rubbed his chest, strength in the flat of her hand. He asked if her stitches itched.

"No. How about yours?"

"A little bit," he said.

"How's it feel to be sterile?"

"Find out. On second thought," he said, "keep your hands to yourself. My wounds haven't healed. . . . And be careful not to breathe deeply. I'm still fertile."

"You'd never know it just looking at you."

"Thanks."

She dug her fingers ticklishly into his armpit. Lurching away, he pressed his elbows tight against his sides. She left him alone, but he wasn't sure how long he would be safe. He was glad he still had on his coat and shirt because one time, before Corby was born, when he was lying shirtless in bed with his intertwined fingers under his head, she had stuck a well-chewed, sloppy glob of chewing gum in his underarm hair. He was sure she had no gum this time but then that time he hadn't thought she'd had any either.

"I guess," she mused, "this will be known as our passive period. Cut off from the real world."

"We're not cut off from the real world."

Her fingertips touched his palm. Tingles spread across his back and over his shoulders.

They lay there silently. The baby sneezed, stirred for awhile then was quiet. She was like a listening yet invisible presence that brought awareness more than disturbance. Awareness of themselves: the pressure of their separateness. This period would not be repeated. They would have no more children. They were entering a new section of their lives. The situation called for reflection, but neither inclined toward ceremony. All they were doing was lying on their bed. Their bed was no altar; it was a place for rest, love and hostility.

An argument had begun outside. Corby was yelling that his father was thunder, and he was too.

They listened to the dynamos. It was spring, and the only thing suggesting sadness was the knowledge that they were more advanced than the season. The return of the energetically sensual life, however, was not far off. They had had such a time. They would have it again. They were in an in-between state, almost like a bodiless condition. They were doing what they often did together, not much of anything; yet now they felt intimate with each other, more intimate, perhaps, than they had felt in months, maybe years, perhaps ever. They knew that many things, a neighborhood brat, a bomb, a wail from one of their own children, a phone call, many things could at any moment wreck their idyll.

She removed her fingers from his hand, and not really thinking about what he was doing, he sat up and pulled off his coat.

"Be sure to hang it up," she said.

Staring into her large and shining brown-black eyes, he felt light. He dropped his coat to the floor.

"Your eyes are green now," she said.

"That's comforting."

"Awhile ago they were blue."

"That's because the bedspread's blue."

She laughed, both at him and at herself. "Come back down here with me," she said throatily, "and I'll make them bloodshot. I will, yes I will, because I will."

He laughed with her. "How?"

She kept the answer to herself.

Kneeling on the bed, he asked her when she was going to get up and fix lunch.

"I thought you were going to go out and get something."

"Maybe next Sunday."

"Maybe next Sunday we won't need food," she said.

"That's unlikely."

"Perhaps."

"What's that supposed to mean?"

"Biter-bugs, love, biter-bugs."

He lay back down beside her, and they were close enough now to feel each other's breath. His hand found its rest on her hip and hers on his. For awhile he studied her nose. It was small and rounded, not quite delicate. Her finger figure-eighting, she explored the cleft in his chin. He wondered if she knew she was tracing the mathematical symbol for infinity.

"Jeanne?"

"What?"

"I itch."

"Scratch."

Instead of taking her advice, however, he tried to hear her breathe, but the sound was too faint to register, and he was scarcely able to see the rhythms of her chest pulsing under her robe and the way her nostrils subtly flared. He kept himself still. He felt terribly self-conscious, but he told her anyway, Thank you for making the rhythms of breath pleasant; only he didn't tell her that out loud, so she said nothing back.

Then someone knocked loudly on the door. It was Corby, full of yells now and demanding to be let in. So Gene, feeling something small inside himself peeling, got off the bed, but on the way to the door he found himself shocked because he was closer to tears than he'd been in a long time.

His finger slid moistly over his eyelashes. He knew why he was moved. Part of the reason was lying in bed. Another part was walking toward the door. He deeply inhaled. There was acid on his breath. It smelled like the wild onions that were growing now in the spring of the yard, the wild onions, scrawny, purple-flowered plants, the wild onions that made up the rest of the reason.

The Embodiment of the Times

In their own collective way, Joe and Sarai were gamers, though sometimes Sarai had trouble keeping the rules straight. They had been at the party a good while but had long since separated. Neither knew exactly when. He was somewhere swallowed up in a crowd, and she was busy with an older woman who gasped:

"Horrible! You can't take your children to the show any more – they're so awful!"

"Who? The children or the shows?"

"The shows," the stout woman sneered, tonguing a peanut fragment from between her teeth.

Sarai examined the smoke wisping from the panatella she was rolling in her fingers. "Who wants to take their children to the show?" she asked. "Listen, Lady, I go to shows to get away from mine."

"Oh," the woman replied, shocked. "Oh," she said and nervously patted her black jerseyed breasts.

"Now if you'll excuse me," Sarai said, flicking ashes in her palm, "I must, if you please, visit the euphemism."

"Come back," the woman said, fluttering, "there's more. I've just gotten started."

"So have I, so have I."

As Sarai edged through the crowd in the den, her husband, stretching over naked collar bones and necks lavaliered with gold and silver icons of the Zodiac, waved and drew himself free toward her. Sarai was irritated: there were too many chatterers and flirts stuffing all the parties she and Joe went to.

They met in the packed doorway leading into the hall. He took her cigar, puffed on it twice then gave it back.

"I see," he said, "you've been visiting my friend."

"Who does she think she is?"

"Aramanda McGillicuddy – our hostess of charm."

"Come on."

"I'm serious," he said. "We do some work for her husband. She goes by that name when she's prowling."

Not interested in tales about business and impatient to get
away, Sarai said, "Here, Joe, take this," and gave her husband the
cigar. "I'll be back." A tiny spray of ashes fell on the carpet. Joe took
her hand but she pulled away, the bistres under her eyes looking like
worn badges of passion.

"She's in love with me," Joe called after her.

"Who?"

"Aramanda McGillicuddy."

"Ha!"

"I mean it."

"Then go in good health," Sarai said irritably, walking sideways away. "She's a lunatic."

Joe started back into the scattered conversations spraying in
the room then saw Aramanda McGillicuddy herself coming toward
him. She walked with a grand stride, and her fish-puckered lips were
silvery tonight. Joe started backing away. The woman, like his wife,
was a threat, both of them in black, both of them at times rather wild
in the eyes. He was into the hall now and, although he could not see
Aramanda any more, he knew she was still working her way toward
him; her after-image swarmed over him: her black sweater, like
Sarai's, tastefully loose, and her floorlength skirt, slit up to her waist,
curtained away from the silver hotpants under it. Her soft thighs
pumped palely past the billowing skirt. She reminded him of Sarai's
mother who Christmas-shopped in Houston each year with a cane
wrapped in barbed wire to help her clear the crowds for her sun-
glassed passage. Sarai was somewhat like her, he mused, only shy in
spite of her candor, in spite of the fact she had been unflappable in
every crowd he had observed her in. Sarai was shy in the presence of
the world she pretended to be above.

The sensation of his own body disappeared. He dropped the
cigar but, fumbling, caught it like a stubby baton gone out of control
before it hit the floor. Straightening but not yet in full balance, he
retreated into the empty livingroom rubbing the burn in his palm with
his ash-dusted thumb. The livingroom was small; its furniture was
dark with age, and, for his taste, too many of its borders were ranked
with fringe. Lumpy but soft and full, the padding was suggestive of
short breath and flab. It also looked inviting.

Suddenly light from cup after cup of the champagne-sauterne
punch he had had earlier, Joe rolled away from the muddied ochre
armchair and revolved, sinking, into its mate. Beside him was a
mahogany lampstand fluted down its leg and brass-toed claws. He

took the crystal ashtray off it and laid it in his lap, a token of defense. He glanced at the doorway but the woman was not yet there. Inhaling the smokeless air deeply, he remembered his son Bryan saying in the aimless confidence of his three immortal years, "I'm not going to die, Daddy. When I get old they're going to put me in a new boy so I can chew gum!"

Joe laughed. He felt older than thirty but happily younger than death, even though his three removable bridges expelled him from the company of chewing gum with his son and infant daughter. Losing his breath, Joe laughed again, because there coming for him, smiling broadly to engulf him, was his old friend and dreammate, Aramanda McGillicuddy. Touching his knee in a gesture of intimacy – or was it conspiracy? – she set herself at his feet.

"I think I offended your wife," she told him.

"I think so too," he said, "but not nearly as much as you're going to."

"How do you mean?" she asked, brushing her wrist across his ankle, which was some twenty years younger than hers.

"*L'oubliez-vous,*" he said, "forget it," assuming that French was somehow appropriate under the circumstances.

She snuffed. "The only French I know," she said, "is *a coucher avec moi.*" She tugged her skirt free for comfort then palming his shoe told him, "I hope your wife holds her punch better than my husband. He's going to pass out. He ought to be milking his ulcer."

"You're not trying to offend my wife, are you?" Joe asked, his green eyes joking with her.

"Of course not. She misunderstood me. And now you did, too."

Rolling up the points of his oxblood suede vest, Joe said, "I doubt it."

Looking amused, Aramanda McGillicuddy leaned back on her straightened arms. "You young ones haven't learned how to be corrupt yet, have you?" Then she threw back her head to give him the stretch of her neck. "The night's young," she said, toying with him and rolling over to face him on her knees. He thought she looked ready to bite his shins. He restrained himself from barking, and she braced herself against his thighs to stand up. She picked a midge of lint off her breast. "If you get lonely in here being a hermit," she said, "don't forget there's a party in the other room. You're welcome to join it," she said, sounding renewed with a bitterness that he welcomed.

"I'll be in soon," he told her.

"Good. They're beginning to dance on the patio, and before the night's over you owe me at least one."

"What do you mean owe you?"

"You owe me a dance for politeness – I'm the hostess. And you also owe me one because you're rude."

He suddenly pressed himself against the back of his chair. He had just noticed Sarai disappearing into the hall as Aramanda turned to go. Sarai, he thought, must have been watching. The image of her, just before she fled, flashed at him, her dark eyes delirious with mockery. Sarai was getting slippery. She was too young to be eccentric like her mother who, for no good reason that they knew of, had left her husband the year before, saying, "There wasn't anything wrong. I just wanted a change. Aren't people allowed to have changes? After all, we're only alive."

Joe sucked the cigar deeply but it was out, then the instant he removed it from his lips a tiny purl of smoke ascended out of the ash.

Earlier in the evening, as Joe and Sarai were leaving the house, their son was showing his little sister an artbook while the sitter was losing herself in a toothpaste commercial on TV. Holding his place with his fist, Bryan called out, "We like naked people, don't we, Daddy? Even if their eyes are crooked. See?" he abruptly said to his sister who, drooling, was trying to crawl over the open book. Joe was sorry he had not stayed to hear his son explain why the eyes of the Modigliani were out of line. The tale undoubtedly involved some entertaining terror.

Suddenly there was music distinct in the room, and for the first time Joe noticed two speakers set in the top of the wall. They were facing him. The music, electric guitars and tom-toms gunning behind them, came down at him. He flinched at the runs which were loud and out of balance. He was staring now at the doorway. An invisible flood of sound poured through it waving over him and drowning him in the crush of its force. Rimshot slaps battered their way inside him, and for reasons he could not yet name the pressure of the sound reminded him of Aramanda McGillicuddy who was whirling now into the room, a train from the party behind her.

"Since you're such a prig," she said, flushing him out of his chair, "the party's coming to you," and she began dancing before him, and shortly he was up and imprisoning himself in her movements. The others dancing near them were somehow like fragments broken off from Joe and Aramanda, and Sarai was with them. They were all packed together celebrating either dreams or nothing or simply breath, all of them crammed together and, continuing conversations that had become, in the noise, incomprehensible; and the masses of their flesh were jerking bumping twisting grinding hooking rolling bouncing, their joints popping mashing pulverizing the accepting spread of carpet which shush-shush-shushed under their feet.

Dancing, Joe told her, "All parties are alike, aren't they?" but misunderstanding him, Aramanda whirled out her arms and answered:

"Yes! It *is* like a straitjacket."

"I didn't say that," he said louder.

"I know but you get used to it."

They kept on dancing, harder.

"You're pleasant to look at," he said.

"I can't hear you," she answered, shaking her head, whipping her joint-breaking hips at him.

"I said you remind me of a crocodile."

"No – won't hurt the carpet a bit."

"Why don't you take off your clothes?" he told her, and rubbing her nose and pounding her abdomen toward him, she said: "Who cares? I'll get it off my nose later."

"You're not even listening to me," he told her.

"You are," she said, "you're a good dancer. Just let your body talk."

"I hope my knee doesn't go out."

"There's still a bunch on the patio."

"Are they as attentive as you are?"

"Some are even better looking," she said, laughing, "but they don't have the fun."

"I'll bet."

"What?"

"I said does your husband know the kind of life you lead?"

Her body still moving berserkly, she gathered his head in her arms and, grinding herself slower and closer to him, said, "Of course he does – he's the one who taught me, but don't tell anybody."

"Why?"

She threw her arms over his shoulders and, keeping up her bouncing movements, laid her head against his. "Hush," she said, "just dance – quit trying to fuck my ear."

He pulled away from her but she grabbed him and told him, "This dancing is making me buzz."

"Don't be naive," the fat man told Sarai, a line of sweat bisecting the side of his face.

"Now now," she said, moving his hand off her rump. The man wasn't going to let her get back in the livingroom. He kept his hand on her arm and, pushing his paunch at her, tried to get her to dance again.

"We're friends," he insisted, "all of us, every one of us're friends."

"Then please," she said, "don't squeeze me so hard. I'm not a damn roll of toilet paper."

"Aw now now," he said. "Let's dance."

"All right," she said, giving in, "but keep your hands up where they belong."

"Nobody," he said, laughing, "nobody's trying to hurt your fanny. There's hardly enough there to fool with anyhow."

"Fine."

"Quit worrying," he said. "I'm not going to spread notoriety about you."

She hated this man and she hated the party, the two were the same: ugly and full of innuendoes no one was really going to act on. All this party-talk was pitiful and tiresome. She was going to give this man a lesson. She was going to call his bluff. She was going to watch him squirm. She was going to make him see what a fool he was, and she was going to get rid of her shyness.

Forcing herself to squeeze his fat, moist hand, she said, "Why don't we go in the back of the house? We could still hear the music back there."

"Good," he said and, taking her arm, started leading her down the hall.

"Let go!" she said, panicking and snatching her arm free and running into the livingroom to find Joe, but he was gone, she thought, she couldn't find him, then she turned back around and the man was still there in the hall, standing in the doorway, eyeing her contemptuously and waiting for her to come back to him. She hurried on into the crowd, but by the time she found Joe she was no longer frightened, she was disgusted at everyone here, especially her husband. And she understood her mother, too. She understood now that she'd had the good sense to junk the whole rotten mess.

Tiny-stepping forward and slicing sideways through the dancing couples, Sarai finally found Joe. He was still with Aramanda McGillicuddy, and their movements, rather slow and not much more than gestures of distraction, now had little to do with the raunched order of the music.

"Your husband's been telling me the most interesting things," Aramanda said.

"I'm sure," Sarai said, "just don't let me interrupt. You two make a lovely pair."

"Oh for heavensakes," Aramanda said, "I know it but Joe's just too damn shy to give me a chance."

Sarai went stiff, her eyes full of anger; and Joe stepped back, for a better view more than safety, he told himself, thinking a catfight might be entertaining and even useful. It might shock Sarai out of her distance; it might shake her loose from her poses. But the mirth disappeared. Sarai's skin, he'd just noticed, looked transparent.

"It's time," Sarai said, forcing herself into a tone of correctness, "it's time for us to leave."

"We've only begun," Aramanda McGillicuddy said.

"Your party was lovely," Sarai told her.

"A young babysitter? Is that why you have to leave?"

"No, she's no younger than you are old."

"Now, Dear," Aramanda said, taking her wrist, "let's not be jealous."

"Who's jealous?" Sarai asked. "I've been with your husband, too, and he's lousy."

"Well, yours sure isn't," Aramanda said, laughing, then reached up and kissed Joe on the cheek. Turning back to Sarai, she said, "Why do you think I've been spending all this time birddogging him?" She looked directly at Sarai and wiped her gums with her tongue.

Putting his arms around them both, Joe said, "We really ought to go."

"For shame," Aramanda told him, "for shame. You both disappoint me. But do come back," she said and kissed them both on the cheek. "It was nice meeting you," she told Sarai, slipping into the distance of formality. "My husband's said awfully nice things about Joe. It was a pleasure getting to know you," she said then slipping her arm around Joe's waist, she offered him her cheek then swayed to Sarai for a peck.

The party was over, at least for them it was over, and Joe felt bewildered.

"That's one of the most aggravating women I've met in my life," Sarai said as they walked to their car across the cushion of lawn. Her voice was shaking. "How'd we ever get involved?"

"We got invited."

"We don't even know them – I don't."

"You do now," Joe said. "So chin up," he told her, putting his arm across her back, but she twisted away. "She told me," Joe said bitterly, "she's the embodiment of the times."

"She might embody yours, she doesn't mine."

"Who knows?" Joe said, opening the door for her.

As they drove home it began misting. The streets looked greased.

He noticed his wife watching him. A shadow smeared most of her face. Her eyes were hidden except for pins of light in them. She stared at him the rest of the way home.

Leaving her at the house, he drove the sitter home; and on the way she asked him how the evening had gone.

"Fine," he lied but didn't mean to sound so sharp, and he realized that what he was feeling for Sarai, at least for now, was more akin to hatred than irritation.

Going back, he hoped she'd already be asleep so their relationship, like the evening, could be momentarily canceled. He drove around to give her more time to go under, but when he got home and into the bedroom he found her awake. The blankness of her eyes suggested terror. He had seen it before, namely in her mother, but also in Sarai who was sitting up, back straight, legs under the bronze comforter. The bedlamp lay a faint yellow pall over the room.

"Before you get undressed," Sarai said, "we need to talk. At least I do."

He sat on the frame surrounding their waterbed. She asked him if he knew what was wrong. On edge, he told her, "No," not knowing really what it was he was supposed to answer to.

"That's what I expected."

"Well?" he asked.

Looking at him straight on, defying not so much him but something in herself, she said brittlely, "I don't think we're going to make it."

Sinking, he asked, "What do you mean?" He was trying to mask, now from himself, the feelings he had driven around with for longer than tonight. "What do you mean?"

"Us," she said.

"What about us?"

"Our marriage."

He stood up quickly then kicked off one of his shoes. A laugh, choked, locked in his throat. He couldn't swallow.

She asked him if he were really surprised.

He coughed the catch free but said nothing.

"I just don't think we're going to make it," she said, smiling bleakly.

"Why not? You get upset about me tonight? What did I do?" He felt as if he were talking to a stranger, the kind of stranger he was not anxious to know any better.

She kept up her smile. "You did nothing wrong tonight," she said. "To be honest, I thought you handled yourself admirably."

"Then what's the trouble?"

"No trouble," she said, sounding almost flippant. "I just don't think we have any substance."

"What the hell are you talking about? What's substance?"

"I don't think there's anything to us. I've been feeling that for some time. Surely you've noticed."

He had but he wasn't going to say so. Long ago he had decided that the conflicts resulting from their gaming weren't to be taken seriously, even if sometimes they knocked them apart. "Okay," he said fliply, "do you want me to handle the legal work? It'll be twice as cheap that way. I'll give us both a discount."

For the first time since early in the evening, she smiled at him warmly, but her eyes were welling. A tear squeezed off her eyelashes and hung at the top of her cheek. She breathed through her mouth, bit her lip. "You're not going to fight me, are you?" she said, the question sounding like a plea as much as an accusation.

"No," he told her.

"You're not going to try to find out what went wrong?"

"No."

"You don't have anything to say?"

"No."

Jerking away from his stare, she asked him where he was going to sleep tonight.

"In our bed," he told her stiffly.

"How can you?" she cried.

"Easy. Just lay my body down and go to sleep. What do you think I'm going to do – sleep on the floor or in some damn motel?"

"But we're splitting up."

"Listen, Love, a bed's a bed. It's been pleasant before – I don't know why it shouldn't be at least satisfactory now."

"You mean you're saying you still love me?"

"That's beside the point," he told her. "You don't have to love somebody to sleep with them." He was refusing to be drawn into her game, if it were a game. He was determined, at least for now, to stay separate from her confusion. "Maybe it's time we started keeping up with the times," he told her, primarily to occupy the silence. She asked him what he meant, and laughing, he said, "Hell, I don't have any idea. I was just making conversation."

He peeled off his vest then opened the closet. He continued undressing, and during the process he did not glance back at her, then a wretched, confused-sounding noise rattled in her throat; and he looked around. She appeared alternately happy and sad in her own way, he thought angrily, half-hysterical; and he knew then that she had already drawn him in.

Stripping off his boxershorts, he told her, "If you keep looking at me, you're going to get warts on your eyelids." In a moment he thought he heard her say she didn't want a divorce, but he was not really sure what she had said, so he didn't answer her. He reached in and got his pajamas off the hook and put them on. He reached back into the closet and straightened the trousers he had looped over a hanger. Buttoning his pajama top, he looked at her, started to say something but involuntarily swallowed. The phrase would not come.

His footsteps heavy, he walked around the bed but instead of crawling under the covers he sat rigidly on the edge, wobbling with the water in the mattress beneath him. Sarai switched off the light.

"What're you thinking?" she asked him.

"I'm wishing I had a fork so I could stab this damn mattress," he told her.

She laughed and he laughed too, but quickly he tensed. She banged against him, her arms in flight around him, and he fell back with her into the heavy mass that jostled and slopped beneath them.

"I'm sorry," she said, suddenly laughing, and he knew that this was another damn game they were playing. "I didn't mean it," she said, but he still didn't answer. He couldn't because he'd begun laughing himself, only another part of him was standing aside and listening coolly to both of them laughing. He had no idea how long this would last, the laughter and the observation of the laughter that killed it. The bed that their marriage lay on and rolled aslush on did not even seem like a bed at all, he thought, but a gigantic serving of Jell-O.

Finally he pulled himself free from her and, upright, but continuing to wobble, he held out his hands and braced himself with her. This was not the first time divorce had come up, but it was the first time it had been taken seriously, by either of them as far as he knew. Laughter returned to them like hiccups, and feeling less sober than his thoughts, Joe wondered if maybe their real trouble was that they were beginning, at thirty, in attitude if not yet in flesh, an amoral time of marriage that they did not know how to handle.

"I didn't mean it," she said, "I really didn't."

"Sure you did," Joe said. "You meant it. So do I sometimes, though I guess I've never said it."

"It wasn't that woman," Sarai insisted. "Really, it wasn't."

"Yes, it was," he told her. "You saw yourself in her," and both of them laughed at that. Joe had no idea where his words were coming from, and he certainly had no idea whether he even believed them.

"You're lying, aren't you?" she asked, wiping her face.

"No," he said, finally getting himself back in focus. "Look," he said, sniffing moisture out of his nostrils, "it's one thing for you to put up a good front before the public, but it's another to break down in front of me. I'd rather you break down in public and keep up a strong front around me. This honesty crap's a bunch of shit."

As if feeling sharp for a moment in her bones, she pulled the lobes of his ears, and kneeling, they were leaning into each other for balance. Her fingers ran past his face and down his arms, and his palms pressed the firmness of the strength in her thighs. Her cheeks were moist and briny on his lips. They listed with the mattress' sway and listened to the chaos they were insisting now on keeping muffled. Their separate motions were scarcely distinct from the dying pulsation of the water beneath them.

Woman of the Region

"I **don't care** how often I get out," she told him. "He's a troglodyte. I can't stand it, not any more, I just can't stand it,"

"Sure you can," he said, pushing his chair away from his desk to face her more directly. "You have to," he said, but his right eyelid began tic-ing.

"I don't," she said then looked away.

He kept his gaze on her, the large willowy collar of her turquoise blouse flaring open as if to receive him. Everything about this woman was forward, and that both frightened and intrigued him, for she was also oblique. He had lived here for five years now and still had not gotten used to the people. They might act embarrassingly humble, or they might look you straight in the eye, purse their lips, say something outlandish and not seem to care if anyone caught the joke or took them seriously. And this woman was worse than any of them. She kept coming in to see him and he still had no idea if she were in love with him, rudely on the make, truly wanting counsel, or idly passing time while he squirmed.

He did know, though, he shouldn't be trying to tell her to see matters her husband's way. He'd already done that; he'd told her that the first time she'd come slow-loping in here to him. He'd told her that to offend her, to keep her away, but she'd kept coming back. She had him trapped. It made no difference that they were in his office and he was – he regretted the fact – teacher of a class she was in. In his mind she was the one with the power.

He tried glaring at her, but laughter kept dancing in her eyes. He had only been married two months, and he knew she knew that, but she still kept coming in trying to install herself in his life, his new home still feeling delicate, his new union not yet habit. Of course, his first marriage, almost two decades long, had not been habit either, he had discovered last year when his wife sailed away with a man she'd remet: one of two boys she'd gone steady with in high school. He'd recovered from the grief but was still punchy from the shock.

He'd begun all this wrong, he kept telling himself. When the woman had first come in to talk to him about problems with her husband – his unwillingness to go anywhere – he should have been merely polite, not so receptive to all the digressions in her tale. Again he looked at her, but this time her gaze lay gently on him. He wished he felt more measured, more comfortably self-contained. That would be much better. Then he could speak thoughtfully to her. In studied consolation his hand could press her shoulder like a blessing, and his arm, like an older brother's, would go around her back, and then the fantasy so ridiculous, he thought the swells and firmness of her flesh would, throbbing and heaving, move wildly against him. But none of that had happened, he reminded himself, and it wasn't going to either.

As if in accusation, she was staring at him, smirking at what she called his carrot-colored mustache. She had even asked him once if he were trying to look like that crazy Friedrich Nietzsche they'd had to read. "You ought to cut that thing off," she'd said. "Anyone trying to hug you'd probably end up scratched to death. Around here we get vigorous when we start hugging."

The way she was eyeing his mouth made her look as if with her gaze she was rooting around trying to find treasure near his large square teeth. She had even said that once. She had said, "Your teeth really are large and square." Then shivering as if thrilled, she had added, "Lord, you must have a tremendous bite."

A little laugh had broken within him, but the largeness of her own laugh had overwhelmed it.

"You're nervous, aren't you?" she asked.

"No!" he told her, both his hands suddenly moving like fly-swatters at dust motes by the lapels of his jacket.

"Sure you are," she insisted, her nostrils flaring, her gray fox eyes needling through him. "You're worse than my husband. Here I'm the one been going on at the mouth when you're the one not getting taken care of. You must've married wrong."

"Now wait," he told her, "I didn't say –"

"And frankly I'm surprised."

"But –"

"Lord," she said, "here I've been thinking what a great gob of rock you are, when it's you hardly married and your sweetie's plumb given out." A raucous laugh burst from her. "I bet what you're really hoping now is for me to just stand right up and skinny on out of my clothes."

He threw out his hand to stop her, though she had only readjusted herself in her chair.

"Now wait," he said. "Just settle down."

She kept laughing at him, then catching her breath, she said, "I bet you'd like that – for me to shake myself loose and farm right out of these clothes. Now isn't that right?"

"No!" he protested, his voice so pinched it sounded like someone else's. "No, it's not," he said. "That's ridiculous."

"Hell," she said, "if I did you'd be a better man for it."

"Now wait."

"Of course you would," she said then abruptly hiked up the hem of her skirt. He gasped then saw that she was only straightening her hose. "I'm sure you don't mind," she said, "you being a married man now. We just have to keep our equipment straight, tug it back in line sometimes."

He looked away until he heard her chipperly say, "I'm done." She fluffed her skirt loose off her thighs. "I did, though," she told him. "I meant exactly what I said."

"Said what?" he asked, never knowing what angle she'd start speaking from.

"I said I'm tired of my husband acting like a damn troglodyte."

"Yes, you did," he said, "I heard," but he no longer had any idea what anything meant. Then, feeling prompted by a lunatic, he said, "You do love your husband. You do, don't you?"

"Don't be naive," she replied, sounding disgusted. "If I didn't I wouldn't have come here to you. I certainly wouldn't keep coming back. I do have some pride," she informed him. "Don't you know anything?"

He just looked at her, dumfounded, as if bolts of electricity were pulsing through him. The sensation, though, came from his telephone buzzing.

"Go on," she told him. "Answer it. I'll wait."

"Yes," he said. "You might, though, wait outside."

"No," she told him, "I prefer to stay."

He picked up the phone. He knew it had to be his wife, and it was. She asked perkily how he was doing, and feeling guilty about feeling nervous, he curtly said, "Fine."

"Oh my," she said, her voice dropping. "That crazy woman's there, isn't she?"

"I'm afraid so."

"What does she want this time?"

"Who knows?"

"Well, you get rid of her and call me back."

"I'll be just a second," he told her. "Anything up?"

"It better not be," she said. "If it is I'll pull it out by the root." He kept waiting for her laugh, but the laugh did not come. "I mean it," she said. "I'll pull it clean out. I'll wrap it around that hussy's neck and strangle her dead."

"Sure thing," he told her. "I'll call you right back."

"My my," the woman said when he had hung up, "I guess the little lady doesn't have much to say."

His confidence renewed by his wife's fine edge, he told the woman it would be much better if she just got up and left.

"But I don't want to."

"Well, you need to. I'm busy."

"I doubt that – big man smart as you been teaching so long, you couldn't be busy. You probably even have your old yellow notes memorized."

"That's –"

"They bore you as much as they do us?" she asked, her eyes sparkling at him.

"Look," he told her. "I have things to do."

"I'm curious about something," she said. "You ever have any lady come in here and just hustle right out of her clothes?"

"Have what?"

"I understand that happens all the time. I sure couldn't imagine it happening in Math, though – not unless the girls looked like frogs."

"I told you," he told her, "I'm busy."

"But my husband?" she asked, pulling a hankie from the V of her blouse.

"Now cut it out," he told her. "You're not pulling any crying stunt here."

"Lord, no!" she said, laughing, then blew her nose hard. "It's my sinus. They always act up when I get upset." She blew again into the skyblue hankie, then looking him straight in the eye, she asked, "What about yours? Your sinus ever act up when you're knocked up against a wall?"

"No!" he snapped at her.

"Mine do," she said, pulling a spitcurl lower on her jawline. "And if yours ever give you grief, I'll let you use this," she said, offering the little flag of cloth. "There's probably still a good-sized corner hasn't got any of my stuff on it."

"Now stop it," he said, helpless as she laughed.

"You know," she said, leaning back in her chair, her knees staring at him from under the hem of her skirt, "the bad thing about sinus is you reach a certain stage. The cracklings up in your nose start itching. They like to drive me nuts sometimes. But you can't just reach up, pick'm out like you could when you were kids – flick'm like my brothers used to. You get a certain age you can't do that. All you can do is blow and hope this time they pop free."

"Look," he said, "I'm busy. I mean it. Please."

"It's my husband," she said. "We live like our house is a cave. Sometimes I think I'll go nuts."

"You already have," he told her, but she didn't reply, or even seem fazed.

All he wanted to do now was go deaf, hide his face in his hands and go deaf. But he couldn't do that. If he did she'd come over to him and slide her arms around him and begin massaging his shoulders and the back of his neck where the tendons got tight. Kneading the flesh in his nape, she would say, "There, there. Now isn't that better?"

He stared at his desk top: scratched varnished walnut, but there was no clutter of papers he could riffle through. There was not even an open book he could underline and jot notes in. There was only a metal letter-opener whose nicked blade was bent at the point. He thought about grabbing it and stabbing her. Perhaps that was the only way to get her to leave. But he couldn't even do that. If he did he'd be certain to hear her say something like "Lord, it's a marvel, it really is."

"What?" he'd shriek in response, berating himself for not having sense enough to keep his mouth shut.

"It's just amazing," she'd say, grabbing her chest where the blade had gone in. "You get excited your nipples turn harder'n peach pits. Those boogers almost stand up and salute sometimes. It's just amazing all the miracles us humans have to give thanks for."

The only other thing he could think of now was to resign himself to despair. That was probably the only way to get rid of her, to retreat so far back into himself that nothing could register, not even the need for breath. Then the chimes in the campanile began sounding, but they brought him no rescue; they merely told him it was noon and he was going to be late for his tennis match. Worse, they said he was already late calling his wife back.

Ready to submit to whatever this woman wanted, anything that might encourage her to leave, he turned around to face her, but what

he saw surprised him. Her hands lay primly in her lap, and she was
smiling at him sweetly. That made him even more nervous. He wanted to swallow or was it cough? He couldn't do either but strangling, he
thought, might be fine.

"You're touching," she said.

A ghost of a laugh came from him in defense.

"I like that," she told him. "No wonder you're such a pushover
can't make up your mind. But most good men are. You're tolerant.
The other kind is mean or too full of themselves and no fun. I used to
be married to one like that. Got rid of the sonofabitch, too," she said,
and he believed her. "But he wasn't anything like you. Not like you at
all."

"What about your husband? What's he like?" he asked to get
the discussion off himself.

"You never know," she said. "I don't. So I guess that's why I'm
married to him but keep coming here. It just hasn't turned out the
way I expected."

"You mean with your husband?"

"No, with you. You're a lot more bound than I thought."

"What do you mean?"

"You don't ever try to make me happy. You just ask questions."

"What do you want me to do? Propose we run off?"

"For heavensakes no," she said. "You'd drive me nuts. I've
just been hoping sometime you'd come see me on my turf, out there on
our farm. The rolling plains are a lot stouter place than you know, but
I guess you're too distracted with your new little lady to ever find that
out. You might, though, give it some thought. I'm often out fishing at
one of our tanks."

"Fishing?"

"Sure. Lots of women like to wet a hook. You'd know that if
you and the little wife had lived here longer and she had more earth
in her than I imagine she does."

"What do you mean? She was born here."

"I'll be damn," she said. "I didn't know that. You might have
more guts than I thought. So bring her out with you when you come
see me because when it's hot there's not much better than scooting
down in the mud by the water and getting all cool and damp.
Unfortunately my husband doesn't go for that much. So it'll just be
the three of us. You might come join me sometime. Will you?"

"Maybe," he said, and seeing the power had shifted back to

him, he took advantage of it and rose. He would usher her out and get on his way.

"Don't worry," she said, standing with him. She picked a mite of lint off his sleeve. "I mean it. Your bride's welcome, too. Who knows? She and I might even turn out friends. She does have a light touch, doesn't she?"

"Sure," he said. "Of course, she does."

"I'd better run along," she told him but didn't turn away. "You just keep being true to all your responsibilities," she said, squeezing the back of his arm. Then dryly she told him, "Some day you might even be glad. Those obligations'll give you something to lean on, especially down the line when, like my husband says, you can't get yourself up any more hard like a hammer."

All he could do was stare at her then quickly she kissed him. That had never happened before. Abruptly she turned toward the door. She cracked it open. Looking back at him, she said, "You might try scooting around in the mud sometime yourself. Most people I know have too much fat on their ass. Mud helps dry the problem out, Mother told me. She says you get too oily the cysts start, and that's no good when you're naked and want to be appealing. I don't know anyone likes looking at a butt full of red risings. But I wouldn't know about you. Like I said, you're a lot more bound than I thought. I will, though, see you later."

"Yes," he said firmly. "Next week in class."

"There, too," she said. "Incidentally, is that little bride of yours thin-hipped or broad?"

"Slightly thin," he said, drawing back.

"That's what I thought. You ought to be careful with her. My husband's built the same way, which may be why he turned into one of those troglodyte deals. Of course, you and I are more prone to appreciate pleasure, both of us tending down there toward the mesomorph," she said, laughing, and he laughed with her.

Then her features froze. Abruptly she turned away. She was suddenly going out the door, but in memory he could still see a smirk fluttering across her lips. She was not really trying to be a threat; she was just being playful. Or was she? Could that sudden look of sobriety or hurt or whatever it was have been another guise? Then he remembered his wife's own outrageous threat: I'll rip it out by the root and strangle her dead. The lady had a lot of earth in her – both of them – more than he'd thought.

Closing the door, he found himself smiling. Good adventure lay

ahead – I mean at home, he said, looking at his tennis racquet standing erect against the wall. In the line of his vision was also the phone,
and his heart was pounding his chest like a hammer.

Night and the Blood Washed Away

It's a beautiful country, he told her. The sunsets. India, Europe: no sunsets like these. Maybe only in Kenya.

She was not saying anything. As she had for so many years now, she was admiring the timbre of his voice: itself an ogive as much as sky: God's dome, receptive like the red wash turning violet through a splash of orange as the evening soaked through the fluid horizon.

He had been a pastor then a bishop. They had traveled the world on missions for the church, then later the government. They had never had children, and she had been the first, only, girl he had loved. Even as a child, he had told her father, the doctor in the small Texas town they had grown up in, that he was going to marry her. They went to college together. He became a minister, then a bishop, then now together with her a watcher of sunsets on the farm a friend had willed them.

Although one of them was going to die before the other, they seldom talked about that. There was no need to. One of them would be in Heaven, and later the other one would, too, but now they watched sunsets.

– The darkness comes, he told her. But morning, too. This sunset's a promise. This farm now our portion. The colors spreading up there, then dying into stars.

The mesquite branches resembled gossamer. A norther was coming. She wrapped her shawl around her shoulders, to let him know it was time to go back in.

– Yes, he said. Yes: to the house.

She pulled the shawl tighter around her. It had been a gift from Nehru.

– The Lord's been a mercy, he told her.

– Yes, she said, touching the back of his arm.

– Isn't this twilight a glory?

– It's lovely, she said, looking at him, then instantly they were facing each other directly.

A jolt broke through them.

— Yes, he told her. The twilight and the mercy of the blessing you've been.

Her thin lips parted. Through them came the shape of his name. He smiled at her. She brushed her hands gently through the fine white hair on the back of his head. His fingertips touched her wrist, where a vein swelled over the spur of a bone.

— I do think it's time we go in, she said.

— Yes. Soon.

— I'm getting cold, she told him. There's a chill coming on.

— Of course. Remember, he said, how Tuscany was in the winter. How the vines in the fields resembled an army of small crosses marching up the hills?

Then another time he was watching a sunset fade. Only a blush of its radiance was left when he noticed her absence. A dampness seeped out from his bones. He began shivering, thinking how strange it was that the chill came up from inside rather than down through skin.

— It's the opposite up there, he said, perplexed. There the night comes from far off and washes away the sky's blood. It's a mystery, he said. With us the chill comes out from the bones.

Patiently he waited for her answer, but soon he was shivering even more.

He pressed his soft arms against his chest. He was not used to being cold. She had always been the one to tell him a chill was coming, that it was time now to go on in. He needed something to brace against. The changeable sky seemed distant. He felt frail as he kept on pressing himself into himself until it seemed that his hands, pushing through the wind of his body, were going to meet.

A Gift from the Scorched Moon

When I woke up, my wife was hanging upside down from the ceiling like a bat. In the dimness her buttocks looked huge until, still waking up, I realized that what I was seeing as the gigantic curve of her rump was really the mounded mass of her back. I relaxed.

I wondered, however, what Marshelaine was doing up there. The sag of her nightgown resembled old skin about to peel off, but I knew this was winter and we had not gone out; besides, we owned no sunlamp, so she couldn't have been molting. But what puzzled me most was how she was holding onto the rafter. Even if she had had grips up there, she should not have been able to hold on for long. Her arms are so weak she can't even do pushups and has trouble with situps. Her pectoral growths, though, are nothing short of magnificent: sculptured fins, gracefully globular.

Her lack of movement began to intrigue me. There was no tremble of strain, no swaying except now and then a ripple in her gownskin, and that was caused, I supposed, by convection currents in the upper part of our room.

I was getting lonely. I asked her what she was doing up there, but she didn't answer, so I asked her again softly; I didn't want to alarm her. Her gown, as if answering, began fluttering. She was awake, but I still could not hear her. Suddenly a sharp pain pricked long through my ears. It wouldn't stop. The pain turned shrill, a terribly high-pitched tone. I went dizzy. Vertiginous, I asked her desperately what she was doing up there. The shrillness kept drilling through me. "Shut up!" I yelled and the pain stopped. The piercing shriek had become my own drumming pulse.

"I'm sorry," she blandly replied.

"That's better," I told her, thankful that she was becoming less and less like a bat. I wasn't up to dealing with a load of guano.

"I thought I heard termites," she said.

"We don't have any termites."

She yawned then informed me, "The moon was too bright. I couldn't sleep." She was as insouciant as a bagworm on juniper.

Reminding myself that she resembled a bat more than a parasite, I asked her, "Why didn't you pull the curtains to?"

"I didn't want to wake you."

"Thank you," I said but wished I were Plastic Man so I could stretch my arm out long enough to whack her gelatinous ass.

"I'll be down in a moment," she told me. "The moon's passed most of the way by already. So go on back to sleep."

"How?"

She did not answer, and it was all I could do not to yell again at her. Actually, that's an exaggeration. It was easy to refrain from yelling, primarily because I found myself suddenly suffering from a temporary case of acute lockjaw. I've had it before, but it goes away quickly. Usually. I asked her if she wanted me to come up there with her. She said she didn't think so, that she'd be down shortly. The vertigo returned. I swung my left leg off the bed so my foot felt the floor. That helped.

"Do go on back to sleep," she said.

So I did, and the next thing I knew she was lying beside me. The closeness of her created what I have to call intimacy. The toenail of her big toe was scratching my ankle, and I knew that she was also asleep. I felt more peaceful than a martyr in the bosom of the Lord. I had no desire to wake up and leave. I mumbled to her, in the moonlight washing palely over our sheeted bodies, that if some disturbance came – knock on door, ringing of phone – that I might not respond but would stay loyal to the respite of our tangential slumber. She laughed, and I swelled large, but not as large as the gigantic spread of the vacuum where we lay. I shrank, then at once I felt tiny and huge, and in that moment I noticed that her toenail had left my ankle. I moved my foot to find it but couldn't and felt, somehow profoundly, the sadness of the foolishness of mortality. There was no vertigo this time to distract me from it. So, being a reasonable man, I went back to sleep.

Then the phone rang. Rang again perhaps.

I woke up.

I imagined my wife's toenail had become a pulpit, a powerful idol. I didn't know any more if I were still hearing the phone ring or only remembering hearing it ring.

I didn't know what to think. I wasn't sure what I felt. The ringing synchronized with my pulse. The two were indistinguishable but at least I knew they were mine. Mine! Both of them. Mine. Phone. Blood.

Held in communion and trust(?) with Marshelaine. Phone and blood, ringing and pumping. I turned dizzy again.

You – whoever hears me – would have, too, because I had just discovered that I had been shot. There was a hole, strangely clean in the moonwash spread through the room, a hole where my left nipple had been. Perhaps, now that I think about it, it *was* my nipple, shadowed. But there was no pain. And the phone had stopped ringing. In memory, however, I heard the sound. It was a cough more than a report. Continuing to hear it again and again, I knew that the gun was no modern weapon but a blunderbuss whose ball and wad had plundered my chest.

Footsteps were coming down the hall. Marshelaine's footsteps. I knew they were hers even though she was trying to trick me, trying to walk like a cripple. She was cackling too. The cackle was living outside her throat, somewhere between her and me.

Brazenly she snorted, "Something wrong?" My wound instantly healed. I wilted, flutters down my chest, up my neck, the disappearance of groin. Her toenail scratched my knees. I wondered where she really was.

My husband's a lunatic. None of this happened. That's why I'm going to

Then I heard the toilet flush and saw Marshelaine coming back to bed. There was a toothbrush in her hair. She was coming toward our bed with a toothbrush in her hair, and a pair of Mortimer Snerd falseteeth bucked out of her mouth. The overbite was remarkable. Fingers clenching hips, she sneered like Dracula through the chompers: "I trink you blooood."

I laughed and, full of play, she threatened me again then jerked her foot up on the bed and began hissing, her fingers clawing, and suddenly I noticed she was stark raving naked, and if I had not been laughing so hard I would have prayed; maybe I did, but all I remember saying was asking her in a stutter if she weren't cold.

She blared out again, "I trink you blooood!"

I told her, "Come lie with me."

"I trink you blooood!"

"Come here, Naked Lady."

"I bite you in the neck, I trink you blooood."

"Shut up and come here," I said, reaching up for her.

Clawing me, she said, "I take your essssence into meeee."

I laughed, as I often do when I achieve, without feeling lusty, the mystical state of tumescence.

"My my," she said, spitting the toy teeth out on the carpet. "My my," she said, admiring the teepeed sheet. "My my my."

Actually it was my knee making the sheet rise. But I didn't tell her that because my knee at that moment was serving a valuable function. It was protecting me from any onslaught she might make. Of course, my knee wasn't really protecting anything. If she had wanted to hurt me, she could have. Easily. Even in play. But she didn't, at least then. She only smiled, warmly, and removing the toothbrush from her hair and dropping it, she said with admirable piety, "Shall I minister to you now?"

I blinked. She was no vampire. She was a saint. We were both in the bosom of the Lord: ourselves. Perhaps we still are, though things are not the same. The Lord's bosom is not as ample as some have reported.

I just read Jerome's palaver. It was noticeably accurate for him. As usual, though, he left out what I call the flesh. He also put phrases in my mouth that I never uttered. For instance, he said that I spoke of ministering to him. I actually said, "Let's screw." I love him. The room was our monastery. For then nothing else counted.

To the flesh!

Our bedroom, as he indicated, has a beamed ceiling. Redwood beams stained richer than natural redwood. The color of deep passion has been frozen on them. Also in the room, as he noted, is our king-size bed. Its sheets are Virgin Mary blue; and our bedspread, accordioned at the foot, matches the beams in color. To the left of the bed (left to whoever's on bottom), under the high windows, are two black-lacquered chests-of-drawers with hunks of quartz at each end; and in the middle, straddling the pudendal crack between the chests, is my jewelry box which Jerome also uses to store his cufflinks, studs and collar stays, along with two steel pennies and an old quarter-sized parking lot token. I shan't describe my jewelry, because I've rarely used it since that night. On the other side of the room is a walk-in closet which Jerome uses and a stand-outside-and-reach-in closet which I use. Shoes clutter the floors of both closets. On the walls is an even spread of paint, the color of rich cream. Somehow it seems nourishing, more organic than the sheetrock it covers. Radiating through the bathroom door are sunyellow walls, a copper-colored bathtub matched by a copper-colored lavatory whose sides plane out severely to the walls. The towels I use are any number of colors. The toilet seat, which you can't see from the bedroom, is black. Jerome calls it Satan's Lid. I've termed it Luther's Grail. We seem unable to accept it as merely a necessary fixture. We need to glorify it, no matter how rudely.

On the night he was describing, Jerome was wearing a pair of limegreen shortsleeve pajamas with boxer-type bottoms. The middle button's missing from the shirt. Maybe that's the wound he referred to, but I doubt it. He wasn't joking about the wound. If he was, however, he shouldn't have. There's a touch of crime in my heart.

Closer to the flesh now. Jerome's chest is fairly smooth. He's not very hairy except in the cranial and pubic regions, the two areas that mean the most to me. His hair, which I trim, is light brown except when he's by the window in the sunlight, and there it turns either blond or auburn. Mine is dark brown and I usually wear it drawn back in a snood. He told me once the bun looked like a chimpanzee's tit bunched in a large rotten pasty. Perhaps it does. I can't help it; I love him. Besides, he was only joking and I enjoy his foolishness. It's about all we have, and sometimes I think it's enough. Sometimes.

I read what she wrote. I don't trust her. And I no longer care who's reading this, a careless diary from a commune of two. We have no children. We shall never have any. And I have no job. I don't need one. Ours is a rarefied existence. At least that's what we tell ourselves. Neither one of us, however, is capable of much truth. No one else we used to know was either.

I can't think straight. I think in circles, and I'm undecided if that's a sign of degeneration or creeping wisdom. What difference does it make? I'm only scribbling on our way to death. We're getting closer. I suspect that not much more remains except embalming.

To the flesh, she said. I don't know whether to admire her or have pity for her. I know very little, except that the air we breathe is fresh enough. I admit, however, that part of me is repulsed by the kind of honesty I've just displayed. Nevertheless I don't know what I was going to say. I can't think straight. I think in circles, and those circles, lopsided like the journeys of Earth around the sun, move, they move! They move like the spiders she and I contain. They are feasting, but their gnawing does little more than make me itch inside.

Whatever Jerome says, I still love him.

She's trying to distract me. I can tell it each night when we go to bed. Each day. We rarely leave the bedroom. She never mentions her friends. I don't suppose I do either. We're bewildered. Our life is calm. Like that night. We kissed goodnight the way we've kissed goodnight thousands of times, and I was struck by the niceness of the gesture and by the sureness of the intense gyrations that followed.

More and more I recognize the absence of stillness in our situation. It's as if we're retreating, not out of fear, but in motion toward some source. I've lost all sense of society. The world has become private, and Marshelaine's the one who's moved me, moved me toward this privacy that seems more and more like a source. I'm not sure, however, that she knows what she's doing. I feel afloat, and she seems distant. We are calm for now, but I don't trust her. The calmness resembles sleep.

For chrissake he's the one trying to fool me. Calmness! Sheeee! He's afraid to admit that I might be destroying him. Not that I am, but he's scared to admit that I might be. Perhaps I am. Perhaps he deserves ripping up. He's foolish. No spiders are inside him. The spiders are me. I wonder if diseases are hiding on the hairs of my limbs. I like to kiss him and to rub myself on him. In fact, I like kissing him as much as I like screwing him.

I itch.

I think he's infecting me with something. I don't care about leaving this room either. We have enough food stored up, and if we run out we can order some more or eat each other. We do that anyway. I don't love him. I hate him.

But last night when he was crawling the walls I laughed. He asked me what was funny. After thinking about it, I told him I was not sure. If he had been crawling up the walls in frenzy, I could have told him, but he wasn't. His progress up the sheetrock was masterful. His confidence was breathtaking. I would never attempt to climb a wall. I don't know how he does it. I'm not even sure why he does it. He doesn't climb walls to release energy. Maybe he climbs them for distraction. Sometime I'll ask him. I think he'd tell me the truth. And if he'd only ask, I'd tell him how I hang from the ceiling. I wonder how he does it. If he weren't asleep now I'd examine his hands to see if the pads are gummy but he's a light sleeper and I don't want to wake him. I'm horny. And I have nothing else to write. The moonwash is so pale I can scarcely see the notebook. I don't know if I've made sense or not, but such is the anguish of those who no longer masturbate. I quit fiddling with myself when Jerome and I quit society.

I should have stirred, because I was also awake and sexually aroused that night. I thought she was asleep. She was mumbling. I should have known she was awake. Maybe it's best, though, that I didn't insert my member in her. I rather enjoyed the tension. It made me trust her, so much so that I told her several times I loved her. I haven't told her that out loud in a long time. I hope she knows it, though. . . . To the flesh, as she says. It's as if . . . No. Not really. I started to say that we seem like strangers, but that's not true. I'm not certain what I mean. There's a rhythm of ignorance running through me. It's related to the spiders which she, for some reason, calls herself. She's wrong in that. She doesn't have anything to do with spiders. She's healthy, but she also gives off an air of frailty. I should help make her stronger. I should show her that I can be rough. I should maul her a time or two. That would be good for both of us. It would help clear the fog. It would also be better than making these goddamned New Year's resolutions out of season. I say they're out of season. Maybe they're not. We don't have a calendar. Just each other's body. I hope she enjoys mine as much as I enjoy hers. When I maul her I'll find out.

Jerome's a liar. We're not in retreat, and if we were I doubt that he would survive very long. He's too guarded. If he ever let himself go, the moonlight would drown him. I might have to do away with him, and soon. If you're reading this, Jerome, my warning is a gesture of love. I want you to try to maul me. That's a matter of necessity. Or repressed hate. Hell! I'm beginning to write like him. I don't know where he got the idea about a source. I don't believe in one and never did. That's not true. I don't know what I believe. I *am* beginning to become like him.

We're ghosts.

Between my last statement and this one we screwed, so we're not ghosts after all. At least we weren't for a spell. We might be now.

I still think I'll have to kill him. To save myself. I won't feel alive if I don't. Perhaps later, when I'm up on the ceiling, I'll drop down and crush him. If I aim right, I'll be able to snap one of his ribs so it'll puncture his heart. Or lungs. That would work just as well, though not as quickly. His pain might even invigorate me into an orgasm; I enjoy them tremendously. There's only one hitch. I'm afraid that on fatal impact he won't ejaculate. If he doesn't, the murder will be in vain, will prove he's not mortal, because mortals leave wet stains, they *are* wet stains, and if he's not mortal, he'll get revenge on me. He won't kill me. He'll harass me. But not bloodily. He'll harass me by doing nothing. Anticipation of the chaotic release of power that's sure to come will torture me mercilessly, so much that I won't be able to stand his acts of kindness: the lovely way he feels my hair, the vigorous way he slaps my butt, the full smoothness of his lips everywhere; and if I tell him to leave me alone, he won't answer, but he rarely does anyway. The torture has already begun, and I haven't even attempted to smash him.

Vaguely I remember telling him I love him. I shiver queasily. I'm not sure if I love him or not. If I don't crush him, I may never know.

We're both on our stomachs and naked as infants, which in terms of moontime we are. We've been stillborn.

She no longer hangs on the ceiling. She whimpers a lot. I thought at first her sinuses were infected or that pneumonia was swilling her lungs or locking her joints. I know now I was wrong. She's afraid there's no source we're heading for. She's mistaken. There is.

Her life is in bed, but she still needs rest. She's not as courageous as I thought she was. The spiders are in her, too, and I understand now how she hung on the ceiling. She wasn't a bat, she was a spider. Her size confused me. She can't hang up there any more. The spiders are inside her. She's controlling them. In the past they controlled her. They were what was making her hang, but now that they're inside her they can force her to do little. Nevertheless, she seems frailer.

Her look is unsettling! She stares at me, but I don't think I register. The brown in her eyes is washing out, and sometimes they appear to be holes through which I can see, however hazily, the pillow behind them. Perhaps it's something else. Perhaps I'm glimpsing a part of her brain. Whatever it is, it's wet.

Something, I think, is going to happen. I have no idea what. I do know, though, that I can't crawl the walls as well as I used to. A lot of times I slide. My hands have become extremely clammy. To keep from falling, I have to press hard. I don't think it's worth it.

Last night I fell. The walls are out now. My area for maneuvering is narrowing, but I feel freer than ever. The sensation, however, is not altogether pleasant. I seem desperate to myself, even hysterical at times, and yet I'm in love with Marshelaine more powerfully than ever. I realize that that might be merely a reflex response. I don't trust myself well enough yet to tell her how I feel. I'm thirsty. Her lips look wet. Or scorched. She's shivering. She's afraid there's no source. She's wrong. We're already at the source, but she's still thinking in terms of a journey. She's afraid she'll never arrive. She already has. We arrived together. The world here is now, without walls that matter. I accept that. Perhaps I even like it.

What a shame. He's more vulnerable than ever and doesn't know it. He's not even aware that part of him slipped into me through the holes in my eyes. He thinks the holes were illusions. They were real, and now they've closed, and he's been diminished. I'm glad, though, that he's begun telling me he loves me. I only wish I had the nerve to try to kill him. But I don't. If I did, I would be equal to the love he pretends.

I can't seem to stop sweating.

She's naked. I love her. She's moist. She's alive. And in good spirits now, too. She was hanging from the ceiling again earlier. And several times she dropped. Almost on me. It cost me my breath, but it made her laugh. In fact, she laughs a lot lately, especially when I tell her I love her. But I laugh too.

Last night Jerome died inside me. He's going to do it again tonight, he said.

Last night I felt a spider leave. Marshelaine took it from me and then discharged it in the toilet. I think we both felt better for the transaction. . . . I keep fogging up. The big event I was expecting has not occurred yet. I'm not sure it will, but I'm getting used to its absence. The fog! Source; source. I don't think the source exists any more. I know it doesn't. Marshelaine knows it, too. She's known it longer than I have; admitted the absence longer. And when she laughs now, she seems nervous.

She's reading this while I write it. She told me to say that she's given up the ceiling. She said the ceiling's as useless as virginity: at best an eccentric pretense. I suppose she's right. She often is. After tonight I'll write no more in our diary. I see no reason to record either failures or successes. I no longer believe in extremes, and whatever happens between extremes is a private matter. She just said I sounded as if I'm in despair. I am. I am also happy. She said that doesn't make sense. I told her I'm avoiding extremes. She wasn't impressed. She did ask me, however, what I thought about love; and I'm telling

her now that I believe more in a kiss than in love. She says I'm wise.
I accept her judgment, however ineffectual it may be. She also just
told me that she'll kill me tonight, and I'm telling her that if she tries
I might once more believe in extremes.

It finally happened. Jerome is paralyzed, and I am now free. I
can do anything to him I want. There are many possibilities; the most
intriguing are sexual. He can only move his toes, but I can move all of
me, several parts at once; and since this morning, when I discovered
he could no longer move, I have done just that. I have danced for him
and on him. I have writhed against him and by his side. I have also
shaved off all his hair. And if I am not mistaken, I think I have seen
him smile a great number of times. I hope I have, because the tears I
can't stop are all for him.

No Accounting Shall Be Asked

I don't know why he did it," Buzzern Erly said, swallowing a lemon-drop, "so quit pestern me about it."

"I'm not pesterin' you. I just asked a simple question."

"And I told you, Homer, I don't know!"

"Sheeeee," taking off his frameless glasses, Homer said, "Harris *is* your son."

Buzzern pulled a wrinkled handkerchief from his hippocket. He snorted in it then rubbed his nostrils red. Squinting, Homer stared at him until Buzzern snapped, "Never indicated otherwise, did I?"

"Well, gawwd-damn, a feller don't break a guy's back with a tire tool for nothin'."

"Didn't say he did."

"Then why the hell'd he do it?"

"Put them glasses back on," Buzzern told him.

"Don't change the subject. I am family."

"I admit that."

"Hell," Homer said, snatching a fistful of dewy Bermuda grass, "no wonder Harris to end up in jail."

"I resent that," Buzzern said, pushing against the arms of his cedar-planked lawnchair. "That bastard grease-monkey had it comin'."

Blowing, Homer fogged his thick lenses, rubbed them clean on his white starched shirt. "How's that?" he asked, satisfied that he was finally going to get some information.

Buzzern dug in his shirtpocket for another lemondrop.

"How you mean?" Homer asked again.

"He's queerer'n a three-dollar bill."

"Awww, then how come Harris to be arrested? I mean if all he did was cream some candy-ass."

Buzzern knuckled at his scorched pale eyes, glazed now with a film. "Harris is too," he said flatly. "Let's go in get our coffee. I feel bound."

Their wives were sitting at the hexagonal oak table on the sunporch.

"And you didn't," Ditie asked her sister, "even get to talk to him?"

Madlin jerked her gray and white flowered rayon dress off her hips. "We didn't even know he was around here."

"Funny. Fella at the gas station last week asked me weren't I related to'm."

The screendoor scratched open.

"Anybody phone?" Buzzern asked.

Nodding, Madlin daubed her thin lips with a napkin. "If we want, we can see Son after noon. They give'm some kinda drug last night."

"To quiet'm?" Homer broke in.

"Reckon."

"Mention any more about the state hospital?"

"Some," Madlin told him. "Nothing's definite yet."

Leaving the sunporch to get two more coffee mugs, Buzzern called back, "Iced or hot?"

"Iced," Homer said.

"Hunh. How Harris has his."

"You leave Son alone!"

"All I mentioned was iced coffee."

"Sorry," Madlin said. "Thought you was referrin' to somethin' other."

A shadow bit across the table, and the screen laid a haze on the yard. Homer sat down but the women ignored him.

"Oh me," Madlin sighed.

"It's all right," Ditie said, patting her sister's wrist, "we're all of us just hunksa dumb meat." Wincing, Madlin broke her stare at the open-necked bodice of Ditie's orange and white seersucker housedress. "Are. Takes an effort to do more'n gobble each other up."

"But I don't know. For some reason Son seemed to always resent me."

"Now don't go seekin' blame," Ditie told her. "He's grown and you're not responsible for what took place."

"Maybe it was just because I'm a woman."

"Fiddle! Now I didn't rush over here to hear you talk crazy."

"I think maybe it is he's got a hatred for women how come all this to take place."

Leaning back, Ditie laughed. "For cryin' out loud, Madlin. If you really wanta know, I can tell ya how back when he was thirteen-fourteen he'd bike over the house'n walk in on me soakin' in the tub."

Homer chuckled but Madlin, sprung rigid, sneered, "If I'da known that I'da hurrahed'm for it no end."

"Well, I did it for ya, but I'm thinkin' now I might not ought to have."

"Hnh. You can see what it led to. Somethin' worse, far as I'm concerned, than breakin' a guy's back. I don't wanta even think about it."

Smiling and rubbing the hang of her bosom, Ditie gazed out at the sun-bathed yard. She ran her palms down the table's beveled edges and looked across at her sister. "You know, Madlin, I reckon it's a crime Daughter was married and gone those years. None'a this might've happened if he coulda walked in on her."

"That's disgusting!"

"Hooey on you," Homer said. Madlin faced him sourly. Rising to meet her glare, he told her, "Aint nobody gonna say Homer Oldfather's daughter's disgustin'. His wife either. I've seen'm both naked and always considered it a pleasure."

Shuddering, Madlin twisted away, gave him the hunch of her back. Already flared across the table, he caught himself on the wooden surface. "Pew! You always have been ice water."

"Homer!" Ditie cried, tugging his trousers to pull him back down in the chair.

Veins broke across his blown cheeks. He thrust himself up again, but Madlin stared flintily at him. He lost his voice, bit his tongue and yelled, then crashed back down to where Ditie was fighting to pull him.

"Homer!"

"She –"

"Settle down!"

"All I was was bein' funny and she goes accusin' me –"

"Nobody," Madlin informed him, "accused you of nothin'!"

"Then I'm sorry," he told her belligerently.

Kicking the door, Buzzern said, "What's goin' on here?"

Madlin snapped, "Homer got testy."

"Huh. Didn't think ya had it inya," he said, thumping down the mugs and scraping his chair to the table.

"Let's go in the other room," Ditie said, touching Homer's thigh.

"No," Madlin told her, but Homer went with her.

Buzzern and Madlin avoided facing each other. Their fingers trailed blindly over the roughness of their stoneware mugs, made by Harris his year in college. That was eighteen months ago. Since then they had rarely seen him. He'd written from Austin at Christmas that he'd gotten a job working sound for a band.

Tucking his chin, Buzzern coughed to clear his raw throat.

"If Son takes care-a his soul," Madlin said, "the Lord'll see'm through and us too."

"I aint worried about us."

"You might be. There's some shame here."

"That what," his voice rose, "that church's been teachin' ya?"

"Don't criticize it, it's been a rock." He sucked loudly off his palate. "It has," she said. "It's been a harbor."

"It's been a crocka sour shit."

"Don't talk like that."

"Has. You been goin' to ruin ever since you got involved."

"I've been in it ... all ... my ... life, Buzzern."

"No ya aint. Harris started gettin' hair on his body and you commenced to go nuts. That's been – god! *years*."

"Hush! I never have nagged you to be saved."

Digging his thumbnail into his forefinger's pad, he said he considered that fortunate. His eyes felt gummy, but he refused to rub them.

Regretting, however, having snapped at her, he forced himself to squeeze her nape. Sometimes, he remembered, she liked that, but this time all she did was sip coffee.

He refilled her cup. They glanced at each other.

"If you'd just open up your heart," she said, "and ask for strength."

Stung, he bellowed, "I don't feel weak."

"Son needs us."

"I aint abandon'm," he said, hearing wind and smelling red clay dust. His tight shoulders ached, but he wrenched back his neck to fight the pain and watched her firmly brush the white flowers on the sunken front of her dress.

"Buzzern?"

"What?" he asked, straining to stay erect and realizing what a great distance there was between them. He suddenly felt small, inadequate in her presence, and noticed how the tip of her nose had begun to hook. She, like no one else, had always been able to make him uneasy. He wrapped his fingers around the cold stoneware mug and flinched when, touching the backs of his liverspotted hands, she told him:

"When you go see Son, I think it would be better if you went by yourself. Don't you?"

In spite of the bad brunch – powdered eggs and lukewarm coffee – he tried to maintain the look of a gentleman. They had taken away his tie, but he kept the collar of his violet and white striped shirt buttoned. He was sitting erect on the cot and staring foully at the blanched lips of the toilet bowl whose porcelain throat was rusted above the low level of water. His dyed black hair, curling over the tops of his ears, came down fluffily on his short forehead. His small wiry body appeared anxious to spring. The soiled hollows around his aquamarine eyes gave him the look of desperate blindness. He smoothed his yellow trouserlegs, smudged with grease around the waistband. Remembering the lovely and powerful twang of bone cracking, he heard a guitar string snapping.

Buzzern came, heels clicking, to the barred door. Keeping his formal bearing, Harris rose. Buzzern twisted his lips, squinted as if he couldn't decide whether to frown gravely or force out a smile.

"Top o' the afternoon's morning," Harris said, transforming to brightness as the deputy unlocked the door.

Nodding, Buzzern came in. The door clicked to, and the deputy left, his keys dangling beneath his belly's sag.

"I'm pleased you came," Harris said.

"Your Uncle Homer's outside."

"Show him in. Please do.'

"Better if we visit alone."

"Then please have a seat," he said grandly, motioning to the sheetless cot, "have a seat, humble though accommodations are."

They sat down, surrounded by the rough gray concrete walls.

"I take it," Buzzern said, "you feel –"

"I do. Perfectly fine. In fact, clean," he giggled, pleating his trousers. "And how, might I ask, are Homer and Ditie?"

"Fine."

"Splendid, they're charming. I'd really love seeing them both. Does Aunt Ditie still have that fabulous body?"

"It's ample. Enough. Up front."

"And down below where wild flowers grow?"

"It'll do to hold on to come a storm."

"Delicious. Just absolutely delicious. I do hope I get to see them."

"You got your own sit-y-ation."

"I do, don't I? But my god, it's not all that serious. I just absolutely refuse to be treated like a whore. I do, however, hope the poor chap doesn't expire."

"Does or not, you got trouble."

"Oh dear – everything so precarious."

Buzzern snatched the lemondrop package from his pocket. "Talk nat'r'l, Harris. You sound like a goddurn fairy."

"I am, Dad."

"Well, I'd prefer you not soundin' like it. Hypocrisy sometimes has its advantage."

"But –"

"Shut up!" and Harris flinched; his features seemed ready to drop off his skull. "Need a lawyer?"

Cringing, Harris said he had one, "and he's Ch- Ch- Christian and st- straight."

"I aint inter-ested in's personal habits. He good?"

"I- I- I had him be- be- before."

"Good," Buzzern said, doubting him and popping his thumbnail against a tartared canine.

"D-d-dad?"

"What?" but Harris didn't answer. Vigorously Buzzern sniffed his nostrils clear, ground his teeth. It hurt him to hear his son stutter, but it hurt worse to think that the only way Harris could keep from it was to talk fancy. For a long time he had tried to discourage the airs, was aggravated that Madlin had never been willing to help him. Glancing at him, he thought his son looked ready to throw himself bawling upon an invisible lap.

Harris trembled, but Buzzern knew it was more out of some weird rage than grief. During the school years, he had seen him like this before, had known of the fights his son had had, with other boys, with the principal once, and a couple times Harris had hit girls; but he had never been trouble at home. He had made things for the house: the oak table, coffee mugs, and some painted pictures that were pretty but didn't make sense. For a time Buzzern had hoped Harris would settle down when he went off to college, but that hadn't worked out either. Harris had said Wichita Falls was just like Decatur: "They should put up a sign saying *Welcome: The Place of the Friendly Dead.*"

Buzzern kept grinding his teeth, and when Harris slumped Buzzern pressed his son's spine and, giving with the pressure, Harris came back erect while Buzzern recalled with confusion that his son hadn't had so many fights. Wa'n't such a fighter no more'n most boys. He's just different. My son goddoggit. But he still couldn't figure out yesterday; they hadn't even been expecting him home.

Harris moved his leg against his, and Buzzern crushed the lemondrop package in his fist. "Hell! There's another'n left in it," he said, feeling the lump inside.

Harris smiled at him, sweetly Buzzern thought, swallowing away the residue of sugar in his throat.

"Have it yourself," he said, stuffing the crumpled soft package at his son's chest where he expected to find a pocket. None was there. Rigid again, Harris took the package from him.

"It wouldn't, by any chance," he said resonantly, "be coated with dope, would it?"

Buzzern snuffed. "If it was, I wouldn't give it to ya." Harris giggled, then knuckling the corners of his eyes, Buzzern told him curtly, "I'da ate it myself."

"Let's go fishin' out the lease," Buzzern said, irritated, walking across the sun-browned lawn of the square.

"There're snakes out there," Homer said.

"Might be."

"Whyn't we play dominoes?"

" 'Cause Madlin took the doubles and made a decoration out of'm."

"Listen, blind as I am, I wouldn't see a snake till I stepped on it."

"Hell, what you need's a dog. Let's go the cafe."

Burned by a windgust, they crossed the street. Homer squeezed Buzzern's shoulder. "I'm awful sorry. My heart goes out to ya."

"Well, where we're goin' they got great pe-pecan p-pie."

Madlin kept trying to get him to go to prayer meeting, but Buzzern said he didn't have any desire for it.

"More'n any other time we need to go."

"I aint anxious for more noise."

"You hadn't even met our new preacher. Young fella."

"I don't intend meetin' him neither. Won't be any different'n the old one'r they wouldn'ta hired'm."

"You ought to at least go for Son's sake. He needs our prayers."

"No!"

"Buzzern, I'm tellin' ya, he needs us to go."

"If you're so damn inter-ested in's soul, how come you not to go see'm?"

"I'm sure you gave him proper advice."

"Didn't give'm any advice a-tall. I give'm a lemondrop which it might be puny, but it's a helluva lot more'n you ever did."

Slapping her navy-blue polka-dotted dress down her hips, she asked once more, "You goin'r not?"

"No! Me'n Homer'll play Canasta. Ditie goin' with ya?"

"I'd hoped so. Why?"

"Hoped you'd leave'r here to liven us up."

"What's that mean?"

"More'n I ever hope to accomplish."

"That's disgusting."

"May be, but I'm still not goin' to no prayer meetin'."

"One of the main reasons you should's in jail."

"Was. Gettin' ready to be took to the state hospital."

"Well, my prayers'll be for ya."

"Fine. But don't make'm loud. Sound carries at night."

Madlin left shortly and took Ditie with her, also Homer, who told Buzzern, "Guess I'll go too. Enjoy takin' off my specs'n listenin' – especially when the meetin' gets stout."

Alone, he walked several times around the white frame structure whose north corner had settled. He walked up on the creaking porch and went back in, noticing a spiderweb above the door. In the kitchen he poured a Dr Pepper and quickly drank it. Sucking ice, he wandered through the four rooms but couldn't find what he was looking for. Maybe it was only distraction he sought, but the old furniture and painted-over wallpaper were too familiar to provide it. Kicking off his shoes, he reclined on the bed, reached in his pocket for a lemondrop, then remembered he'd given Harris his last one, and the drugstore was already closed. The only other place carrying them was a Fina station on the highway.

Agitated, he pulled himself up, stuffed his feet in his shoes, and left the house. On the way he'd be passing the station where Harris had had his trouble. A breeze fanned him through the dusk. The walk

was downhill. His shins began aching. Cars hushed past him. Noticing
that buttercups had sprung up in the yards, he stepped off the curb.
The flowers had always reminded him of yellow soundless mouths too
delicate to scream.

Turning a corner, he noticed Mary Martha Carter, stooped,
white hair frizzy, watering her purple phlox.

"Hidy," she said, shooing her cocker spaniel away from her
house-slippered feet. "Madlin gone to prayer meetin'?"

"Has."

"Well, I'm prayin' for y'all too. Harris been always one of my
favorites." He nodded thanks. "Y'all take care now." She squirted the
dog.

Stiff and sore, he continued in the gutter. Father the most
unusual son in town, he thought, but that didn't affect much. Might
be a widower too'n not know it. Some disaster could've happened on
the way to church. Whatever, he knew he'd do what he did: walk
toward the highway for lemondrops; go to the bank to cash his Social
Security check; continue to work part time at the lumberyard; think
about playing with Madlin on the bed but not doing it except on an
occasional Wednesday night when the prayer meeting was more glorious than usual. Looking up from the pavement, he saw a service station attendant, corpulent and tall, standing in front of the pumps. He
sauntered toward the street as Buzzern came nearer.

"Evenin'."

"Evenin'," Buzzern answered.

Ambling past, he heard the man call, "Hey!" He turned to see
him wave him back. "C'mon over here."

Buzzern tensed. "I will," he said, "you sell lemondrops."

"I said come over here."

"What for?"

"You Mr. Erly?"

"I am."

"Then come over here. I gotta watch the pumps'r I'd come
across the street for ya, with ya."

"I see," Buzzern said dryly, briefly amused to think that his
son would've already crossed the street, clobbered the man with a tool
or fists or feet, and called the police and ambulance himself. Spurred
by the notion, he started across and the man, seeing he was coming,
headed back toward the pumps. They met beneath the shelter.

The man, much larger than Buzzern, growled, "Name's
Deacon, Jermyn Deacon. Thought I recognized you."

"Don't recollect we've met."

"Aint. I just had this place a month. Been livin' in Alvord. How I recognize you is because your son favors ya. He been around here a lot last couple weeks."

"Has?"

"Nights. Five-six times."

"I didn't know that."

"Well, he has. Didn't think we had his kind around these parts."

"How you mean that?" he asked Deacon's solidly massive belly.

"Fairy," Deacon said and spat.

"Don't think I heard ya."

"Said fairy. Sissy ass."

Looking down, Buzzern grinned. The gentlemanly thing to do, he thought, would be to insert a two-by-four down this Jermyn Deacon's throat and ask him to speak around it.

"Sissy ass, hnh?" he said, glancing up.

"I allow I said that" came through colorless chapped lips.

"If that's so," Buzzern said, straight up at him, "what's that make your fella who's gonna have trouble walkin' forever?"

"My nephew."

"I see," Buzzern said, surprised. Recovering, he told him, "Reckon that makes at least two-a them kind we got around here, don't it?"

Dean spat out a brown viscous wad. "You know I'll have to kill your son, don't ya."

"How's that?"

"Have to kill'm. Courts fuckt up all our justice."

"Psh," Buzzern laughed, "people like you, Deacon, are just a bother. You're gonna make me sorry my boy didn't get you in the bargain too. But fat a man as you are, a tiretool'd probably just get lost in ya."

"Wanta try?"

"I don't have to," Buzzern said, looking toward the road. "Don't need a tiretool. Match'd do fine."

"Huh. You'd be the first to go up."

"No, sir. I can move. I aint a lard-ass like you. Now what'd ya want? I'm gettin' anxious for my lemondrops."

"Nothin'. Just wanted to caution you about your son – what might happen."

"Anything else?"

"Naw."

Buzzern started away.

"Hey, Erly," Deacon called and Buzzern turned around. "Your son does favor ya – talks just like ya," his voice rose. "You see what it got him, don'ya?"

Buzzern hacked his throat clear and spat, refused to back down to Deacon's glare. "He's walkin'."

"Not very far he aint."

"Well, you'n me aint coverin' much territory ourselves, are we?"

"What'd you say?" Deacon sounded vicious. Swallowing, Buzzern felt sick. "Hawnh?"

"Y-you heard me."

"C'mon back here."

"Move yourself, Fat-boy," and suddenly Buzzern lost a feeling of connection with his son. He couldn't understand the homosexual thing at all. He thought he'd rather hug most anything than someone like Deacon or his nephew, but he also couldn't dismiss his son as queer, whatever they call'm. That stuff, far as he could see, didn't nail him. Harris was his son and he loved him. Like Madlin, he thought. Loved her longer. Don't feel no clearer for it, though.

"Ya know, Erly," Deacon said, slouching up to him, "hear 'at affliction your son's got runs in families." He bumped against Buzzern, who jammed his hand in his trouserpocket. "Git ya hand outa there." Buzzern looked down at the pavement, black-ribboned by tiretracks. "What ya got in 'at pocket? Portable beaver?"

Buzzern ground his teeth. He smelled oil, then jumped when he felt Deacon's hand clamp his nape. "No, you fat sonofabitch, I got in it a antique Kentucky longrifle."

Gripping the back of his head with his huge callused hand, Deacon said, "What you call me?"

"You heard me."

"Take it back, you goddamn shrimp'r I'm crushin' your head."

"No!"

"Take it back!"

"NO!" and Deacon kept squeezing. "NO!" Ice needled down his spine. He was afraid to try to run and, whispering evilly, Deacon kept telling him to take it back, take it back, take it back:

"I aint quittin' till ya git down on your knees'n apologize."

Resisting the dizzying pain, Buzzern remembered telling

Madlin he didn't feel weak, but now his moment of integrity seemed cheap. It was worse, though, knowing that Deacon probably wasn't even planning to hurt him terribly. His heels left the ground. Puffing, Deacon was seeing how far he could lift him with one hand. His neck popped, and Deacon said it was sure a great pleasure hearing a sound like that.

"Now, apologize, you little bastard!"

"No!" Losing balance, Buzzern was going blind. "No." Deacon's breath was hot with tobacco-stench against his face. "No." He kept repeating the round puny sound which was keeping him conscious. Frightened, he realized that Deacon didn't have the sense to know when to stop. On the highway cars flik-flikt past them, and Buzzern knew that he and Deacon looked as if they were only chatting. He felt rotten. Deacon's grip had become a dull pressure, flinty all the way down to his groin.

"Awright, Erly, in just a bit I'm lettin' ya go," but Buzzern knew he was going to be pushed flat on his face against concrete the moment Deacon loosened his grip. Queasy, he thought of Madlin and Harris, and the ways in which they'd abandoned themselves to urges. The pressure ceased and Buzzern exploded and, hearing a sick yell, realized his vein-thick fist had flashed hard up into the softness of Deacon's crotch. "I'll kill – ahhh." Deacon settled onto the pavement, arms slashed between his legs.

Buzzern looked down at the crumpled uniformed hulk. Weakly Deacon lunged at his feet. Startled, Buzzern kicked him under the chin, crack of hard leather on bone. The blow sent shivers up his leg, but Deacon scarcely moved. Buzzern backed off, then Deacon toppled sideways, his uneven breaths rasping loudly. Buzzern didn't know whether to help him up or kick him again. It scared him not to know what Deacon might try.

Desperate, he ran to the pumps and snatched an empty oil can from the bin, unhooked a hose, and splashed gasoline down the container's hole. He went to the other pumps then ran inside and got a packet of matches from the tray by the cash register. He snapped one off and started back toward Deacon who, pale, was getting back up on his knees.

"Goddamn! You're gonna kill yourself!"

"No I aint," Buzzern told him.

Staring blankly, Deacon worked himself to his feet and managed to say, "That oil not gonna burn."

Buzzern tilted the can and jerked it. He struck a match and

dropped it on the wet stain which popped and burned longer than he expected. Bent, Deacon limped backward when Buzzern snapped off another match.

"Whatta you think you're doin'?"

"What I started for," Buzzern said, hitching up his baggy pants, "finish gettin' my lemondrops. And I'd recommend you to quit botherin' me."

"You're crazy."

"Shut up," Buzzern said, slopping gasoline at him, but he knew that for the gasoline to protect him he'd have to risk blowing himself up. He didn't see any way to avoid that, so he started off for the Fina station which sold lemondrops and, on the way, kept looking back to make sure Deacon wasn't following him.

After buying his candy, he went back home the same way he'd come. When he got to his block, he sloshed out the gasoline in the gutter and, walking across the parkway, noticed the cracks in the sidewalk where weeds came out raggedly. He spat at them and cut across his driveway whose ruts were gravel straddling a lane of grass needing mowing. He was shaking. As hard as he could he threw the can into the open door of the leaning frame garage. He crushed the lemondrop with his back teeth and sucked the rough fragments down. He stepped up on the porch. Junebugs attacked his face. Cursing, he lashed at them. Still shaking, he saw Madlin and the others drive up in the Studebaker.

"Missed a good one," Homer called cheerily, getting out of the car. "Got so ever'body was leanin' and moanin' all over each other."

"What ya been doin'?" Ditie asked.

"Suckin' lemondrops."

"Honey, you got a real habit," she said, squeezing his shoulder, and went on in the house.

"Don't s'pose," Madlin said, "there was any news on Son."

"No." He took another lemondrop.

Wiping his sweat-damp, brine-colored hair, she told him, "There're'n awful lot of people prayin' hard for us."

"They includin' Harris?"

"Not out loud, but in their hearts they are."

"What I expected," he mumbled, sucking up candied phlegm from deep in his throat. He swallowed it.

"You seem awful contrary," Homer told him.

"Usually is," Madlin said, slapping the door shut behind her.

Chuckling, Homer said, "Thought all them lemondrops'd

sweeten your disposition. How come they don't? Hunh?" Wiping his chin roughly and feeling like smudging Homer's thick glasses with his thumb, Buzzern smelled gasoline. "Hunh?" Homer kept asking, "Hunh? How come?"

The junebugs were rattling the screens behind them, and with both hands Buzzern clenched his belt, the buckle digging into finger-bone.

"Aw hell," Homer said, "you shoulda gone with us steada stayin' here doin' nothin' but stirrin' yourself sour. Madlin asked ya. Why didn't ya go? Hunh?"

"Because I aint very smart," Buzzern said softly, thinking how aggravatingly continuous life was.

"Aww, come on now."

"I aint, and if anybody says my knowin' that makes me some kinda hotshot, then he's a g-goddamn fool."

Turning The Deer Free

She had already begun her presentation – lecture laced with poems – when a tall and imposing man came into the auditorium at the Instituto and sat down by himself on the back row. He nodded at her as if to apologize for being late. Seeing his gracious gesture, she smiled; but finding herself nodding back more enthusiastically than she had intended, she stiffened, then resumed her talk. She had no way of knowing at that point that his gesture of politeness had only come from a mighty attempt to suppress a grand belch. He and his ex-father-in-law, who had made the trip with him, he would later say, had been drinking beer since leaving Monterrey eight hours before.

The woman, short and brunette and rather jerky in delivery, continued her talk which in some ways was a series of lengthy introductions to poems she was reading during the evening. Her theme, the posters and handouts had announced the previous week throughout San Miguel, was "Woman As Sage, The Poet As Woman And Knife."

Her voice was small but there was an intensity about her which came from earnestness modulated by gestures of sweetness. *And when cutting my sick breast away,* she read,

> *he found my transparent heart.*
> *In it were olive trees*
> *and a white stucco farmhouse*
> *perfect for making love in*
> *after we had climbed down*
> *from the Sierra de Los Angeles.*

She went on, and for awhile it was hard to tell which remarks were poetry and which were exposition. It was also unclear if she were describing her own operation or affecting a persona. She told the audience that the surgeon was both rapist and life-saver, a man both loving and unreachable. She related the situation, a mastectomy – her response being the drama – to woman's complex involvement with the male. The urge for love, like the urge for health, she said, "made me see clearly what I had always felt, though fitfully: that the fear of going under another's control is a metaphor for that instant of violation – that sudden loss of self – that precedes the sweet transcendence of loving, the most marvelous courage of all."

One person near the front clapped. The man who had come in late nodded again, but this time at the floor sloping before him. Squinting, he readjusted himself in his seat, little bucket of a butt-rest designed for people smaller than him. He slumped until his propped up knees made the chairback squeak. He made it squeak again, and then again. She glared at him but he was looking at the side wall now and could not have seen her. She went on with her talk.

Her voice now smooth, she had the tone of seasoned maturity common to the respectably educated New Englander. Her moments of acridity were masks for shyness, and her openness came from an enthusiasm for learning. In short, part of her was still a student, still a girl from Middlebury prone to crushes on her teachers; but, as she had always been, she was satisfied to let those crushes remain lyrical daydreams. A poem or two might still come from them.

Once more the man squeaked his chairback. But was he really trying to be disruptive? She noticed him twisting, as if struggling to find a comfortable position. The space he was in was too small for him. The rows *are* awfully close together, she thought, sliding into another poem.

She glanced down at her husband. He looked content but she wasn't sure he looked really well. Or was it the lighting here that gave his skin an ashen cast? Fifteen years older than her, he had worked as an editor for two decades in New York and Boston. He also had published a short stack of novels, and one of them had recently been reissued in paperback. "Of course, that's satisfying," he had told her, "but I think I'll dabble in verse for awhile." Was that another way of saying he was preparing to retreat into death?

Ten years before they had come to Mexico to write and live quietly, free from the adolescent bustle of the States. She was afraid, though, they might have to leave soon. Her husband had been having trouble again with arrhythmia. "Don't worry," he had told her. "The world has it, too."

"Bones speak their own truth," she said. "It's the bones I find helpful to remember. The bones and the water, especially the sea, for the bones are form, the core of shape itself, and the sea draws us home, into a center that is always shifting:

Hidden in the sea a sunken self waits.
Gulls are drifting overhead.
A girl by herself rows her own dinghy,
her chapped cheeks glowing.
A cold wind fills her mouth.

She looks down into water,
sees a face rising toward her.
A ghostly body shimmers into shape.
She would reach out to him
if she could only believe once more
he would return to land with her.

She paused then said, "Thank you." Throughout her body she felt wonderfully light. But was her talk over? Or had she just finished a poem? She didn't seem to know herself. She tried bowing but her body would not cooperate. For a moment her head seemed to be bouncing on her neck. Yes. She was through. The place, though, had not exploded into the sweet violence of applause. It should have. She had rehearsed her conclusion a lot. Just this morning, in front of the mirror, she had realized what a fine conclusion she had made. Something, though, was wrong. Perhaps, she thought, they want more. But nothing happened. Then she found herself slapping shut the hard-backed notebook her poems and remarks were in. Closing her eyes in a gesture of gratitude, she clasped her hands to her breast and applause finally came.

Smiling, she bowed to her people, then affecting an air of modesty, she held up a palm to bring quiet, though the applause was already dying. "Yes," she said, then heard herself telling them, "Thank you."

She told the group that she would be glad now to take questions. At first no one had any, then again she heard the loud chair-squeak in back and saw that the big man back there had raised his hand high. A shiver went through her. His largeness of attention was thrilling.

"Yes," he said. "Back here. I have one." Clearing his throat, he stretched his left leg out into the narrow aisle and, laughing, said, "Damn cute place here, but they must've made it for the goddamn pigmies." The crowd looked back to see who he was. "What I want to know is," he said, "what it is you think you are."

"I'm sorry," she said, tensing. "I don't think I understand."

"What I want to know is what it is you think you *are* – I mean when you write. What do you think of yourself *as*? Understand?" he added impatiently.

Belligerent gestures had always upset her, but she was determined not to show that, not tonight, not even to herself. This man, after all, did not really mean to sound so hostile. He was, she preferred to think, simply inarticulate. The slack rasp of his accent even said such. She wanted to tell him she understood that, but stiffening to counter the unsettling sprawl of his posture, she coolly explained, "A poet, Sir, has many masks."

"I said I want to know about *you*," the man snapped back. "Who are *you*, damnit, I mean when you write."

Quickly waving her free hand palm down, she signaled to the group to hush its squirming and whispering. There was no need now to get agitated, she had things well in control. The crowd settled back in their seats.

"Many ideas, of course, go through one indeed," she told the man, her lips pursed, her phrasing clipped. "Memories – fantasies – quite a few different cognitive rhythms actually," she said, smiling to tell him she found their play delightful.

"I don't want that psychological crap," he said quickly. "I want to know about *you*."

"Please," she said. The crowd was stirring again. "Please," she said, looking down at her friends. Twisting and frowning, they were craning to see who the crude man was. But her husband, she noticed, looked calm. He was not shuffling and muttering the way the others were. He was keeping his eyes forward, and that soothed her.

A little laugh flipped in her throat. "Perhaps you have some interesting point," she told the man, "but for the life of me I don't know what it is." Laughter rose welcomely from the crowd. She had stung him and some of her people even clapped, and with enthusiasm, too, she was thinking. Her dark eyes sparkling, she turned to a different part of the audience and asked – they were such fine people – if they had any questions.

"Damnit," the man said, yanking her attention back to him. "I'm not through. You're not going to brush me off," and suddenly she found herself smiling. There really was, there was something thrilling yet childlike about him. It had been an awfully long time since she had been around anyone so insistent, someone who made her realize anew what fine powers of control she still had. She would play out her line just a little more then snap it taut, she thought, and pop his head off then cradle his remains in her bosom as she sang a few rounds of some old brave Sinn Fein songs she had learned years ago in college.

Snapping out of her reverie, though, she was no longer smiling. The evening was getting out of hand. For a moment she had felt as if she and the man were the only two in the hall. There was a firmness of flesh in his length. In spite of his inexcusably brazen manner, a rough tide of connection had been forming between them. She had felt it. For the sake of a possible image she had considered surrendering to it, at least for awhile. But she had caught herself up short. As if to assure him that this was really not betrayal, she glanced down at her husband. He looked unflappable, just as he always did, and that, she knew, kept her moored, lightly moored.

Once more the man spoke up, this time surprising her by apologizing for his clumsiness. Rudeness you mean, she thought, feeling nervous again. He said he hadn't meant to come in late, "but I've been driving eight hours drinking beer with my old ex-dad, and my son came with us. I've been to these reading deals here a bunch of times and you seem different from the others I've heard, so tell me. Goddamnit, tell me."

"Tell you *what?*" someone snarled.

"Ignore him," another said.

Sauvage, the French call it, she thought, pleased with herself. The crowd here was with her, and however unformed the man back there seemed, she knew he was most likely gentle, and the sprawl in his posture said he was wonderfully good friends with himself. She liked that. So few were.

"Go on," she told him encouragingly, and again a little laugh leaped in her throat. "But just one question. There are others here with us."

"Fine. All I want to know is when you write your damn stuff, how do you think of yourself as? Wife? Lover? Hermaphrodite, or just goddamn wind-whistle?"

Good heavens, she thought. The man was actually curious about her situation. He was not going to accept cocktail chatter either. Surely, though, she thought, he's not really trying to flirt – not in front of all these people. A feeling of terror was surfacing in her, and with it a memory that seemed like a dream. She was a girl again at summer camp in the Berkshires. She was crossing a stream on a long rope bridge. She slipped and fell but she never hit bottom, not in her memory, and at times that bothered her more than the rocks on the bank below. The rocks had been real, and though the fall had not been far she had broken her ankle and fractured her collar bone one dew-slick morning. In her dreams she still fell, but the falling always quickly became a sensation of purposeless drift. There was no bottom, no hard clear point of stoppage, only a drifting in a fog, and no unicorns lived there now.

She looked up from the floor at the man. He was still waiting in the hugeness of his impatience. Her lips began parting as if to let out a sound, some word she did not even know had formed within her. But no sound came, only the gesture of a gasp gone mute.

"Well, whatever the hell it is," the man boomed, standing up, "don't change a damn thing. And don't ever listen to the frozen people here. They're all tasteless shits," he said, turning and striding up the aisle straight out the door.

Standing by herself on the stage, she felt raw inside, as if that crazed odd man had scraped away some part of her. Regathering herself and nodding to her friends that she was all right, she felt as if the man had lain down like a dead weight on her. As she thanked the group again, her faint voice broke. She hugged her notebook to her chest. A prickly sensation shivered up her nape and down her left arm. *Frisson*, she muttered to herself.

She felt dizzy, but forcing herself to speak, she suggested they all retire now to the reception. Her friends began applauding. Several were already coming up to greet her. Descending the stage, she wanted to throw her arms around them, they were all so dear, even the ones whose names she did not know. They made her feel ready to take on all questions, anyone's questions, but there weren't any. There were only mumbled congratulations, and the people who came to her seemed to pull away from her, even before they had finished speaking. Something had gone wrong.

She had always looked forward to the post-reading time. She and her audience would melt together and, purified by their appreciation, she would rise above them in glory then float back down among them and fold herself languorously around them. But this was also the time she always forgot to dread. The time was never as vibrant as she had hoped, or as tricks of memory would later recall. She felt empty and adrift and her husband, damn him, was keeping his calm face forward.

Years ago she had thought that these awful sensations of removal might yield some fine verses, but they never had. It was different, though, after sex. She had made many poems then, as if making love freed her from confusion, freed her from herself, opened her attention to the marvels of small things around her, and large things invented. Memories blossomed up out of her then, or swarmed down upon her, leaving her blithely indifferent to self.

Her husband was coming toward her, to hug her as he always did after readings, but when she reached out toward him she felt paralyzed. That confused her. She wasn't paralyzed. She wanted to jump up and down. She was happy. She had to be. She and her husband were the same height and even almost the same weight. They fit together nicely, and wonderfully calmly. She despised it when she heard women say they liked their men towering over them. That was as stupid as men going crazy over big vulgar breasts.

"You were lovely," her husband said, and the sound of his voice freeing her, she desperately kissed him fully on the lips. He jerked back in surprise, saying, "Goodness!" then laughing gently, hugged her again.

"How was I?" she asked.

"Fine," he said, "splendid. But you always surprise me."

"How?"

"In a lot of sweet ways," he said, tossing the subject away.

That piqued her, but the fit didn't last. Compliments were coming down on her now like a fine autumn mist, and pulling away from her husband, she received her dear friends.

The bustle at the reception seemed oddly anonymous, but now feeling neatly detached, she could be as coolly observant as her husband who, she knew, was in another part of the house visiting. She was by herself and that, she assumed, was fitting. She just wished these people were more demonstrative. She had, after all, achieved a modicum of prominence. O my goodness! she muttered, her fingertips quickly covering her lips. That man – odd giant of a man – was here, across the room by the fireplace. A number of the crowd seemed to know him, though he was not keeping his attention fixed on any of them. It looked as if they were vying for the attention that he was not yet ready to give them. Of course. He was looking directly at her, yet he did not act, she thought, as if he had seen her.

Someone immediately came up behind her: Dolores, the hostess for the evening. She often gave parties after events at the Instituto, and now she was rapidly giving her friend some cautionary advice: "Listen, Hon, you turn your eyes the other way. I don't want you and Terrance going at it again. Once a night's enough."

"Terrance who?"

"Terrance Durand — the smart-mouth lunk who almost destroyed your reading."

"Who is he?"

"A Houston art dealer. He's been coming down here for years. I'm surprised you've never seen him, though he never stays long. Right now he's all hot on some crazy ex-Marine who's a mean tequila drunk who paints these odd canvases and everyone of them has a big hole in it. He's here, too, but don't meet him. Just get a drink and flirt. You've earned it, Sweet." Then she was gone.

Feeling airy now, she tried to find her big adversary, Rockhead Terrance or whatever his name was, but he was nowhere around. Oh yes, he is, she said, surprising herself, her spirits brightening — there he is — and she began walking directly toward him. He did not look, she thought, as if he'd been drinking and driving all day. Standing up, he looked more dignified than he had sitting down. Sidestepping through the chattering crowd, she hurried up to him, got his attention by laying her hand on his wrist and introducing herself.

"No, no," he said, stopping her, his large hand rising at her face.

Smiling, she pulled his hand down and said, "I insist. I want to thank you. Your remarks," she said, "I found them interesting—rough-hewn," she added, "though some of them were."

He looked soberly down at her and told her, "I apologize, Lady." Thinking she was using her wiles to control him, she met his gaze directly. Then without blinking, he said, "You were hearing a drunk."

"I certainly was not," she said, correcting him, "I certainly was not. You made, in fact, some searching remarks."

"Look, Lady, I apologize. Just let me off the hook."

"Not till you make sense," she said, touching the side of his arm.

"Damnit, Lady, I was drunk in your talk, and I'm still a bit drunk."

"Oh hush," she said, touching his arm again.

But he did not smile back at her.

"No, no," she said, knowing she had made a mistake, she should not have come over, but her hand had not moved away from his arm. "No, no," she kept saying, "no, no."

"I said I was drunk," he snapped back at her.

"Oh no, you're not," she said, and again she felt strong. A keen sense of power had risen up in her, like a flame she was ready to dance on through. She would stand up to him and defy him if she had to. Lummox or not, he would not control her, but the longer he kept glowering at her, the fiercer his gray eyes seemed; they were lupine now in their look, and she felt as if they were driving her off balance, as if her feet had actually risen off the floor. Then placing her palms together, she told him she appreciated his attention.

"Good!" he shot back, "and I appreciate the fact I'm drunk. In fact, Lady," he said, his voice rising, "it's the only damn way I can stand yourself."

That stunned her, but surely he didn't mean it. He couldn't, she thought, unable, though, to laugh off his inexcusably crass rudeness. People here didn't appreciate that crude, that insanely tactless kind of humor.

"You're not funny," she told him. "You're just cruel. I'm surprised you're even interested in things like art. You're cruel," she told him, tears welling in her eyes. "You're cruel, there's no excuse —"

"Look, Lady, I said I was drunk. And I also said that's the only damn way I can stand your damn self, so leave me alone!"

"You are!" she said, fighting off her tears. "You're just nasty and cruel. And I came over here to help you feel included in the gathering, but you turned everything ugly. And I expect an apology, too. I'm not used to being treated like this."

"Then shut up and leave me the fuck alone," he told her.

She felt as if she'd been clubbed. Everyone around her had gone quiet. The room was no longer aflutter. People were staring at her. They weren't glaring at the man either. They were staring at her, as if she had been the one to cause the scene. But she hadn't. They were wrong. They didn't understand.

The man continued glaring down at her, and again — but perhaps only in memory this time, she couldn't be sure — she heard him say the cruel thing, that he couldn't stand her unless he was drunk. Her chin was quivering. She wanted to break down and cry, break loose and run, but she didn't dare. She was going to try to face him down. She had to. If she didn't everyone would think she was pitiful. And she would think that herself, too. Then she caught sight of her husband, but he was not coming toward her. He did not look upset either. He was keeping his gaze calmly forward. Then abruptly, without saying anything more, the man turned away from her: He was leaving, walking straight for the door, and no one was following him out. No one was telling him goodbye. She had won! They were glad to

see him go, but she still wanted to scream at him. She wished she had
slapped him. But that had not happened, and her little sense of victory had already passed. Her legs shaky, she felt empty and weak, separated from these people who, not so very long ago, she had imagined
were her friends. But they weren't. They had not come to her reading
because of her. She knew that now. They had only come because the
evening had promised some pleasant distraction. She should have
known that, she thought. After all, the promise of pleasant distraction
had brought her and her husband to San Miguel in the first place.
Nothing else: just escape from the adolescent bustle of the States, that
and a few other attendant illusions. But they could not stay in flight
much longer. Her husband's heart was weak, the beat of it increasingly irregular. She felt like a heel.

She hated these receptions. The people were fickle and indifferent. She hated being associated with them, people who cheered you
then dropped you, and their cheering wasn't much either. She wished
she were home. She wished she were alone, having just left her husband back in bed. She wished he were sleeping, deeply, so he would-
n't even have a chance to be aware of her presence in the house.

Alert, she would have risen from beneath the thick covers. She
would have put on her robe. She would have closed the door behind
her and gone to the dining room table. She would have sailed by now
so far beyond any sensation of self that images would float down upon
her like snow, and the flakes would leave tear-shapes on the table top,
the ghosts of pearls. The moon would be shining through a veil of
clouds; and coming through the stand of pines at her side, water
would lap around her ankles, then swirling, it would rise above her
knees, and a deer would run down through the mist, then veering
back, disappear between trees. Someday, maybe soon perhaps, she
would have enough nerve to free it from her woods, to let it change
into a unicorn.

Fingers in the breeze would pull her hair loose, and the current
of the water rising around her would sound like sensual moaning.
Somewhere near here lovers were lying on a fragrant bed of pine
boughs. The sounds drifting from them would squeeze around her
tightly then push on inside her, like that man who, if she had let him
have his way, she imagined, would have backed her roughly up against
a tree and bruised her with his lips until they both were crying.

But he was gone now, and she was nowhere near a forest, just
alone in a crowd of stingy-hearted, auto-exiled acquaintances. She felt
aghast: to think she even wanted to tell her husband about these

things the man had burst loose inside her. She knew, though, that she would keep them to herself. There was, after all, no need for confession. She had not betrayed anyone. Besides, if she told him, her husband would not understand; he thought too much in causally chained strings of events. She wasn't like that. The world, when it blessed her – who cared why? – flooded randomly. She wiped her eyes. That man, Terrance Durand, had not given her a poem. He had just bitten his way inside her then left. She felt ashamed. For a moment she had even considered turning him into one of her muses. If she only had a quick tongue on her. But she never had, and she envied the glib: people protected by flippant, fast wit.

"Nice talk," a man said, passing by her.

She wanted to laugh but said, "Thank you." The man, however, was already gone.

"Loved it," the woman trailing him said.

"Why thank you." But she, too, was gone.

The image of the man pressed against her again, kept lumbering all through her, then the size of him swelled until his features became as rough-edged as boulders. The sprawl of his force was massive. She felt small and substanceless, nothing more than a moist high cry of delicate pain.

"What're you thinking?" she heard her husband ask, his hand touching the small of her back.

She was having trouble catching her breath.

"I asked you a question," he repeated, needling her, she knew, in a foolish attempt to tease her back to him. "Well?"

"Nothing," she told him, pulling away. "I'm just upset."

"I know," he said, "but you really handled yourself well awhile ago. I think you told him off. That's why I didn't come over," he said, hugging her and telling her she had a fine lip. She shrank away from him. These illusions of his were offensive.

"I didn't tell anyone off," she said coldly.

"Maybe not, but at least he and his drunkenness are gone."

Suddenly she was quivering again and finding it hard to catch her breath.

"It's all right," her husband told her, gently touching her back. "He just got to you there for awhile, but he's gone now. And don't forget: all these people here are on your side. You're the star of their night."

Pursing her lips, she closed her eyes. She felt like spitting, and at her husband, too, his damn calmness a sign of fear and weakness, not kindness. "I just wish he were still here," she said, spewing.

"Oh no," her husband told her. "You don't wish that at all. None of us does."

"Why not?" she asked.

"His being here wouldn't change anything. Besides, I'd probably be the one to get in trouble," he added chipperly.

"How?"

"I'd try to bite his ankle, then we'd all be sorry when he really did go out of control."

She turned to look directly at him. "I wouldn't," she told him. "I wouldn't be sorry at all."

"Why not?"

"Please," she said. "Nothing," she said, still shivering. "Please. Just leave me alone. I want to go home."

"Okay. Sure. Let me give everyone our goodbyes and we're off."

"No, I don't want to tell them anything. And I want to go home by myself."

"Are you sure?"

"Yes."

He took her arm.

"No," she said, "by myself."

"I understand. I was just going to walk you to the door."

"I don't need that."

"Okay," he said, backing off. "Fine. I'll see you soon. I won't be staying long either. Kiss?"

She gave him her cheek.

The thin night air was chilly, and she was sorry she had been curt to her husband. He had done nothing to hurt her. In fact, as he always did, he had treated her with respect. He had not rushed up to defend her from the dragon. He had assumed she had the proper gifts for defending herself. He obviously saw her as a woman, she thought, not some child who had to be taken care of. He had never said such, but she knew quite well what his attitudes were, and they were admirable, though not very inspiring, she admitted, and now with his health failing she had fewer and fewer occasions to leave their bed with the ripe moist feeling of genuine freedom that lovemaking brought. But that wasn't his fault, and she was glad she was not trying to pretend it was. She had been having her own distractions: that sense of idle floating that was coming upon her more and more, along with the difficulty of catching a good deep breath.

She was almost out to the street now, but she stopped to touch the trunk of a tree just past the tennis court. She liked the rough texture of the bark on her palm. She took a deep breath. Yes. There was the smell of rain in the air. There might even be a downpour. She hoped so. She kept breathing deeply but not to taste the smell of rain. She needed something substantial filling her lungs, but the air here was thin, though there did seem to be a fog of a mist about. Then a tear fell down her cheek, and several more tears rolled. Her world wasn't anything more than the promise of a few slim books, and it hurt to know there was nothing in them that went to the quick of anyone's heart.

A good hard rain would be nice, she thought, with thunder as loud as cannons and lightning as bright as the sunlight here at noon. She really had been too hard on the people, she thought, and again she felt substanceless. Without meaning to, she had been aping that bitter drunk man. She felt characterless, as if there were nothing inside her, not even remnants of dreams. She had let the man lead her astray, but that would not happen again. She'd be sure of it. This was too beautiful a place for anyone to try to run down. Her time of escape here, however, was coming to an end; and she knew that. Her husband was dying. They needed to get back to the States. She would take her memories with her, but most of them now would be peopleless.

She sat down at the base of the tree trunk. There was a bench on the other side of the tennis court, but she did not want to walk that far, not yet, maybe in a moment when her strength came back. All she wanted to do now was remember what the world looked like when the sun came up after a rain. Here all the tile roofs turned copper and gold, and the parochia turned luminescent, and the deep red petals of bougainvillea danced like angels up and down the thick earthen walls and even over the roof tops. She needed to stretch out, just for awhile. She needed to sleep, but just for a moment. The grass felt good, her head resting now on the little pillow her hands made. The air was thin here, awfully thin, but that was because of the altitude.

Her eyes were closing and the feeling in her legs was disappearing. For a moment, though, she had the sweet sensation of floating above the world.

A Bit Of A Bitch

G o on," she told him. "Get it out. Say it."
"Say what?"
"Whatever it is making you hate me."
"I don't hate you."
"All right then whatever about me's bothering you so much."
He bit the punchstem of his ballpoint pen.
"Say it!" she shrieked. "I can't take much more of this."
"Who's asking you to?"
"Do you want a divorce? Is that what you want?"
In and out he punched the point of his pen.
"If you do," she said, "I'll be more than happy to give you one."
"I didn't ask for one."
"Well, I'm about ready to."
"Fine," he said. "Whatever you want."
"Damn you. Say it!"
"Say what?"
"I want to know what it is making you so awful."
"Who's awful? You're the one raising your voice."
"Come on, Dan. What is it?"
"All right," he said, tossing the pen at the sofa she was hunched into.
Brushing the nastily tubular thing away from her onto the carpet, she told him, "I'm listening. I told you I'm listening," she repeated and began rubbing the tiny gold cross hanging from her neck, rubbing it hard.
"We'll start with that sword there," he snapped, glaring at the pendant. "You and that born-again hooey of yours don't give a damn about me or anything else."
Haughtily she laughed at him.
"Come on," she said, "don't tell me you still feel guilty about that escapade last year."

"No!" he shouted. "I don't feel guilty. It's probably the most decent thing I've done in my life."

"Decent?"

"Yes, decent."

"You didn't even know her last name," she said. "At least you said you didn't when I found that dumb journal and you got all broken up."

"Don't be so judgmental."

"Who's being judgmental?" she asked. "You're the one racked with guilt. Love and compassion my eye! If you're calling that love and compassion, how do you describe your relationship with me?"

"I usually don't try."

"Well, that's a nice thing," she said, "to find out after well over twenty-odd years."

"Damn odd, though it *was* rather nice," he said, beginning to tremble, realizing once again how much easier it was to be silently bitter than to drag up these confusing things about themselves. He was nowhere near old but felt senile, and adolescent, too. It was terrible to realize he had no grip on her. This arguing was enervating. It never led to a proper explosion, and certainly never to anything resembling clarity. Then he heard her asking him what he wanted out of her, but he had no idea how to answer.

"Listen, Dan, if it's guilt you're feeling "

"It's not, Emma," he said, emphasizing her name in some oblique form of rebuke.

"If it is, just stop it. I forgave you months ago."

Staring at her, he said, "Forgave me? What's there to forgive?"

"Don't play games. If I'd done the same thing, you'd've gone berserk."

"Maybe, maybe not. So what?"

"I'm getting tired of this," she told him.

"So am I."

"So why don't we be civilized and just call it quits?"

He felt like an ass. Everything about her was laid out in horribly reasonable options. Sin called for forgiveness. Pain called for control. Trouble called for counseling; but kissing her, especially at night in bed, was like putting his face in a pad of cold, chlorophyllic grease. He hoped their two sons, who were in Italy now, were having a better time of the flesh than he was.

"Well," she said, "I'm listening. Is there something you'd like me to do?"

"Yeah. Something indecent."

Stiffening, she told him, "I've never denied you your pleasure."

"My God, Emma." He slurped down the rest of his Chivas neat. "Your very existence denies me of my pleasure."

"Well, you finally got it out. Listen, Buster. I could say the same thing about you – only I don't need to get my courage up with whiskey."

"That's what I like about you, Honey – you're a real straight arrow."

"I've had enough of this," she said. "I thought we might work out an understanding, but apparently not. I'm going to bed," she said, getting up.

It pricked him when she didn't even glance back at him. "Fine," he called to her, "and be sure you lock the bathroom when you change, because when I get drunk I get randy."

"A lot of good it does," she sang, sailing away.

"I'm going to the club," he yelled, bouncing out of his recliner, but she didn't answer. "I said I'm going to the club."

"I heard you," she called from the back of the house. "What do you want me to do – sign a quit-claim deed?"

He grabbed his jacket and topcoat and whipped open the door to the porte-cochère. When he got in the car he sighed, though a grin broke across his face as he turned the key. Once again Emma had fallen for his ruse. He sped out of the driveway and, tires squealing, struck out for the glories of fleshly understanding.

Her name was Beatrice. She was six years younger than he was, and her dark brown eyes were depthless. Half a year ago he had handled her divorce, and now he was handling her. Her lips were full and her body, when she moved, loped with delicate roundnesses; and he took it as one of her sweet gestures that she was dressed tonight in the purple lamé caftan he had given her last summer as a token promising warmth for the coming winter they were going to spend some of together. Her auburn hair, frizzing at her ears, was swept back in a frenchroll. The effect, he thought, was dramatic yet neatly contained.

"I was wondering," she told him, pulling him inside, "if you were going to make it."

"*Semper fi*," he said, hugging her.

She kissed him and asked if he'd like her to fix him a drink.

"Sure. Are you having one with me?"

"Not yet," she said. "I've already had four."

"Let's stick with coffee then – though a Chivas neat on the side might be nice."

She went to plug in the percolator, and he ambled back into the den whose parquet floor was corrupted by her sons' dissembled hot-wheel track, a spread of broken and peeled crayons spilling out of a shoe box, and three patent-leather shoes: two black, one red. Tidy by habit, he bent down and poked under the sofa and coffee table to find the fourth shoe. He finally noticed it perching on the bookshelf above the TV set.

"My, you look dignified," she said, coming in.

"I thought the kids were spending the week at your mother's," he said, getting up.

"They are. I just haven't got around to cleaning their mess. Anything on TV?" she asked, sitting down across the room from him.

"No idea," he said, stretching out on the sofa, aggravated now to find himself wishing she were better about keeping her place tidy. Drawing her legs up into the seat of her padded chair, she scratched her shins.

"Don't get any ideas," she said, catching him looking up under her hem. "I still have that infection."

"That's what I was afraid of."

She pulled her ankles up under her hips and tucked her robe modestly beneath her knees. The flash of underthigh he had seen looked as kneadable and pink as Silly-Putty.

Smiling, she got up and came over beside him. She laid her head against his chest. He brushed her cheeks with the back of his hand.

"You didn't," she asked, when his palm pressed her breast, "you didn't say anything tonight to hurt her, did you?"

"We did get a bit steamy."

"Don't be ugly to her. Please. I'd hate it if I made you mean."

"Don't worry," he assured her.

"She is, though, nuts. You do know that, don't you?"

"Sure," he said uneasily. He disliked talking about his wife with Bea; it made him feel unclean.

Laughing, she rolled over and stretched out against him, sliding her fingers between the buttons of his shirt. She scratched him in circles and, reaching over her, he squeezed the back of her thigh.

"I wonder what it's going to be like when we're old," she asked.

"Not much of anything if you don't get rid of that nasty disease."

"Don't talk like that," she said. "Please. Not when I was feeling happy thinking how nice it was we can talk, just lounge around and talk. Please," she said, "please. Don't try to scare me – even if you think you're just joking."

"Then get something that'll make you well."

She pinched him, near the mole by his navel, and he jumped. He was frightened she might have made it bleed.

"Careful!"

"No wonder Emma gets kooky," she said. "I would, too, living with you."

He looked at her directly, and shortly her eyes became a flood upon his gaze, but she did not snuggle against him. Instead she asked him if he were ready for his coffee.

"Yeah, I guess," his reply little more than a movement of lips against the tickle of hair covering her ear.

Twisting to kiss him on the throat, she said, "Let's have our coffee *con ron*."

"Fine," he said and reluctantly rose with her.

Brushing a lock of hair off his forehead, she told him, "I'm glad you quit using hairspray."

"Why?"

"It got to be like wallowing on cardboard."

Later, as he refilled their cups and got himself a beer for the road, she told him, "You'd better hurry. Your club closed half an hour ago."

"Who cares?"

"I care. I don't want her getting suspicious. Mainly, though, I don't want my eyes scratched out."

"Don't worry. Violence isn't her style."

"Does she think she's too good for it?"

"No!" he said sharply. "She has other ways she deals with trouble."

"Please," she told him, "be careful. We're neither one ready for drama."

"I am," he said, not sure which woman he was more aggravated with.

"You're sweet," she told him, and he had an impulse to hit her; but instead, when he leaned over to kiss her goodbye, he kicked the leg of the breakfast table. Coffee sloshed out of both cups. "Nervous?" she asked, playfully smiling, and walked him to the door. "Have fun," she said and blew him a kiss, but the gesture was disappointing. She wasn't nearly as wonderfully aggressive as she had once been.

The chill in the night promised an early morning frost, and the streets were slick with mist. He punched on the radio, but what came out was static and some sappy country ballad. He punched another station but all this one gave was an androgyne wailing. Turning the noise off before he acidentally hit a Gospel station, he wondered if his wife were having an interesting dream. Sometimes she did. But he sure wasn't, and a part of him wished that Emma would meet him at the door and ask if he'd had a fine evening. If she did he'd kiss her and lie and say yes.

Turning into the driveway, he saw that she had switched off the carport light, probably out of Christian revenge, he thought. Getting out, he noticed a letter taped on the screen. He peeled it free then fondled the wall till he remembered there was no outside switch.

Opening the car again, he strained to decipher the green-inked letters. His throat turning scaly, he read:

> *Dear Dan,*
> *Most women I know wouldn't still be around if they found themselves having to write this. But I'm not most women. I don't hate you for what you're doing. I am sorry, tho, you have to lie. I'm even sorrier if you think your belligerence tricks me. I am not, tho, going to mention anything this time about forgiveness. In fact, if I turn the other cheek, it won't be the one on my face. You can laugh at my religion if you want, but if you think I'm a martyr you're wrong.*

He flipped the page.

> *You're going to get some Scripture tonight whether you want it or not. Proverbs 7 (you can find the verses yourself): "For at the window of my house I have looked out thru my lattice, and I have seen among the simple!!! ... a young (?) man without sense, passing along the street near her corner ... at the time of night and darkness. And lo, a woman meets him, dressed as a harlot.*
>
> *   E.*
> *P.S.: If you decide to come on in the house, be quiet because I'm probably sleeping. If I'm not, I still don't want to be disturbed. One other thing: can you imagine anyone committing*

suicide or turning alcoholic over someone as simple & trans-
parent as you? I can't. It is easy, though, to forgive the weak.
They're such a small threat.

He fell back against the fender. The paper was such a blur now that
he didn't know how he'd ever read it. He kept trying to swallow but
was too cold to do anything but shake and laugh at the wonder of her
gall.

He wanted to storm in the house and rouse her for a rite of cel-
ebration, even if it turned into murder; but things like that, he knew,
worked best left alone in the pointless rhythms of fantasy. He didn't
know what to do. He had left the house tonight thinking he was clever.
Now he was not even sure he had been the one to foment the argument. Maybe she had been tricking him all along. But why?

Defiant, he decided to go on in and say nothing, either tonight
or tomorrow, about the letter; and if she asked if he had found it, he
would lie and say, "No."

The door groaned open at his push. The house was dark. Toe-
stepping forward, he bumped into a wall. His movements tentative
now, he made his way to the bedroom, thankful that Emma wasn't the
kind to set a booby-trap or let a poisonous snake loose in the house.
Some women were.

As he inched through the doorway a light flashed on.

"Is that you?" she asked gruffly.

"Yes," he answered, "the Good Humor man's back."

"Oh." She sounded disappointed. "Please – if you'd not clomp
around. You have a loud foot." Then she flipped the light off and,
twisting over, bunched herself back into an attitude of sleep. He
remembered seeing in the momentary glare a moist sheen on her face.
It did not come from tears. It came from some damn tube or jar.

As he undressed and hung his clothes in the closet, an urge
burst in him to call Bea and not even try to keep his voice low. Even
if she were full of mean bacteria, she'd be a good romp tonight. But
that wouldn't work. She wouldn't understand. Looking down at
Emma in the gloom of the night, he suddenly started shaking. Bea
wouldn't understand, he kept thinking, she wouldn't, but his gaze
stuck on Emma, he snarled down at her, "And you wouldn't either!"

The Scapegoat

I heard them.

"How long you gonna keep on doin it?" Cravens asked.

"Till it by god gets right," Elwood told him.

They were standing outside the cafe where a lot of us stay when the weather's right. It's often not.

"You're just a goddurn nuisance," Cravens said.

"Can't help it," Elwood told him. The sun was in my eyes, and I think Elwood also flickered out a little smile, the kind that makes serious people angry.

"You better help it," Cravens insisted, not sounding like the lay preacher he acted like he was on Sundays.

"Why?"

"We're gonna run ya off if you don't quieten down. We might even hang ya."

"I never had thought of it that way."

"You might start. I'm not the only one thinking such."

"How come you to tell me all this?"

" 'Cause I don't wanta hang ya," Cravens said, winding back down. "So please. Just be quieter."

"Can't. My project demands noise."

"Then quit your damn – just give us some peace for awhile."

"Can't. Pipe and hammers make noise. Some of it might even be good for you."

"Damnit –"

It bothered me to hear them talk like that. My folks, the old couple took me in and brought me up, always said I was short on spine, but Cravens' belligerence and Elwood's taunting him back were making me feel raw. I knew that Cravens wasn't joking about their getting Elwood. I just didn't think they were actually going to hang him. Sadder than that is the fact that the poor devil almost got away; at least one person around here, for a time, even said he did. That was Amarilla, and for awhile she was right, too. Her enterprise around here was pleasure: mine included.

Cravens hadn't been bluffing. In fact, the time they got Elwood I'd just left Amarilla's place – it's just outside town – and was smiling and laughing all through my flesh from what me and her had been doing. It was dark and I heard a commotion out in the field. There was all sorts of yelling and carrying on. Someone had a torch and had set what looked like a big cottonwood afire. The light from the blaze looked like glory. The tall grass in the meadow even quivered, like it was thrilled or frightened by the hot light. At least four men were out there carrying on and maybe even fighting each other. Also a coondog I couldn't see was barking itself hoarse. Then a rifle, then a shotgun went off. That stopped some of my curiosity. I got the hell out of there and didn't hear what else happened till the next day, and some of that was contradictory.

"Ole Elwood got what was by god comin to him."

"For a fact. Moment that rope jerked taut he let out a smell stronger'n –"

"Heard some even fainted."

"I heard the same, though we weren't exactly there, directly there, when it all occurred."

"This mornin over coffee I heard you were."

"My heart was out there with'm. So was Szczepinski's."

Theo Szczepinski had the most hatchetlike face in town and passed for Will Cravens' best friend. I never liked either one of them.

"I be dog, Cy. You mean you weren't out there among'm either?"

"Was for awhile, but I had to get back. My nephew's been having some fever."

"Then who the hell was out there?"

"There was at least several."

"Who?"

"Too sonofabitchin dark for me to see, but ole Elwood got it. Popped his head clean off his neck."

"Then he didn't have to suffer."

"Hell have to suffer! He got what he by god had comin. Keepin everbody up like he was. Project he called it. But we got him. Things're gonna be different, too – just us'n God'n the scenery now. No noise."

"Then I don't guess either one of y'all heard."

"Heard what?"

"That rumor sayin Elwood weren't even there. Somebody at the grocer's told somebody he got away."

"Hell he did."

Some others've been talkin about it, too, down at the cafe."

"That's a by god lie."

"It aint either, Szczepinski. I've heard more'n one say the same."

"Then they wasn't there. How the lord could they know? We got him. I saw it."

"While ago you said you didn't."

"You just ask the ones there the whole time. We got him. And there aint gonna be any more racket durin the night either. Elwood's project is through! gone! Just flat out done!"

One of our town's problems – anybody should've known this – was that nobody here knew exactly what Elwood's project was. They just knew it made noise. The second problem was that a couple nights later, the racket all began again. It sounded like a locomotive running over a mess of broken, warped track – that and the wind howling like God or somebody big had the asthma. The pounding, too – irregular like all the other noises. It had no rhythm you could adjust yourself to. But I didn't think the racket was all that bad. I will admit, though, I was away during most of it. I'd gone down to Austin to get myself checked. Doctor here said I had heartworms, but the two I saw in Austin said only dogs have that malady (as a rule). They thought, though, they ought to check over my liver. So they poked around my belly and said I was all right, except for gas; but that's from goobers. I aint giving them up either, even if they do cause wind. Nor am I giving up pitching washers for wagers. I don't care if Cravens does say gambling's a sin.

It was when I come back I heard about Elwood which I've never been close to, him or his project either. That night when the racket started up again, after his apparent passing, a lot of the men got riled. Some of the kids spooked, too, but the women didn't react to the hoorah. When I asked, my sweet friend Amarilla said she would not comment on the project. The women and the men, neither one, she said, understood it. She indicated she was probably the only one in town knew what Elwood was trying to do, and how come he wouldn't tell anybody was because he intended on getting rich and didn't want anybody, he'd say, stealing his bygod damn idea. That's what she told me, and also that they might get married – a fact I disliked, but I didn't let on. I kept my simmering to myself.

"What was he tryin to do?" I asked. "And did they get'm or not?"

"Which one you want to know?"

She was trying to be teasy with me, but I wouldn't bite.

"Both," I answered.

"They did and they didn't. And he may or may not recover."

"You mean you know where he is?"

She didn't even look at me. She just stayed lying there on her bare back with her ankle on her knee. I couldn't even tell if she was avoiding my question. But she did mention what Elwood had been about: trying to make some kind of cattle-screwing machine. Seems he'd heard somewhere about the possibility of breeding being increased. He was trying to make a machine to help the bull out, and I guess the cow, too. But mostly his own pocketbook.

Notions like that plumb amaze me. I wouldn't even know how to start. Apparently Elwood didn't either, but he kept on banging his hammer on the pipe all night trying to adjust what hadn't even been put together right in the first place.

"Then how come all that racket after they hung him or whatever?"

"It wasn't Elwood," she said. "What it was was someone trying to finish up what he'd been trying to get started."

"But you said nobody knew."

"Somebody might've seen him. Probably all it was, though, was somebody finding his stuff and trying to figure out what it was he'd been after. I imagine it'll be awhile before we hear anything else from his gear. But what I'm curious about is if you plan on sleeping over."

"Indeed I do," I told her. She needn't never asked, her knowing how partial I was to waking up in the breeze of the morning and hearing them yellow-bellied freckle-breasted meadowlarks singing and me feeling all blowsy with them, like I'm swimming up out of some crazy dream to find my sweet lady slow-loping my mule.

We had another drink before sleep, but when I woke up in the night she was gone. She wasn't anywhere in the house. The back door was wide open. I couldn't find her out back either, so I figured she must be tending to Elwood, wherever she had him hid. I found out later I was wrong. Someone had threw her down the well.

It's just extraordinary how a mind'll pull your ninners. Here I was half in love with her and grateful she hadn't suffered pain from her fall, her death having occurred before. Some bastard had planted an ax in the middle of her back, right near the spot where my fingertips used to meet when I clutched her and we got so lathery neither one of us cared about the poop-noises our bellies made against one another.

But she was gone and I swore I was going to get revenge. I didn't care who I had to hurt. I was so angry pissants were crawling all inside my craw. She hadn't ever done anything but help poor people feel better. I swore I'd get whoever hurt her. And I did, too. Got both of them, and quicker than I thought, too, me not even ever having pretended to be swift in the head.

What I did was find me that contraption Elwood had been working on. They did hang him and he did die, but not at the same time. I staked his outfit out for two nights, but no one showed up. Fact, the only one came near it was a scrap-buyer in the middle of the day and he didn't know what to do with it any more than anybody else here in this curly dogtail place did. Nobody came around the well either, except maybe a pig or two from over Szczepinski's farm. I asked around the cafe and saloon, but nobody said anything more'n what a shame it was all this carrying on and disaster. But you can't tell with folks around here whether they're telling the truth or not. I don't think it's because they're so clever. I think it's because they aint figured out themselves what the truth is. I have heard outsiders come in and call them sly like a snake, but those are the suckers coming through town and buying the trinkets kids make out of sticks and nails and ribbon when they're playing hooky. The kids tell those sports the doodads were made by Indians living over by the bluff. It was a pig, though, broke the ice and let me undrown the crime's awful secret.

Szczepinski didn't help either or that jackass Cravens who I myself heard threaten Elwood with hanging. It was that young sissy dude, Heinz Fretlinger, who hadn't never done anything fit to talk about other than try to gamahuche a goat. I caught him attempting the same thing with the pig, only he didn't notice I was around. He didn't have any luck either – the pig kept biting him – young Fretlinger cussing and crying and swearing he'd get an ax. That's when I started taking notice. Folks around here don't use axes except to chop wood; they don't even have any ax-throwing contests the way they do in some places, like Austin and San Antone. Swinging an ax is just damn hard work except apparently for Fretlinger who's always been a sissy. He lives in a shack back of Cravens' wheatfield. I followed him home and early that evening found on the handle of the ax at his place all the evidence I thought I needed.

When he went out that night I slipped in his shack and found a yellow ribbon tied on a nail in his wall. I knew where it came from: way up high on Amarilla's thigh: garter you call them. I lifted it off but when I put it in my pocket I started feeling sad all over and missing her.

There wasn't any place to hide so I went outside in the dark till Fretlinger came back. I figured he'd be drunk, but he wasn't anywhere close to it. He just walked in and lit a lamp. I stayed outside watching through a window, then noticed a coil of rope on a pile of clothes in the corner. The end of the rope was a noose. Somehow, I realized, Elwood was involved in all this, but I wasn't sure how. Fretlinger couldn't've done the hanging himself, or firing the shot either. He was too weak for the first and too lily for the second. Still, something told me everything was tied together, that I was just too damn crazed with grief to know how, only that's not the way I felt. When Fretlinger finally let the secret out, everything was all taken care of – only not in the way I'd planned.

Thinking he'd get scared, I chunked pebbles at his window, but all he did was raise the window and ask if anybody out here wanted him. Like a fool, I said yes.

"Who ith that?"

"Somebody knows what you did, Fretlinger."

"Who ith it I thupposed to do?"

"I know – a bunch of us know. We're gonna get you for it, too."

"You juth come on in. We'll talk about it."

Thank god I stayed hid and he didn't have an ear worth a damn. He poked a shotgun out and pulled the damn trigger, only I was in the other direction from where the blast went. I admit it, I was scared and must've lost control and yelled because he whoopeed and came running out of his shack. I kept hugging shadow. When he finally gave up looking, I'd snuck around the other side and would've give anything for a couple rattlesnakes to toss up on that little pecker of a porch leading into his place. He went on back inside and blew out the lamp, I don't even think scared. And rattled as I was, I wasn't even sure any more he was guilty. I thought about the ax handle again, saw it up close in my mind. What I thought had been blood was just paint. I'd put it there myself a couple years back, about a month before it had disappeared from Amarilla's tool shed. Fretlinger might've been a thief, but I don't think a killer.

Next day the story circled, the story about Fretlinger shooting me, only they didn't know who I was, just that there had been commotion. I was delivering groceries back to the cafe's kitchen when I heard Sally Cravens say, "Husband told me something like this'd happen."

She was standing outside the dry goods store between me and the woman she was talking to so I didn't know who it was. I could just hear their voices.

"You ask me, it all goes back to Elwood," the other woman said and I agreed. "I think he got away and killed her." But I disagreed with that. "He's the one had the ax," she said. "They didn't hang him. He got away."

She was right. Nobody but me now knew what happened to his body.

"Got away? How?"

"Someone helped him."

"Who? Young Mr. Fretlinger?"

"No. At least not directly. I think it had to be the woman herself – maybe Fretlinger with her."

"Fiddle! Heinz Fretlinger never had anything to do with that woman, or any woman. Just Elwood and all the other damn men. But they sure didn't hang or kill anybody."

"How do you know?"

"The atmosphere around here'd be tighter than it is."

"But Cy was upset and so was your husband Will."

"They're always upset. The noise ever bother you?"

"No. I heard it but I didn't think it was that bad. I don't ever lose sleep less a baby's crying sick or such."

"That's what I mean. I don't know a woman in town that that noise bothered."

"Then why the men?"

"I told you – that woman. Oh, they were upset with Elwood all right but not about his noise. Not mainly."

"About her then?"

"Her and him both. Him hogging her. And someone else, too, but I'm not sure who it'd be. Just mark my word – Heinz Fretlinger's a victim. He's no more guilty than we are."

I'd better back up. Long about then I drifted out of earshot and couldn't be sure if she'd really said Fretlinger was a victim or if she'd said Fretlinger was gonna get'm. The sun was in my eyes and if I can't see good I have trouble hearing.

Confused, I started feeling sick in my stomach and somehow guilty, too, and cheap for what I'd been ready to do to Fretlinger, titty that he was. Then it struck me: I didn't have a damn friend left, and maybe never did, at least the way I'd thought. For awhile I even wondered if I might not've invented about that ax and Amarilla doubled up at the bottom of the well. And even all the things me and her used to do – did I just dream that? And if I did then how come everthing fell smack-dab in their sonofabitchin places?

So there I was: one moment convinced Fretlinger was a rotten damn killer then the next minute realizing he didn't have anything to do with it. And what's worse: even ready to give up memories I wasn't even sure any more me and her had ever had. And them women to blame. They'd messed up my notions, and not only that: for the first damn time it upset me to realize how spineless I was. Talking to themselves and not even shining my way – face or butt either – they threw the truth on me. It was hotter'n a brand stuck up in my face. There was only one person I hadn't even considered might've did all the trouble, and that unlucky bastard was me.

I had a reason, too: hatred of Elwood and hatred of her: that grief I hardly even told about, or faced myself either, till then. And Heinz Fretlinger didn't even own an ax, except the one he'd stole a good while back– stole or just hadn't returned. I had put it there on his place as evidence but just in my head. I threw the real one in the salt cedars down by the river, which was dishonest. The ax wasn't even mine. It was hers and I was mixed up. Then it happened – her getting killed that last night I was with her, when I woke up and found her gone.

I'd gone outside, gone out to the barn where I heard hay or such rustling and a loud cranky squealing. She'd been hiding Elwood up in the loft. But it must've been just a short while before that she'd found he'd passed. I say that. I don't know. The noise was coming from his weight putting a strain on the rope that pressed against the pulley as she lowered him in jerks back down on the ground. I stayed back and watched. She drug him out in the clearing. She piled down on him hay and the wood I'd chopped. She slopped kerosene on the stack then struck it all up in a big damn fire. All she had on was her nightclothes. I watched her through the shadows and glare. I watched them toys on her body I sometimes played with – me and ever damn sonofabitch man around here. Even Elwood, dead and dumb as he was now, popped his eyes open at her when the wind blew a flip up under her gown and pressed it fast against her.

It wasn't just jealousy stirring me. It was the fact she was burning him with a look on her face showing a lot more agitation than sorrow. That's when I knew that if something similar had happened to me, she'd've set me on fire, too, and not even broke a sweat digging a hole. That was the kind she was, and I hadn't known that. That was just damn hard to take, and an awful lot worse than being thought spineless. She didn't think I was anything, except something to piddle around with so I'd do her damn hard work. I wasn't anything to her, and Elwood wasn't either, except a chance to get rich. It wasn't even pleasure we'd had together. All it was was convenience, and something like that rips deeper than anything can ever scab over. That's the way I felt then, and I didn't get over it till I put the pain – thought I'd put it – plumb out of my squirrely damn mind.

After she stoked the fire a lot more than I ever thought was necessary, Elwood wasn't no more than ashes. You couldn't tell what was him from what the wood used to be: everthing mixed together, except for charred staves that could've been bones. But pretty and nasty and unruffled as ever, she went to the well to wash her damn hands. And that's when I started thinking myself into fits. I thought that if I was still asleep she'd have done the same thing she just did and come on back to bed, acting like nothing had happened. I couldn't stand that. I knew what she'd been fiddling with, and I don't mind saying it either: I aint enough man to be casual about being played with by a hand that's just been messing with a corpse. So I gritted my teeth and went back to bed, but not before first I allowed myself to set that ax down deep in her back.

When I woke up I felt like I'd been having another one of my squirrel-headed dreams. I went outside to find her but couldn't. I didn't know where she'd gone and hoped I hadn't really done what I'd just dreamed I'd done. I was sure I hadn't. So I went over to the cafe for coffee, which for a month or so I'd been having in the morning instead of beer. That was near the time when I heard those damn two women chattering. I still don't know why but somehow they made me start facing what it was I'd done. In spite of their cussing their men, they were part of a good world I'd never known, and that made me feel small and to blame – and separate from everthing, even myself, because those people, tidy as they think they are, hadn't cared any more about Amarilla than she'd cared about me. I wasn't even sure any more they cared about each other. Life felt cold and I felt to blame, like a damn blue norther had crawled in like worms and crickets under my skin. That was the misery I was going to have to face: nobody around here cared shit, not about me or anybody else. Only I was the one who'd used the damn ax – they hadn't – and on somebody

I once considered sweet and still even love in my drizzle-headed way.

I could've escaped. I could've just left and nobody cared, everbody used to me lighting a shuck, and they sure not going to go to any trouble or grief either over a lady like Amarilla. Even if the men had been inclined, the women wouldn't've let them do anything open about it. So I could've got away. But I didn't. I went back in there at the cafe and confessed. Only nobody believed me, except in his own crooked way Will Cravens, who like I said's a lay preacher; and here that's bigger than sheriff, which we don't even have.

"Well, if you really did it," Cravens said, "we oughta hang ya."

I stood stout like a man and admitted I deserved that.

He said he wasn't one to judge but if it would make me happy he'd be glad to get the boys and some rope and pop my neck off my shoulders for me. He hollered them all over, but, laughing, they said they were going to buy me a drink first, and a fresh hot plate of fried eggs. They made me sit down at a table, and ole skinny Cy Szczepinski held the fork and fed me faster than I could even swallow. I think he was trying to strangle me.

"When you want us to string you?" Cravens asked.

My mouth was so full I couldn't answer so just shook my head to tell him I didn't know.

"You want it later on this afternoon or just wait till morning?"

Scrunching my chin down to force some gas out, I indicated I didn't care, and they commenced laughing, one of them even suggesting they pull my pants off and run me out in the street. Everbody thought that was a fine idea, except Szczepinski who said that when I saw the women if I got a bone on he'd cut it off with his big Case knife. Finally able to swallow my throat free, I told him not to worry, that even if that snakelike joke in my drawers tried to rise I wouldn't ever let it do damage. Then someone poured a pitcher of beer over my head, and all of them piled on me, stripped my britches off and chased me out the door – hitting and kicking and throwing onions and ever damn thing they could find. Even the picture of the naked lady on the wall which looked a little like my friend, deceased now, and theirs, too.

Outside, like I feared, was a cadre of women, but except for showing a bit of disgust they didn't pay much attention to us. The men chased me down the street and pushed me down in mud puddles by the watering troughs. They knocked me up against horses, which got skittery, and ripped my shirt off and even some of them rubbed hockey in my hair. They didn't hang me, though. They just run me out of town.

And Cravens, who's got breath smells like corn that's been pissed on, shoved his stout belly up against me and knocked me stumbling over a big fanning spread of prickly pear. He told me I was a liar, that Amarilla hadn't died in any well, she'd just moved because her place was going broke and there wasn't anything or anybody here to hold her.

What they were doing to me hurt. If I could've cried I'd've leaked tears all over the dirt, but I didn't. Worthless and spineless, I just sputtered and choked and heard Cravens saying again how much a liar I was and how they couldn't stand or put up with such trash. And everbody hurrahed him, or maybe they were all now just hurrahing me.

Finally getting a hold on myself, I knew there wasn't any point arguing with them. They don't listen. People like Amarilla don't either. They just take what they want and go, and no feelings of loyalty or staying still with someone ever hit them. She pulled some good work out of me, and pulled a chance at a fortune out of Elwood, too. She pulled some life out of everbody here except Fretlinger who'd rather court a damn animal and Cravens who's rank and stove up with talk. But they were all kicking me now and beating on me and yelling at me to hurry up and leave, which I did, in spite of them being all over me and grabbing me back down. Naked and bruised as I was, I scrimmaged out from under them, and spineless or not, I ran.

"Catch!" one of them called. I turned around and jumped, but it wasn't a snake Cy was throwing at me, just a piece of rope. He hollered at me to hang myself, that they didn't want to take the trouble, then they all started after me again. I ran. They yelled at me to stop and come get my rope, but I kept running, and feeling as gutsick as I'd ever been, I wasn't going to slow down or go back. I was quit of them and free — free of them and free of everything. All I wanted was a cliff to jump off of, and I would have, too, if I'd found one.

There was only one thing left: keep going and, first chance I got, steal some clothes.

When I did look back they'd all gotten small. A few of them were chunking rocks at me, but the distance between us was smart; and before the day was over I'd swiped a pair of overalls off a clothesline.

What I'm doing now is living out in the woods near the river. I don't mind it either, being cut off. I don't mind it damnit at all. My dreams have started coming back and, silly as some of them are, they do me good. When it's dark I don't even have too much trouble hearing the sounds of Elwood pounding on his pipe: things back the way they were. I do, though, miss my sweet friend. Most people like her live only near town, and I can't go back there any more. I can't ever just plop myself down near where she is. I'm to blame, too. I feel bad about what I think I probably did with that ax. It would've been more mature to have planted something else in her. Sometimes she let me do that.

It seems funny now. Afterward she'd start carrying on about how stout Will Cravens' preaching was – she did go to church now and then – and how, though most of the people where we lived didn't know what sin was, she said, there really was such a thing, and women knew about it better than men, which didn't mean, she said, that women sinned more; it meant they had a more practical sense of what it was, they being less prone to hoorah and such, and having more practice with forgiveness because of the men.

I never did understand what she was talking about those times – which is another reason I miss her and why, as time ripples past, I get the notion more and more that I really wasn't the one stuck that ax in her back. Sometimes I'm certain I didn't. But I don't believe she just moved. I wouldn't've invented about her being dropped down that well. I couldn't've come up with something like that any more than I could've ever come up with that idea and that contraption Elwood was making everbody miserable with. But somebody got her, and the more I think about it, the more I don't have any idea who did it. I don't even know if she knew. But I still feel to blame, and I can still feel that ax's oak handle solid and hard in my hands. I don't care whether Cravens believes me or not, the blade would belong to him: wedged right between his eyes.

But I do remember one time her saying when I was cleaning up her place, her saying how come most people don't pay attention to me is because I'm so much like them, only me and they don't notice it. She always did have a way of talking and thinking funny. And I wasn't one to ask her to explain herself either. The reason for that being the questions never occurred to me till a long time later. One time I even told her such, but she just laughed and wiggled her body which somehow reminded me of clouds. We have a lot of them around here – all kinds. We just don't have much rain. And the songs those freckle-breasted meadowlarks sing beneath them in the morning, when the clouds are red and purple or even just gray and blue, always seem to me sweet but sassy enough that you don't even mind how ridiculous they are, and how different they are from what they sometimes look like: them birds I mean – all puffed up soft in front like my friend and making you want to dive on in and just lose yourself blind in their feathers.

The Way the World Is

The afternoon hot, the traffic light, convection currents waved off the pavement, and only a few people interrupted the green stillness of the lawns he bicycled past. His hair, when the sunlight struck it, flared golden. Fighting the crosswind pushing him toward the curb, he pumped his yellow racer faster. His chest thudded, his back and crotch soaked. He was on his way home to his two daughters.

His heart pounding out a deep rhythm, a gust of wind knocked him skidding against the curb but, quickly listing left, he jerked the handlebars to keep from tumping over. His back tire skidded as he shot back out into the street. The glare was dizzying. Mirages ahead were unreachable oases.

A Volkswagen Beetle, parked on the street blocks ahead, shimmered its sand-colored bulk at him. Stinging drops of brine washed his eyes. The substance of air-filled lungs and blood pumping ballooned his chest. The rapid quivering of his tires rattled up his spine, and at that moment a grand smile of satisfaction – he had no idea what it was in response to, other than the momentary wonder of existence itself – appeared on the glistening features of his face. His arms no longer trembled with fatigue; they, like his legs, felt strong again. Asphalt hummed beneath his tires.

Because his eyes were mostly on the road, he could scarcely see now more than light and shadow waving amorphously into and out of each other, but he brought back out of memory the various architectures of the houses on the street feeding toward his own. They were one- and two-storey, split-level, brick, some of them with siding on them; his, though, was stucco. The trees – sycamore, pine, and troublesome hackberry – thickened. Jonquils and irises and hydrangeas leaned over the monkey grass and wandering jew that bordered the beds they had been planted in. Patches of light, spilling down through the tree branches, were petal sprays his tires hissed over and between.

"Jefry!" someone called, and he saw it was Vestal Leit, a retired bus driver who had the finest lawn in the neighborhood, though maybe the poorest house.

He angled across the street and, stopping at the curb, met the old man who was resting against the handle of his hoe. Tools poked out of every pocket.

"How's it goin?" the old man asked.

"Fine," Jefry said, aggravated. Vestal tended to chatter.

"Saw on my walk you about got all that crabgrass out."

"Most of it," Jefry said. "It'll take awhile longer to get the rest."

"Better hurry. That stuff comes back like mites on a bird."

"I'll get it," Jefry said.

"Probably not all of it," Vestal told him. "How're the kids?"

"Fine," he answered, catching Vestal's flinty eyes needling at him.

"You been chief cook and bottle washer nearly three years, aint ya?"

"About that."

"You ever hear from the kids' mother?"

"Sure. She checks in with them now and then."

"Ha! Your generation don't know how to handle their women. I broke mine proper. Women and horses both do an awful lot better when they're broke. They respect you for it, too, and they also ride a lot better, which is the main deal. Break'm right and you won't have much trouble. You might think about that when you hook up with a new one."

"I wouldn't worry," Jefry said flatly. "We're all doing well."

"Maybe so," Vestal said, shifting his weight. "There're just a lot of sickies loose. A lot of damn sickies. That's why I approve of war – keeps people occupied and out of trouble."

Pulling out his handkerchief to wipe his face, Jefry scooted back on the seat and found himself laughing at the asphalt below him. This encounter was absurd, but then nonsense had its own delights, too.

"I don't mean just the young," Vestal said, insisting on keeping his chatter going. "I mean ever'body. A war now and then'll cut out a lot of this crap gets outta hand. You agree?"

"No."

"Didn't think you would. It's probably a generation-type deal."

It intrigued Jefry that the old man, no matter who or what he was criticizing, never appeared truly angry, as if talk and notions were simply ways to occupy time, and nothing really to live or die for.

The old man wiped his bristly cheeks. He'd told Jefry recently that one way he kept his skin smooth was not shaving every day "Realized that soon after I retired. Hell, I don't care if three out of ever four days it looks like sin. On that fourth day I'm smooth as a baby's butt, and me and Gladys don't hug around any more reg'lar'n that anyway. Women, you'll notice, tend to get damn dry."

"How is Gladys?"

"Except for that growth on her elbow," Vestal said, "she's fine. Hell, here I am goin on about my wife and you don't even have one. I'm not making you lonely, am I?"

"Not really," Jefry said. "But I really ought to go. The girls are waiting and I need to get the sitter home."

"All right," Vestal said. "You just go and do what you think you need to do."

Feet back on his pedals, he cycled out into the street. Glancing back, he saw Vestal Leit waving at him with his upraised hoe. Shadows were smoking the old man's face.

"The way they mostly are, your children were just fine," Mrs. Biggs said, shivering, "but the air conditioner got too cold. I hope Brady and Cammy don't get the sniffles – or worse," she added. "Pneumonia can kill you. There's some of that going around, too. I think you ought to be more careful than you are."

"The thermostat," Jefry told her, "is right behind you there on the wall. You should've adjusted it."

"I saw it, but I don't like doing other people's machinery."

"Good lord, Mrs. Biggs, you were the one here all day."

"Most of it. The girls and I played on the swings awhile. And it squeaks. You ought to oil it some. If you don't it'll rust on through and one of them might break an arm – or neck. You ought to watch out better for hazards like that."

"Where are the kids?" Jefry asked.

"Out back," she said, then told him it was too hot in this weather for him to be riding that fool bicycle of his. "What do you want to get – a stroke?"

"I'm all right."

"That's what my second husband said," she told him, "exactly what he said about a week and a half before he had his last heart attack."

"He wasn't riding a bicycle, was he?"

"Of course not. He had a motorsickle, but I made him get rid of that, too."

"Let me tell the girls I'm home," Jefry told her, "then we'll be on our way."

"You're not going to take them with us?"

"If they want to go."

"I don't think it's a good idea to leave children unsupervised. Too much could happen."

"Then we'll take them with us," Jefry told her, smiling.

"I hope," she said, "you don't think I'm interfering."

"Not at all," he said, patting her shoulder. She reached up and took the check out of his hand. "Any messages?" he asked.

"Just one," she said. "Your friend Wheeler called but didn't say for you to call back. You might, though. Some people don't say what they mean or want. Some folks don't say that at all."

"Anything else?"

"Couple envelopes in the mail but I didn't open any of them. The girls wanted me to, but I didn't think I should."

"That's a lie!" sang Brady, leaping into the room from the patio. She was six.

"It is not!" Cameron cried, running in behind her. She was five.

"Nunh-unh, Daddy. Mrs. Biggs said she'd open every single piece."

"Brady! You're going to Hell," Cameron said. "Liars go to Hell."

"*You* are."

"Shut up," Jefry said, "both of you."

"She's the one started it," Cameron insisted.

"Cameron!"

"She did. She started it."

"I'm being quiet," Brady said. "I just came in to hug Daddy, but you're going to get your fanny toasted." Then he heard her whispering, "Asshole."

"Brady!" he cautioned her.

"She said it, I didn't," Brady lied. "She's been playing with that nasty Lindal up the street. Talks like him, too."

Suddenly Jefry realized that Mrs. Biggs was staring at him, saying in effect, You ought to be shot for not cuffing these little ruffians.

"All right," Jefry said, "everybody settle down. Let's get in the car."

"We going to Dairy Queen?"Brady asked. "If we're not I'm not going."

"Hush!"

Mrs. Biggs was scraping her fingernails with her blue house key. Laughing as he backed out of the driveway, Jefry asked her if she'd like to put in another shift.

"You call me," she whined, "when you need me. And, you girls, be good."

"We'll try," Cameron said, "because when you try to be good you go to Heaven."

"Not me," Brady said, "I go to Baskin-Robbins, and not you either 'cause you'll be in Hell. Just me and Daddy and our peppermint cones – the only two of us in Heaven."

Immediately Jefry slung his arm over the seat and caught Cameron's hand before she hit her sister. He kept a hard grip on it. "Now settle down," he said. "Both of you." And they did.

When he got to Mrs. Biggs' house, he told her, "I'll pick you up Monday."

Mrs. Biggs slammed the door behind her then turned back and told the girls through the window, "Switchings is what you need – switchings," but both girls swarmed over the back of the seat and, tangling their arms around their father's neck, told Mrs. Biggs, as they kissed their father's ears and, giggling, licked his neck, that that wouldn't happen.

Wheeler had called about a tennis match, and Jefry was pulling on his shorts when the doorbell rang. Thinking the girls would answer it, he buttoned his pants and sat on the bed to slip on his socks and shoes. Voices from the television set in the girls's room fussed. The doorbell rang again, and then again.

"I'll get it," he complained, and slopped down the hall in his untied shoes. At the door he pulled his red jersey over his head.

It was Vestal Leit, chin tucked and looking depressed.

"How about me comin in to visit?" he asked, then shook his head as if there were something awful he couldn't understand.

"I'm getting ready to play tennis," Jefry told him, acutely aware that Vestal had never approached him like this before, but Vestal said:

"My business won't take long." The old man looked rotten. His eyes were red and bags puffed under them. His head and hands quivered.

Both confused and curious, Jefry told him, "Sure, come on in," but Vestal hesitated.

"I'd better not," he said. "You've got your own doins to take care of – tennis and such."

"Listen, why don't you come with us? We can talk on the way. And if you get tired waiting around, it's just a short walk back."

"Who'll be carin for the girls?"

"They're coming with me."

"I'd better not," Vestal said. "What I came to talk about, it wouldn't do for them to hear."

"So why don't I just call my friend and cancel?"

"I don't aim to interrupt," Vestal said, backing away. "You and me can talk later."

Jefry stepped out into the carport and took the man's arm, the muscles in it stringy, the skin soft.

"What's wrong?" he asked.

"Forget it," Vestal said, his voice high, a desperate look glazing his eyes. "There ain't anything wrong."

"Come on in," Jefry said, assuming the old man was lying. He dragged him in to the doorway. "I'll call Wheeler and call the game off."

"I won't let you do that," Vestal said, but Jefry had already picked up the phone. "No!" Vestal said. "Put that damn phone down."

"For heavensakes, I don't mind."

"I won't allow it."

"Then come with us."

"Not with those girls. No! I didn't have any right comin here in the first place."

"But you did!"

"And I regret it. Now let loose of me." He snapped his arm away, then Jefry noticed both girls had come out of their rooms and were staring at them. He told them to go back, but they kept standing there.

Vestal was shuffling toward the door. Jefry tried again to shoo the girls away but they refused to go, then he heard the door creaking, and a loud report. Vestal had snapped the spring on the screen-door against the shuttered frame.

"Wait!" Jefry said.

"I've waited long enough," Vestal said. "There's goin to be some, goddamnit, regret!"

Jefry caught up with him and, unable to convince him to stay, got him to agree to come over after supper.

"I will, even though it might be all over by then."

"What?"

"Not with your kids around, I'm not gonna talk about it."

Finally Jefry went back inside, and immediately Brady told him she didn't want to watch him play tennis.

"I'm not leaving you here by yourself. Now get your shoes on."

"I'm not going either," Cameron told him.

"Now both of you, get your shoes and get in the car."

"You're mean," Brady said.

"Why can't we stay?" Cameron asked.

"You heard me. Get in the car. Both of you."

They kept arguing but, trying to ignore them, he bent over and tied his shoes. They kept saying they didn't want to go.

"Shut up!" Jefry told them. "Just shut up and get in the car," and suddenly turning agreeable, they did just that.

"Daddy's going to win," he heard Cameron say.

"I know," Brady told her. "We got him fired up, and Wheeler's gonna get creamed."

As usual, Wheeler was late showing up. When he did arrive, he bounced out of the car wearing a broad-brimmed leather hat, one side tacked to the crown with a diaper pin. Leg muscles rippling, he hop-shuffled toward Jefry. The tails of his faded green, paisley sport shirt flapped off his wrinkled tan walking shorts.

"I got new shoes, too," he said, snapping his ankles together in midair, but what Jefry noticed most were his black socks.

"You look like you got outfitted at the D.A.V. store."

"No, no, man, these are Adidas." He dropped a yellow ball and swatted it fast across the net at Jefry who twisted to keep from being struck in the groin. As quickly as possible Wheeler hit his other two. Jefry sailed the first one over the fence, then forgetting about aim, sent the next one straight at Wheeler's head.

Rallying, they criticized each other's play and dress.

"Where're the girls?" Wheeler asked, backhanding his shot.

"Out on the soccer field. I told them we wanted to be alone."

"Love me, love my dog."

"You're doing all right," Jefry said, "for someone with a withered arm."

"Anyone'd do well playing with someone wearing a sissy red

shirt like yours."

"I picked it out myself."

"I can tell."

"Like your black socks, too," Jefry said, their rally moving briskly now.

"Change what?"

Now and then varying the pace with lobs, they were making each other run, and they kept up their chatter.

"What strap?" Wheeler said. "I'm not wearing any strap. Got it tied to my leg."

"What with – dental floss?"

Before long the couple in the next court was staring at them, but Jefry and Wheeler kept bantering while they played. The man, pushing, when he moved, his bulbous belly and splayed feet, seemed more aggravated than the woman. Her dress, tight at the darts, was powderblue and her auburn hair was swept back into a pony tail. Finally the man had had enough. The woman told him to ignore them, but when Wheeler didn't stop his play to retrieve a ball that had rolled up against his and Jefry's net, the man dropped his racket, stuck his hands on his hips and said, "I said a little help, please. A little help, please."

"Sure," Wheeler said, letting Jefry's shot sail past him for a point. "Just keep your elbow straight," he said, going for the man's stray ball, "and don't take your eye off the sphere. Feet on the big sphere, eyes on the little sphere," he said, bouncing it back at him.

"Thank you," the man said, "and would y'all mind quietening the chatter down a bit?"

"Be glad to," Wheeler said.

"I appreciate it," the man replied, returning to his own court and nodding to his partner that he'd taken care of everything, and everything was now in control.

"Your serve," Wheeler said, pitching Jefry a ball.

"Play these," Jefry called over his shoulder as he turned around quickly the moment he got to the service line.

"Wait!" Wheeler said, pulling a cigarette from his shorts pocket, sticking it in his mouth then lighting it. He adjusted his hat, and with the cigarette still between his lips told Jefry, "I'm ready."

Squinting at him, Jefry said, "You're not nervous, are you?"

"About getting beaten? Not by a spastic like you."

"You don't usually start smoking till the second set."

"I'm building up strength," Wheeler said, glancing at the

woman in the next court, and Jefry sailed an ace by him.

"Fifteen-love."

They split the first two sets and were three-up in the third when Brady and Cameron stormed onto the court, saying, "Daddy, let's go home, we're hungry."

"As soon as we finish this set."

"That's too long," Brady said.

"I'm thirsty," Cameron said.

"We'll just be a minute."

"We're not going to be quiet either," Brady said.

"Just get under the umbrella out of the sun and hush."

"I wanta pee," Cameron said.

"So go on ahead and pee."

"No, I want to do it at home."

"Me, too," Brady said. "You've played long enough."

He and Wheeler went back to playing, and the girls kept badgering him, and having lost his concentration, Jefry missed point after point, but often narrowly, and he found himself laughing at the chaos his daughters kept stirring. They wanted a drink. They wanted to pee. They wanted candy. They said they were sick. They said they were tired, and both of them threatened to vomit, and half the time, Jefry knew, they were playing and having a wonderful time figuring out new ways to tease him. Finally, though, Jefry told Wheeler, "Let's quit. I'll see you at the house."

"What time?" Wheeler asked, his wife and son out of town for four days. "Eight?" which, Jefry knew, meant any time between eight-fifteen and nine-thirty. "I'll bring the drink."

When he got home Jefry found a note stuck on the door. Its faint letters quivered across the scrap of brown papersack they had been penciled on.

"Who's that from?" Cameron asked.

"Can I read it?" Brady asked.

If you're not tied up, the note said, *call me. V. Leit. Even if she answers. She don't know yet.*

The girls kept saying they'd rather go out to eat than have leftovers. He told them to go watch TV. They said there wasn't anything on.

"I'm hungry," Brady said.

"I am, too," Jefry told her, "but let me take a shower first, and

I'll fix us all something."

"We don't have to wait for Wheeler, do we?" Cameron complained from the bedroom. "He might not ever get here. Besides, the TV's not working right."

"Go fix it for her, Brady. You know how to work it better than anyone."

"No," she told him then leapt up into his arms. "I like it when she's bored."

He kissed the top of her head then made a motorboat sound on the back of her neck before putting her down.

"Run along," he said, "I need to get undressed and shower."

"Fine," she said, sashaying away, then snorting out a deep laugh, she said, "I don't even want to see your old hiney."

Jefry pulled off his shoes which he had not even bothered to untie. He glanced at the radio clock which clicked and rolled its minute wheel to the next number. He remembered the plates on the drainboard. They were covered with dried slabs of uneaten sandwich parts from lunch: cracking smears of peanut butter and strawberry preserves. Two of the glasses still had milk in them. On the stove top was a dirty tablespoon and an unwashed pan. Somewhere else in the kitchen, Jefry knew, were two cups stagnant with the mucous of old cream of chicken soup. Mrs. Biggs didn't do dishes.

Unable to decide whether to call Vestal Leit, Jefry leaned over the tub, and as he turned on the water, he remembered hearing the old man's feet hissing along the floor. The absurdity of the earlier encounter struck him. Vestal had never come over here in need or anything else, and he had never left a note either. *She don't know yet,* the note had said. Know what? Maybe the knot on Gladys's elbow was malignant, but that didn't make sense. The temperature of the water was right now, and he stepped into the spray, then as he started lathering himself, the bar of soap slipped out of his hand and caromed off the light blue tile. Bending to pick it up, he noticed brown streaks of mildew on the grout. Knowing the weekend called for serious scrubbing, he hurried through his shower.

Hair still wet, he went to make the call.

"He's not here," Gladys Leit told him.

"This is Jefry. I was . . ."

"Who?"

"Jefry Cross. From down the street. He asked me to call him."

For awhile the woman did not say anything. Finally she admitted, "He's out back."

"Okay. He wanted me to call. If you'll tell him I called."

"I can't," she said, then he heard her crankily add, "He hung himself."

Rushing outside, he met his daughters running in. Talking fast, they told him what they had seen. Squatting, he put his arms around them and said he'd just heard.

"We were in the alley," Brady said, "playing, and he was up on the roof and we asked him what he was doing – fixing something?"

"We did," Cameron said, "but he wouldn't talk back to us."

Jefry hugged them to try to squeeze away the horror, but they pulled away, as if they were too excited to slow down for affection.

"It was like he was deaf," Brady said.

"He had a big old chain," Cameron said. "I mean *big!*"

"Then bam! He disappeared," Brady said, "right off the roof."

"You didn't go around behind the garage then, did you?" Jefry asked.

They shyly nodded that they had.

"But he still wouldn't talk," Cameron said.

"Let's go in the house," Jefry told them.

"You don't wanta go look?" Brady asked. "We did, and he doesn't look scary either, just kinda weird."

As he hustled them back inside, Cameron asked, "Is he dead?"

"Of course," Brady told her. "He wouldn't answer you, would he?"

"Well, he wouldn't answer up on top the roof either – and he didn't look dead then, Fartface."

"Hush!" Jefry snapped at them.

"Why'd he do that?" Cameron asked.

"I don't know," Jefry said.

He told them he wanted them to settle down. He asked them to stay in the house until he got back. "I'm going across the street, and if Wheeler gets here before I'm back, let him in."

"What if it's someone else?" Cameron asked.

"Then we don't let'm in, Stupid – unless," Brady began giggling, "they're strangers offering us candy and money."

On the way out, Jefry turned the oven down to warm. Shutting the door behind him, he heard Brady squealing victoriously, "See! I told you he'd go look."

The Leits's cottage was covered with white siding. The shutters and trim were glossy black. Two large sycamores shaded the rich St.

Augustine lawn, but curtains and shades blinded the windows and made the place, in spite of its tidiness, look abandoned; and he remembered Vestal once saying, during one of their chats in the yard, "That's the way the old lady likes it. Keeps out the heat, she says along with the peepers."

Jefry stepped up on the porch. Two pots of acuba pinched the doorway. He pushed the buzzer but no one answered. Then he heard footsteps inside, but they were not coming toward him. The creaking ceased. He pushed the buzzer again and heard flatfooted steps slapping toward him.

"What do you want?" she called from behind the black wooden door.

"It's Jefry," he said, "from down the street."

"What do you want?"

He told her he'd come to see if she needed help.

"I don't need any aid. I already called who I want."

"I'm sorry," he told her. "If there's anything I can do –"

"Go away. I already called the only kinda help I need."

"I mean it," he told her, "if there's anything I can do to help, let me know."

"What is it," she shouted, "you want?"

"Nothing!" he found himself snapping back at her.

"Then go away."

Feeling strangely stained, he turned around and stubbed his foot against a pot, then he heard the cracking sound of the door opening behind him. He glanced back but it crashed shut.

As he walked back across the street, he turned back around and saw the taut length of chain hanging from a pecan tree in the Leits's backyard. The man had tried to make contact with him twice, but he still had no idea why, and all he could do now was face Leit's aggravating blankness.

Keeping his eyes on the graveled ruts, he strode defiantly up the driveway. If Gladys Leit cried out, "Where do you think you're going?" he wouldn't answer.

He came to the gate of the stockade fence and, tripping the handleless latch, pulled it open and saw the pale bare feet slanting toward the lawn. Scuffed maroon houseslippers lay beneath them. He took a deep breath and looked up. A button had popped off the frayed white shirt, and a furry belly puffed out of the space. He ran his eyes up the bulk to the face. Rimless glasses teetered on the edge of the nose. Vestal's eyes were open but they looked no more lifeless now than they had a few hours before. Spasms of a breeze came and blew the rank, fecal smell away, then dying, let it return.

Before long he heard an automobile coming into the driveway, but he didn't look around. He wasn't sure what he felt and had no impulse to decide on a thought. Something in him, though, said he felt an odd reverence in spite of the fact that another part of him said that this thing before him was nothing more than a bag now hanging from a towchain. Noticing that the body wasn't swaying at all, he thought about his daughters and their oddly rambunctious attitude after seeing the man jump. He also found himself thinking that he was glad they knew he loved them, and he was glad to know himself that their own tendency toward chaos didn't leave him feeling threatened.

Before long, when a policeman asked him if he were a member of the family, Jefry did not take his eyes off what he now called the carcass. He heard a wail coming from inside the house. The gathering milling around the yard now was chatting, swapping jokes and oddly distant information, but none of it seemed to have anything to do with Vestal Leit. Then again there came the sound of wailing, and the policeman addressed him again:

"I asked you before and I'm asking you now – are you a member of the family?"

"No," Jefry said, "I just live nearby, and I ought to get home," he said, feeling the enormous but simple strangeness of the world. "I need to fix supper for my girls."

Waiting for Rain

The morning sky bleeds as the neighborhood's cadre of joggers and walkers drones by, the soles of their shoes whispering like gossip over asphalt. Standing on her front porch across the street, a woman in an orchid housedress watches the spray coming off the rotary sprinkler clicking in her yard.

A rolled newspaper – its gray tint matching her hair – lies tucked under her arm. The last of the joggers passes, a small bearded man without shirt, the length of his feet slapping the street's surface flatly. A breeze brings the smell of moisture over to me as I glance at the thinness of cloudcover. There seems to be no chance for rain, although the sailor's saw, "red sky at morning," teases me into hoping we might have a shower by dusk. Drought is desiccating this region.

In the octagonal planter, pink and blue larkspur petals quiver at the edge of the sand-colored stalks gone to seed. Not much green is left in the yard, though there is a sizable, amoeba-shaped patch around the tiny pine we've struggled for three years to keep growing. The soil, where weeds have been pulled, is still dark from last night's heavy watering; but the fescue I sowed last week shows no sign of sprouting. Birds have even quit gathering there.

As I watch the woman gaze at her sprinkler, the electric night-lamp goes off. I forgot to turn the coffee on. I need to get back in, need to do calisthenics to loosen my back, need to take the trash out and bring a cup of honeyed coffee-milk to my wife who finds it hard to rise early, "or even at all," she has said. Her heartbeat's arrhythmically arrhythmic.

Much of the lawn has turned to straw. Crickets whistle. A mockingbird sings like a sparrow, then chortles like a grackle before sailing off into a high-pitched trill that ends with a comical sputter. Cicadas begin whirring. During the last week they left their brown shells hanging by claws on the fruitless mulberry leaves. Yesterday my son brought a batch in to scare my daughter, both of them here for their summer visit. As long as Damon kept them more than an arm's length from her, Gaddi wasn't bothered. She even pointed out that some of the hulls, stacked, looked as if the cicadas had been mating. Damon swore he hadn't tampered with them. "Sure," Gaddi said, mocking him, "sure."

With my old Boy Scout hunting knife I dig up crab grass and johnson grass. The long ivory tubers seem to be independent of the first stage of roots: claws tangled in topsoil. For two hot days I have been digging them out and have filled two trash cans and a plastic garbage sack. My next door neighbor, a retired Air Force colonel, tells me that weeding is futile unless, like him, you use Chemlawn. The other next door neighbor, a psychiatrist and Cuban emigré, gave up trying to nurture his thinning bermuda; he paid to have his yard tilled and reseeded. But more weeds than grass are germinating in the sandy loam he purchased. Scratching nape with the knife's dull blade, I decide to keep trying.

Last month, while pulling out another load of weeds, I cramped up so much I walked stiff-legged for a week. To relieve the pain, I got my wife to walk on me while, paralytic and prone, I sprawled on the burnt-gold carpet in the den. This time, though, I'm not getting so stiff. The knife works better than the V-tipped weeder.

Stabbing the clayey earth and ripping through it, I notice that I'm also not having after-images as much as in years past. In another house across town, I saw little, after working in the yard, except illusions of weeds and strawy grass. Once even a friend's face suddenly became a tumble of clover, goatheads and grassburrs. That was disconcerting. She was going through grief, but it's hard to look sympathetic when your friend has stickers for eyes and a tangle of weeds for a face. In time, though, both of our fits passed.

Dirt, which has gotten into my leather gloves, feels gritty. Specks of dark soil freckle my forearms. Sweat drips down my face and enlarges the stain on my shirt. I used to call this process driving out the poison. Happily, terms of corruption don't seem to apply any more, at least not as often as they did. Or so I like to think. Leaning back on one arm, I mop my face with my shirt. My son comes out and asks if I want a glass of iced tea.

"Sure," I tell him.

Smiling, he says he already has it with him and pulls the glass from behind his back. I foolishly ask if he wants to stay and help me.

"It's too hot," he says, drawing back.

"Be good for you," I tease him.

"I'd rather work on stamps."

"If you change your mind, come back out."

"How much longer are you going to be?" he cautiously asks.

"Nineteen hours," I lie to leave him free.

"No way," he says. "Want some more tea?"

"Maybe later," I tell him.

As he walks back to the house, I see my daughter watching us from the door. I wonder if she's dressed yet. The waxleaf lugustrum keeps me from seeing what she has on. I do notice, though, that she hasn't brushed her hair. She says she doesn't have to get dressed at home so she shouldn't have to fix up here, or do anything that's not her idea. Sometimes, though, she'll hit tennis balls with us, or go shopping, if Mary or I ask, but she prefers to spend her days watching game shows and soaps.

The dog gets between us. My two children have been taken to the planetarium by my father. My wife is lying on the carpet in the den. Acting as if I'm relaxing, I stretch out beside her, but our Samoyed wants us to romp. But we won't. We'll just wait for my wife's mother to finish the thirteen-hour drive to see us. Uncertain, however, that she's actually coming today – she is, after all, erratic – I kiss Mary behind the ear. "That tickles," she complains.

The dog again noses between us. Thinking about a woman I saw test-munching grapes at the grocery store, I get up and pour myself a glass of water. I ask Mary if she'd like something, too.

"No," she says, then, sitting up, welcomes the dog back into her arms. I sit down at the dining table and open the new copy of my alumni magazine. My parents lent me theirs. Somehow I've been dropped from the mailing list. Flipping to the back, I see that my classmates haven't reported doing anything, not even dying. The surrounding classes, however, have some new bank presidents, births and marriages. I feel on edge.

Before long Mary goes upstairs. I know there'll be a crisis if I follow her up, and there is, though it's a moderately civilized spat: charges about my moodiness, about the fact that that's a sign of repression. I suggest there's another point of trouble: her disinclination to be a spur-of-the-moment voluptuary. With more than a dash of pepper in her voice, she disagrees; and the argument's over. Sounds of the children returning are now with us.

Before long the four of us are back downstairs watching television, then having supper. Mary and I talk some more, this time about the coming presidential election. No one seems to have good things to say about our candidate.

After I wash dishes we have coffee together. Damon has ridden off on his bicycle.

"Already learning to tomcat," Mary says, sounding aggravated or maybe amused: I don't know which. "Just let the sun go down and he's off."

"He might find something interesting," I say, defending him. She smiles indulgently at me. Gaddi has slipped away upstairs, perhaps to draw or maybe just pout.

Mary tries calling her mother to make sure she's left, but there's no answer. I try calling myself, then we go upstairs and stop at the entrance to our bedroom. Mary has plans to read: tales of our time's compatriots back in the 14th century: buboes, chancres and a lust for magic. Although we're affectionate in the doorway, I keep quiet about some fantasies I'm having: a sybaritic life with her. She tells me she loves me, and I say I love her, too.

"Do you really?" she asks.

"Sure," I say, clasping my hands behind her waist. "We wouldn't be doing this if I didn't."

"You don't hate me – think I'm horrible and unresponsive?"

"No."

She pulls away and goes into our chamber. Thinking I ought to gather up my daughter and watch TV with her, I go toward my study. I do, though, first ask Gaddi if she'd like to come with me: we could draw or read together. Scarcely glancing up, she says, "No."

When I finally come downstairs for a drink, I see that my son has returned from prowling.

"Guess what?" he says, then tells me he's just discovered that one of his stamp-collecting buddies is a member of our church. He seems glad about the fact and unmindful of the vicious fights he's put up about having to go.

I squeeze his shoulder.

"Can I go now?" Damon asks, pulling away from my hand.

A friend, who's leaving tomorrow to visit his family in the East, comes for dinner. He's tall and red-headed, and his eleven-year marriage has recently been annulled. I congratulate him on his sect's enthusiasm for illusion, but he won't take the bait – possibly because the state says he still has fifteen months of payments left: his non-bride's half-share of the retirement funds he and an insurance company accumulated.

For supper I barbecue spareribs and Mary prepares spaghetti squash, green salad, then lemon meringue pie for dessert. After eating, we retire to the den where we watch a program on that French-American-Scotch-Irish writer of crocodilian extract: Brother Bill. John says he hasn't yet really worked Faulkner into his studies of Plato, Heidegger, Nietzsche and Derrida. I tell him he should: the South's weird-talking folks are closer than he thinks to Odysseus and Priam, Isis and Arjuna. He says I ought to hire out to write blurbs; I say I have then switch the TV back to convention coverage. Mary keeps getting up and leaving to take care of something in the kitchen. I ask her what she's feeding in there – a ferret?

She says she's going to turn the sprinkler on in the front yard. When she comes back she waters the plants in the living room then sits down on the sofa beside me. Soon, though, she gets up to put the dog out. Before long the children come back from the show. They went with the paper's Fine Arts editor who they and I used to live next door to. They scarf down their pie. Mary rises again, this time to load the dishwasher.

During the weather report, John suddenly asks what we think about Structuralism. Noticing that Mary is smiling, I tell him there are only two kinds of people: good ones and bad ones, that the good ones are those still capable of having their hearts broken. He says that's interesting, and I remind him I haven't answered his question. "But why don't we have a drink?"

Mary declines but John and I have Irishes on rocks. As the evening passes I have several more. The children go to bed about the same time the weatherman says we'll have more clouds but probably no rain in spite of the hurricane moving toward the coast. Galveston's going to get creamed.

Their last week with us, we take Damon and Gaddi to Santa Fe; and Mary's mother comes with us. She and the children quickly spend all their money. Suckers for adventure, we also take them to their first opera. High on the grace of mountain air, they sit (for awhile) on the edges of their seats during a fine production of *Elektra*. Gaddi says the huge waves of blood painted on the raked floor of the stage look like gigantic smashed strawberries. She also says that when she gets more money she's moving out here and she and Damon are going to build a mansion. Damon says he'd rather have one for himself. Laughing, Gaddi accuses him of having bad manners. Whispering to them to hush, I tell them intermission will be here soon.

At the airport, Mary looks worn as we kiss and hug the kids then tell them goodbye. Their arms wave like flags until they disappear into the tunnel.

As Mary and I walk toward a window to watch the plane taxi off, I see a woman releasing a little boy to a flight attendant. The kid has a paper heart pinned to his shirt; he's clutching an unwrapped stick of gum. When the pretty attendant takes his free hand, he grins. Looking lovely in her grief, his mother starts crying.

Home now, Mary and I rearrange two of the upstairs rooms so a larger sense of space now prevails in our chamber. Feeling hyperactive and lunatic, I find myself anxious to tell the kids about it, but I hold off calling them. I don't have the stomach to tell them there's something else that's different from the way they remember it. No. That's not true. I just don't want to hear them say they don't care.

The Last Campout

The boys, those of them who could swim or weren't afraid of water moccasins rumored to be in the water, splashed each other in the lagoon that evening while their fathers sat around the campfire drinking beer and spilling stories about their times in Vegas and Crested Butte. One of them, though, a professor named Aran, said he liked Mexico better.

"Acapulco?"

"No. Mexico."

"Acapulco's Mexico."

"Not the part I have in mind."

"So what part are you talking about?"

"Atotonilco."

"Never heard of it."

"Then you've never been to Mexico," he said, glancing over to see the commotion of boys running up into the camp, the kids slinging their dripping arms and laughing as they tried to get the men wet.

"Settle down," a father said.

"Gah!" a boy said, and another one explained:

"We just wanted to see if supper's ready."

"That doesn't mean hotdogs and marshmallows either," a boy said.

"Hush, Todd. We're having venison."

"Not me. Barbequed quail might be okay, but not venison. That stuff'll rip your teeth out the way *you* cook it," he said, giggling and running out of range of the towel one of the men popped at his bottom. Then other boys leapt forward, daring the man to try to pop them.

"Missed!" a boy said, then another one twisting out of range said:

"I want to know where the big sandy beach is. This place is a gyp."

"It's right here," his father said: "Sandy Beach at Possum

Kingdom."

"Yuk! My bathroom's bigger'n this dinky place."

"No, it's not."

"Bummer!" another boy said. "I thought we were gonna surf."

"This is a lake, Joel, not the damn ocean."

Running up into the group, another boy whispered in Todd's ear.

"Really?"

"Yeah," then the boy whispered something else.

"We'll be back later," Todd told the men then ran with his friend out into the mesquites and salt cedars to the beach.

"Did you see that look on their faces?" a father said.

"Did indeed."

"Wonder what they found."

"No telling," he said, then stopped. The other Indian Guide fathers hushed, too. This was the second overnight campout they had been on with their sons, and it would also be the last.

Looking at each other then glancing toward the promontory the two boys had run toward, they noticed another boy, then another, stealing away toward the point.

"Did you hear a couple motorcycles awhile ago?" a father asked.

"I think so."

"Did you see who was on them?"

"No, Harry," he said impatiently, "I didn't."

"You all just keep talking," Harry said, "I'll go check on the boys."

"Hell, they're all right. You ain't their damn mother."

"I know," he said, grinning.

"What's up?"

"If it's what I think, it might be their peckers."

"Hell, they're too young for that."

"I'll be back," he said, brushing dust off his Levi's.

"Damn!" another father said. "Sit back down and leave the kids alone."

"I'm going with you," another one said, getting up.

"Stay here, big Al," Harry told him.

"Don't think I will," Al said, smiling. "I saw'm, too."

"Saw what?" another father asked.

"You all just stay here," Al told them. "Harry and I have to talk business."

"I'm going, too," Harry's son said.

"No, you're not," his father told him.

"I sure am."

"No, you're not. If you do, we'll both be in trouble," Harry said, laughing.

"Not me," the boy said defiantly. "I saw them first."

"Who?" a father asked.

"You just stay here," Harry said. "Make sure supper gets cooked right."

"No! I'm going. And I know why you want to go, too."

"Why?"

"Because those two girls are out there swimming and one of them has bigger deals than Mama."

"Do *what?*" one of the other men said.

"Those two girls on motorcycles," Al told them.

"They don't have anything on either," the boy said.

Unwinding himself up off the ground, one of the men said, "I'm getting kind of stiff. Think I'll take a walk."

"Me, too," another said, getting up."

"Good idea," another one agreed.

"Hike'd do me some good."

"I know what you're doing," the boy said. "You're not going for a walk. You're just going to try to see those two women swimming."

"Listen," one of the fathers told him, "stay here, Son, and take care of the campfire. And try to make sure the tents don't burn down."

"I know what you're doing," the boy said at the men leaving the campsite. "But all they are is naked."

"That's often enough," a father told him.

"You're gonna get in trouble, too, when I tell Mama," he told his father's back. "First thing when we get home, I'm gonna tell."

Before long, all the men except Harry and Al had drifted back to the campsite lamenting not being single again. Others were aggravated that their sons had had to come with them on the outing. A few of the boys, though, said the fathers were the ones in the way. Finally Harry and Al came back, saying they'd made a deal: "We agreed to throw them their clothes," Al said, "if they'd come drink coffee with us tonight."

"Omigod," one of the men said, "you didn't invite them up here, did you?"

"Sure. Why not?"

"Because, damnit, half the women are staying here at the lake tonight in your cabin."

"So?"

"What if they come down and those two are with us."

"They won't. Besides, if they do, they won't see anything. We'll just be drinking coffee."

"And maybe a little beer," another one said.

"Besides," Harry told them, having just poured himself a stiff bourbon, "we'll have the boys for protection."

"That's just going to make it worse."

"I know," Harry's son butted in, "I'm gonna tell. I won't even have to wait to get home. That's what you get for not letting me go down there with you."

"You just keep your little mouth shut, Son."

"No! If you'd let me go with you, I might. But you wouldn't. You made me stay here so I'm gonna tell."

"No problem," another father said, sounding as if he'd found a fine solution. "The women come here, we'll just tell them the girls are Aran's friends. He's not married."

"Where is he?"

"I don't know. He and his boy went back near the road to try to catch lizards or something."

"Joke's probably on us. He's probably down at the point making arrangements for later."

"I hope so. It'd be a damn shame if we all had to go home dry."

"Trying to catch a damn lizard!" another man said in disbelief. "Sonofabitch probably really is. That's probably, too, why his old lady left him."

"Don't be bitter," Harry said, pouring himself another drink. "He's the only one of us who can't even get in trouble."

"Lord," one of them said, "thinking about that tall one out there makes me want to die. Getting up on her would be like climbing a damn mountain."

"How do you know? You didn't even see her up front. They wouldn't even get out of the water."

"Doesn't make any difference. A man sees the stern, he knows what the prow's like."

"Bullshit."

"It's true, and not only that, you get a good look at a woman's nose, you get a good idea what style of nipples she has, too."

"Goddamn, Fred," Harry said, laughing with the others, "you're the craziest damn sonofabitch I ever heard."

"I may be," he said, keeping a straight face, "but the shape of the earlobe'll give you some fine information as well, especially about a part you don't often get a good look at."

"Goddang, I'm ready to start sampling the beer."

After supper the taller girl did come to accept Al and Harry's offer for coffee. She was wearing jeans and a red-vested, black leather-sleeved jacket. Although it was fastened half way, she seemed to be bare beneath it. Squatting around the fire with her, several of the men nervously asked her what kind of blouse she was wearing.

"I'm not," she replied, then smiling mischievously, she clicked shut another snap of her jacket.

"What're you studying?" Fred asked her.

"Radio and TV."

"You going to be an actress?"

"No, advertising, unless I switch to nursing or law."

"That's a weird combination."

"Maybe now," she said, "but it won't be later."

"Why?"

"I'll only be involved with one of them."

"You date a lot?" Al asked.

"Some."

"Anybody steady?"

"Not any more."

"You ever dated any of your professors?" Harry asked.

"Sure," she said as Aran walked back into the campsite with his son.

"Aran here's a professor," one of the men said. "You ought to have a date with him."

Amused, Aran and the girl introduced themselves to each other, shaking hands above the flames, then Aran and his son Damon sat down across from her.

The boy asked his father if they had any more candy or sandwiches. Aran said no but added he'd be glad to split an orange with him. "They're in the box inside the tent."

"You get it," Damon said, his gaze wandering out toward the darkness. "I'll keep your place."

"Better hurry," Harry told Aran. "Damon's going to shoot you out of the saddle."

Ruffling his son's hair, Aran left and the girl asked Damon if he wanted to come sit by her. He shook his head no, but she asked him again as she patted the ground by her crossed legs.

"I'll come sit by you," one of the men said.

"There's plenty of room on the other side," she told him, but laughing nervously, the man stayed where he was. "Come here," she told Damon again, and this time the boy came to her.

When Aran got back he had the orange already peeled and split into sections that were cupped in his palm. He sat down next to his son. Damon took several sections then Aran offered the girl some, and when she bit into hers, juice squirted on her chest. Instantly one of the men jumped up and reaching back into his hippocket, said, "Here, let me help you – I've got a handkerchief."

"That's all right," she told him. "You might miss," and the other men laughed, some of them asking her if she'd let them try their aim. One of them assured her he'd been a crack marksman in Nam.

"No, he wasn't either. He just flew choppers."

Daubing herself with a tissue she'd pulled from a pocket, the girl leaned in front of Damon and asked Aran if she'd gotten all the juice off.

"Just about," he said, smiling back at her.

"Thank you," she said and patted Damon's knee, then one of the fathers asked his son if he might not like to go sit by her, too, and get his knee patted.

"Naw," the boy said.

"Go ahead. She'll let you. You'll be doing me a favor, too," he said.

"Don't do it," another man told the boy. "You'll be up all night – your old man trying to get a whiff off your knee."

Before long Aran asked the girl where she went to college. When she told him SMU, he said that's where he had gone. He mentioned a few professors he'd had, and she'd had one of them, too.

Trying to stay in the conversation, one of the men said, "You know, Aran here's had some plays on Broadway."

"Really?" she asked him.

"No," Aran said. "A couple in New York, but not on Broadway."

"Off-Broadway?"

"That's close enough," he told her.

"I'm impressed," she said, then a flood of headlights exploded on the area and the men, jumping up, said, "Omigod! The wives are here!" and hurried out into the darkness, some of them grabbing their sons and saying, "Let's go see if we can catch some fish."

"No!"

Cardoors slammed and there were only a few of the men left standing around the campfire with the girl who insouciantly stayed where she was. The women were laughing and joking until they saw her.

"Where's Al?" one of them snapped.

"I think down at the lagoon with Mark," one of the fathers said.

Some of the women had already rushed out into the darkness barking the names of their husbands who tried to sound happy to see them.

"What's that girl doing here?" came an angry voice in the night. "Who is she?"

"Girl?" Al said, his own voice loud. "What girl?"

"The one at the campsite. Who the hell is she?"

"I don't have any idea," he said. "Mark and I have been out here all evening. We've been fishing."

"So where is he?" she demanded.

"Out here somewhere trying to hide from me. He's mad because I won't let him go swimming this late. I told him you and I had a rule – no swimming after dark."

"You damn liar!" she said. "Where is he? I'm gonna find out what's really going on."

And another woman in the dark was asking who that girl was, and after coughing awhile Harry said flatly, "I don't know. I think she's one of Aran's friends."

"What's she doing out here?" his wife wanted to know.

"I don't know that either. She and her husband drove up on a motorcycle. They just got here a minute ago. Wasn't he back there at the fire with her?"

"No!" she told him. "He wasn't anywhere around there."

"Then I don't know where he is – probably taking care of their kids somewhere."

"I want to know what she's doing here."

"You got me. They're all Aran's friends. I've just been out here collecting firewood for morning. Wanta help?"

"No! We'll talk fire – we'll talk fire tomorrow," she told him.

Shortly after that the women regathered at the campfire then glaring once more at the girl, they left, but only after looking inside their husbands' tents to check if anyone they'd missed might be hiding in there.

Grinning wryly, the girl said she hoped she hadn't gotten anybody in trouble. Trying to sound confident, the men assured her she hadn't. Getting up, she said she'd enjoyed the visit but really ought to go, her friend was waiting for her at their own campsite.

"Bring her on over," one of the men said. "We'll all have a party."

"Maybe later," she said and some of the men started clearing their throats.

"That might be a good idea," a few of them mumbled, sounding uneasy.

"You going swimming again?" one of them asked.

"I might," she said brightly, turning to Aran. "Why don't you come see our campsite?" she asked him. "We can have a drink or go swimming if you like. Maybe even both."

"We'll see," he said.

Damon started scowling as she left, and Aran asked him, "What's wrong?"

"Nothing!" the boy said angrily.

"Come on. What is it?" Aran asked him, pulling him away from the others.

"It's not fair," Damon said.

"What?"

"I didn't get invited."

"Invited to what?"

"To go swimming."

"I'm not going swimming."

"Yes, you are. You'll wait till I go to sleep and then go. Well, I'm not going to sleep. I'm staying up all night."

"You'll be awfully tired tomorrow."

"I don't care. It's not fair."

"Tell you what," Aran said. "We'll go to their campsite tomorrow, and maybe they'll let you get up on one of their motorcycles."

"And ride it with them?"

"Maybe."

"She probably won't let me."

Laughing, he told his son, "That's what all these other guys have been saying."

It was late when the fathers got their sons to bed. Most of the men went to bed, too, a number of them saying, though, there wasn't any point in it: "I never can go to sleep on the ground."

"That's why I brought my camper," another said.

"Anyone want more coffee?" one of them asked, pouring a fresh cup from the smudged blue pot.

"Sure.'

"Not me," Harry said thickly. "I'm sticking with bourbon."

"Hell!" one of the men said, "can't even go on a campout without the damn wives coming over to spoil it."

"I'm turning in," Aran said.

"You sonofabitch!" Harry yelled. "If you go in that tent, I'm killin' you. Damn! The only free one of the bunch and you're making us all suffer for it. You damn bastard, get your ass over there and get yourself some."

"Yeah," one of them said, "do it for Harry. Little fat big-mouth needs a favor."

"Right – because he damn sure ain't gonna get any when he gets home."

"Listen," Al said, slapping Aran's back, "you ever get any offers at school?"

"Some."

"Young ones or old ones?"

"Sometimes both."

"Damn!" Harry said, "and my old lady thinks she has to interview ever'one of my damn secretaries. She even checks up on the bookkeepers."

"Life's rough," Aran told him.

"Damn sure is," Al said. "You think they might let me and Harry get on part-time out there?"

"I doubt it."

"That's what I was afraid of."

"Hell," Harry said, "they wouldn't even have to pay us. I'd work for free, long as there was some anxious poontang around."

"See you in the morning," Aran said.

"Sonofabitch," Harry told everybody, "I'm going swimming!" and storming up off the ground, he clumsily stepped through the fire, knocked over the coffee pot, and tripping, fell against a tent. A boy inside yelled, and scrambling back up, Harry lost his balance again, and as he fell backwards there came the whine of nylon tearing, and the rage of an angry boy, then another, and squealing and shouting burst from other tents, too, boys in T-shirts and underwear popping from the openings, and their fathers crawling out with them, but Harry didn't pay any attention to any of them because Harry had just passed out. The orange fold of the tent coming down on him looked like a huge birdbeak ready to peck his insides hollow.

Leaving the chaos, Aran went to his own tent where his son had gone awhile ago.

"What's going on?" Damon asked.

"One of the guys slipped and knocked a tent down.'

"Was he drunk?"

"What've you been doing – listening?"

"I couldn't go to sleep. You going to stay here?"

"Yes."

"All night?"

"Sure."

"Then how about giving me a back-rub?"

"What about you giving me one?" Aran asked.

"Maybe," Damon said, "but you probably don't itch as much as I do."

The next morning while the men were drinking coffee and frying bacon, a group of boys went to the girls' campsite. Soon several of them came back asking if they could ride the motorcycles. Some of the fathers said that would be all right, but others refused.

"At least let me watch."

"You can do that, Son. Just don't get on them. Your mother'd skin us both."

While the girls were giving the boys rides, Aran walked through the stand of mesquites to see if Damon were with them, then he saw the boy, just finishing his ride, waving at him.

"Daddy, you wanta ride?" Damon said, hopping off from behind the girl.

"Not now," he said. "We're ready for breakfast."

"Can I ride again? Can I?" Damon asked the girl.

"Not today," she said. "We're getting low on gas." Then she looked at Aran and asked him, "Where were you last night? You didn't come over for a drink."

"I couldn't," he said, nodding toward his son.

"I thought you were. We were here and stayed up late. It might've been nice."

"I know."

"You ever come to Dallas?"

"Some."

"When you do, give me a ring."

"Okay," he said, squeezing the back of his son's neck as two more boys came running up begging to be taken for a ride.

"One more," the girl said, "and that's all."

"Me! Me!"

"You've had your turn."

"It was just a short one."

"I'll tell you what," she said. "There's room enough for both." She helped them on, then nimbly lifting her leg over the handlebar and gas tank, she told Aran she'd see him later. As she drove away, two cars turned onto the dirt road then quickly stopped, their windshields reflecting a bright spray of sunlight. Tires suddenly spitting up dust, the cars sped forward, angling toward the tents down the way.

When Aran and Damon got back to the campfire, the women were fussing at their husbands. They wanted to know why they were so stupid to let their little boys get on those damn fool motorcycles. They wanted to know what those girls thought they were doing out here. They wanted to know a lot of things, and they said they were going to find them all out, too. Aggravated, one of the men said he hadn't let his son get on any damn motorcycle, the kid had done it himself, then another man said the same thing had happened to him: his boy had gotten on and had his ride before he even knew about it. Then another one said, "Hell, I didn't think it would hurt anything."

"You don't talk that way to me – the boy could've broken his neck."

"Well, he didn't."

"You know," another woman said, "we don't allow motorcycles in our family."

"What I really want to know," still another one said, "is how long those women were here last night. You didn't tell me they were spending the whole night."

"Look, I didn't know, and besides, nothing happened. The only one who came up was the one you saw, and she left right after you did."

"Damn you, Harry, they didn't have any business being here in the first place. And I'm finding out what went on."

"Damnit, nothing went on."

"Well, I'm finding out. "

"Listen," Al said, trying to ease the atmosphere, "would you all like some breakfast?"

"Shut up!" his wife said. "We've already eaten."

"Well, I'm getting ready to break a few eggs," Harry told them. "Be glad to have you join us." Then he asked his wife if she had a cigarette.

"Take the whole pack," she said with disgust as she reached into her purse, crunched the package with her fist then tossed it on the ground by the fire. "We're leaving," she said bitterly. "We'll see you this afternoon and I mean early."

"Nothing like Sunday morning, fresh air and freedom, is there?" Al said, stretching by the fire and farting.

"Goddamn," Harry said, "something must've crawled up inside you and died."

As the group was finishing breaking camp, one of the men came up to Aran and in a low voice asked him if he had gotten over to see the girls during the night, but before Aran could tell him, the man said, "Damn!" then taking a deep breath and grinning as he walked away, he looked back and told Aran, "you know, you're a sly wicked sonofabitch."

The Circus

1.

Emerging from the arrival tunnel, the boy and girl looked distractedly around the waiting area until they saw the two who had come to the airport for them. Rushing to meet, the four of them hugged each other.

"How're you doing?"

"Fine."

"I've grown, Daddy."

"I can tell."

"Gaddi acted up on the plane," the boy said.

"I didn't either. You're the one spilled Coke."

"Just because you kept wiggling and bothering everybody."

"You cut your hair, Mary," Gaddi said, swept up for a kiss.

"So have you."

"But it's getting longer."

"Daddy, can we go fishing today?"

"We'll see," the boy's father said.

"I sure hope we get to go today or tonight."

"We've got to drive back home first and go out to eat," he said, ruffling the boy's hair and squeezing him to his chest.

"I didn't think we would, so I got up at six this morning."

"To fish?"

"Sure – before we had to get to the plane. I go every Sunday, but I didn't catch anything. Last week I almost caught one that weighed thirty-five pounds."

"That's all right," his father said, squeezing his son's neck. The boy smiled at him crookedly. "We've been missing you."

"We've been missing you, too."

"Daddy, I want a hug," Gaddi said, and her father, who had already kissed her many times, took her from Mary's arms, and the girl bit his nose then giggled and tried to bite him again.

He tweaked her tummy, and the four of them walked chattering toward the baggage area.

"I only have to stay a month," Gaddi said, "if that's all I want to stay, but I don't have to stay two if I don't want to."

"They know," Damon said, irritated. "It was their agreement, too."

"If I want to go home after a month, I get to. That's what Mother said. How long're you gonna stay?" she asked her brother.

"Probably two." Then looking at his father, he asked, "How often do you think we'll go fishing?"

Mary and Aran looked at each other. Both of them knew that buried in the question was a threat.

"I've gotta pee," Gaddi said. "Bad!"

Aran put her down and, as Mary took her, he asked Damon if he had to go, too.

"N-hn," he muttered, shaking his head. "You know she went twice on the plane and got locked in the toilet. She was a pest the whole way. I hope we get to go fishing tonight, or at least tomorrow at the latest."

Shortly after they arrived home, the phone rang: the children's mother, calling to see how the trip had gone. The summer before she hadn't called or written until they'd been with Mary and Aran for three weeks. This summer, though, was obviously going to be different. Damon had already mentioned that his mother was getting him a digital watch and Gaddi had been promised a silver and turquoise bracelet.

During that first evening, the girl kept reminding them that she only had to stay a month. Her manner was as teasing as it was threatening. In the spring Aran had asked to have his children for two months in the summer. The decree provided for one month but because they had moved and he'd only get to see them twice a year now, he wanted to have them longer. But their mother had raged and said his only interest was getting free from child support payments for another month. He told her that if she didn't agree he'd get a lawyer and take the matter to court. "All I have to do," he'd said, "is show up and I win. The burden of proof's on you because you'll have to show it'll be harm to them to be with their father for two months." After several weeks, however, she told him on the phone, "Let's be adult about this. Why don't we leave it up to the kids? If they want to stay two months, that's fine. Okay?" He agreed, but he didn't trust her. After all, the middle-aged woman who was to be a live-in maid with them in Laredo, a woman hailed as having spent years taking care of children, had turned out to be nineteen and a Mexican who spoke no English.

Three days later, the children's mother called again, to tell Damon that she'd gotten the watch, then Gaddi got on the other phone and sang, "I'm taking swimming and want to go home yesterday, Mary's teaching me 'Seven-Song' on the piano."

"It's started," Aran told Mary.

"You didn't think it wouldn't, did you?"

"No. I'm just curious to see how she tries maneuvering them."

"It was a mistake to leave it up to the children."

At supper, Gaddi asked to say the blessing. She recited a jingle. When Damon was asked to say the blessing, he usually refused, said he didn't know any.

"Just say what's in your heart," Mary told him but, uneasy, he refused.

"I wish we were having something good," he said, wincing at the bowls of salad and zucchini. On his plate was a pork chop and a lump of mashed potatoes. "In Laredo we have T-bone steak."

"Every night?" Mary asked.

"At least three times a week."

"Eat your pork chop," his father said.

"It's got stuff on it."

"You haven't even tried it."

"It doesn't look good."

"Just try it."

Halfway through the meal he said it was good. Gaddi wolfed down her meal and asked for a second helping. "The only thing I don't like," she said, "is worms, 'cause they look like boogers and a dumb kid at school eats his."

"All right now, hush."

"He does. Yukky," she said and gave a throaty laugh.

After supper they played badminton. Gaddi had trouble hitting the shuttlecock but kept saying, "I almost got it. I'm good. I almost got it. Didn't I? I'm getting good. See?" she said, missing it again.

Later the four of them watched television and colored for awhile, but when it came time for bed, both children fussed, said they didn't have to go to bed in Laredo until they wanted to.

"You're here now," Aran said.

"If I don't want to," Gaddi said, "I don't have to stay but a month."

"You said that," Damon told her.

"How long're you gonna stay?" his sister asked him.

"I don't know. Probably two months if you let me fly back," he said, turning to his father. "Because that'll be my fourteenth time on a plane. Are we going to fly back?"

"We'll see," Aran said.

"If I don't get to, I may go back after a month."

"We'll see."

"I don't want to drive. It's too hot."

"You get yourself ready for bed."

"Do we play tennis tomorrow?"

"The lessons start next week."

"If it's hot I'm not going to play."

"Get yourself ready for bed."

"Who's going to read the story?" Gaddi asked, and Mary said she was. Damon said he wanted his own story and Aran told him he'd already planned to read him one.

After the stories, both children complained about having to sleep alone.

"You always do, don't you?"

"Yeah," Gaddi said, "but you all get to sleep together."

"We'll be right down the hall," Mary said.

"I want a kiss. Leave the light on."

"We will," Mary said, rubbing her back.

"Down lower," Gaddi said. "My hiney itches."

Aran came in to kiss her goodnight. She smooched him hard then tried biting his nose. She told him she was scared: "Somebody might get me."

"Nobody's going to get you."

"They might. I want a kiss."

He bent back down and she leaped to bite his nose.

"That hurts."

She giggled. "Again," she said and bit him once more.

"That's enough. Now you go on to sleep."

"I'm scared. Mother always sleeps with me."

"No, she doesn't!" Damon yelled from his room. "Now go on to sleep."

Rising, Gaddi told him, "Well! Just kiss my grits."

"Settle down."

"Kiss again," she told her father.

Damon yelled that he was thirsty and Gaddi cried that she was, too, then Damon said his head wasn't comfortable. Mary went in and gave him a massage.

"You do it better than Daddy," he told her. "He uses fingernails."

"Okay, now sleep tight."

"I love you," he told her.

As Aran leaned down to give Gaddi a final goodnight kiss, she threw her arms around him and pulled him down upon her. She told him he was going to sleep with her. He kissed her and she whispered, "I love you, Daddy, kiss my grits."

"Night," he said, laughing.

"Just kiss my grits," she sassed him.

"I'm going to spank your grits."

"Do it," she said, arching her bottom. He patted her. "Harder!" she demanded.

"Now get to sleep."

"I'm scared."

"Nobody's going to hurt you."

"Why?"

"Now go on to sleep."

He leaped to free his nose from her teeth. Getting up, he saw Mary waiting for him in the doorway. Shaking their heads at each other, they smiled. Mary put her arm around his waist, and he hugged her to him as they walked downstairs for a glass of wine.

The phone rang. Mary pulled away to answer it.

"They're already in bed," she said. "Yes. I'll tell them." She hung up. "Guess who that was."

Glancing at his watch, Aran said, "She ought to know better than to call this late."

"She's really started in, hasn't she? They've been here scarcely a week and the pressure's already begun."

"At least they were in bed."

"Who was it?" the children called out.

"Just a friend," Mary said.

"Who?"

"Now go on to bed. It's late," Aran told them from the foot of the stairs, but it was sometime before they quit insisting on drinks of water and more massaging and kissing. Finally the children bantered back and forth with each other, fussing and giggling. Going back upstairs, Aran told them, "Bedtime." He kissed them both and before long they were curled asleep.

"No!" Damon shouted. "No!" he sobbed, "no!"

Logy, Aran opened his eyes and listened, but his son went quiet. Moaning, Mary rolled over against him, kissed his shoulder. He kept listening for another nightmare shriek.

That morning the tennis lessons had begun and Damon, who was fussing about the heat before the group session began, drank a Coke and threw up in the middle of the lesson. That afternoon he told his father he liked tennis but needed to have his lesson earlier. His father explained that it was the Coke that had made him sick.

"Yeah. It was hot. But I wish I could take earlier."

"You'll be just fine," he said, stroking his son's back and remembering now the two summers when he had taken his son to the Mayo Clinic for bladder surgery: walking him after the operations around the nurse's station, the boy and himself dragging tubes, the boy screaming, and the time he'd called the boy's mother, then his wife and her agitation: she'd been eating a bowl of cereal: "I'm sorry," she'd said, "I don't like being disturbed. It's nothing personal. I was busy. You know I can't stand being interrupted. I'm sorry. That's just the way I am."

Lying in bed, he remembered that it had taken him fifteen months to pay off the bills from the last operation, which had occurred the summer after the divorce. She hadn't paid a dime. But with six months to go on the loan he'd taken out, she moved to Laredo, her salary doubled to an amount equal to his, but no money came. He hadn't asked for any; and for the first two months after the move, he'd kept both children with him so Damon could finish second grade without having to change schools. He remembered her later praising her own generosity for not having insisted he pay child support the two months they'd stayed in the apartment with him. He resented her rhetoric about what a fine and devoted mother she was, how much the children "need my ability to relate to them."

He kept listening. Again Damon started shouting; he was raving, and Aran got up. Going into his son's room, he saw Damon sleeping calmly. Perplexed, he watched him then went into his study to work on some reviews. Damon screamed. The sound, gurgles ratcheted deep in his throat, was animal-like: the voice of a terrified preconscious force. Rushing to his son, he lay beside him. Damon jumped up snarling and Aran kept asking what was wrong. Damon kept spewing, his body convulsing, then he fell back on the bed. Aran put his arms around him, told him everything was fine: "What's wrong?"

Suddenly Damon's eyes opened and, slinging himself against his father, he pealed, "I love you!"

Aran hugged him and the boy kissed him then snuggled beside him. Aran stretched out and stayed there until the expression on his son's face had stayed soft for a long time. He kissed the sleeping boy then went back in his study. Soon, though, he realized that working was impossible and went back to bed. Mary was sleeping deeply, he thought. Adjusting himself carefully under the covers, he heard her ask if he'd been working.

"Damon was having a nightmare."

"What about?"

"I don't know. He's okay, though."

She twisted over to kiss him and went back to sleep. Hands behind his head, he watched the ceiling. In the morning Damon crawled in bed next to him. They kissed each other and Aran dropped back into sleep with his arm around his son. Soon Gaddi waked them all up by coming through the door and plopping herself down on Mary, then leaping over to hug her father good morning, and wedging herself between Aran and Mary, she told her brother, "Get off the bed, Damon, there's not enough room for you. What's for breakfast?"

2.

Home at 1:30 from teaching. Checking the mailbox, empty, he walked through the front door: smell of sausage pizza rich in his nostrils.

"How was your day?" Mary asked after they'd kissed by the oven.

"Fine," he said, patting her bottom, enjoying the workably lovely softness of it.

Seeing him, the children got up from the carpet in the den where they had been working on a model space center and paper dolls. Bending to kiss them, he asked how they'd been doing, and they began telling him about friends they'd made that morning at the swimming pool.

"Damon went off the low board," Gaddi said.

"Great."

"And I can almost somersault under water."

"You're doing all the good," he told them and kissed them in turn on the head.

"My friend's going to come over later," Damon said. "Can he spend the night?"

"That's a possibility," he replied then glanced at Mary who nodded it was fine with her.

"Can he?"

"I think so."

"What about me?" Gaddi asked. "Don't I get anybody?"

"Honey, next week you're going to have a friend stay for four days."

"And Damon doesn't get anybody then, does he?"

"I don't have to. Larry's spending the night with me tonight."

"I get somebody four nights."

"That's not fair, Daddy."

"Settle down. You'll both be taken care of."

"Look what I picked in the garden," Damon said, jumping up and showing his father the basket filled with tomatoes and beets and zucchini.

"I did some of it, too," Gaddi said.

"No, you didn't. You skwushed your tomatoes."

"Yeah," she said, "but I *almost* got it without getting gooey."

"You can't do anything," Damon told her.

"I didn't break anything the way you did out there."

"Okay, darlings," Mary said, "we're about ready to eat. Wash up."

"Why?" they often asked.

"That's what we do before meals," she told them.

"We don't have to in Laredo," Damon said.

"Mother doesn't ever make us wash," Gaddi said.

"This is here," Aran told them.

"What if I don't like the pizza?" Damon said. "What kind is it?"

"The good kind," Aran told him.

"I like pizza," Gaddi said.

"Good."

"I'm not going to eat it if I don't like it," Damon said.

"Then you're going to take your nap hungry," Aran said.

"I don't want to take a nap. I'm calling Larry to come over."

"After your nap."

"I'm not going to take a nap."

"Yes, you are, too."

"Mother doesn't make us."

"Honey, naps are good for you," Mary said.

"They're not good for me."

"You're taking one," Aran told him.

"I'm not either."

"Damon, you're taking a nap. And let's just cut out the arguing. This is mealtime."

"If I don't like it, I'm not going to eat it."

"Just sit down."

Sulking, Damon plopped in his chair and defiantly crossed his arms. Giggling, Gaddi said, "Damon's gonna eat like a dog."

Mary began setting the table and Aran took the pizza from the oven, laid it on a trivet on the drainboard and sectioned it.

"Here, Sweetheart," Mary said as she placed Damon's glass of milk in front of him. His scowl diminishing, he looked up at her and she blew him a kiss. Tucking his chin, he blushed.

"Do I have to take a nap?" he asked her.

"Yes. We all are. Doesn't your mother think they're good for you?"

"Yeah, she says so, but I can always talk her out of it."

She and Aran looked at one another.

"Why're you rolling your eyes?" Gaddi asked her father.

"Nothing."

"Yes, you were. You did just like this," she said, mimicking him.

"Nothing," he told her. "I was just winking at the spiders."

"There aren't any spiders here," Damon said.

"Sometimes there are."

"Where?"

"Never mind," he said, bringing the pizza to table.

"Yummy!" Gaddi said.

Aran sat beside his son and squeezed his thigh.

"I think I'm going to like it," Damon said, "but I still wish I didn't have to take a nap."

In the middle of the afternoon the doorbell rang. In the den with his son, Aran went to answer it, but Damon leaped up from his model, knocking over a capped jar of paint. "I'll get it!"

It was Doug, one of the friends he'd made at the pool. Damon rushed outside, and Aran saw a car was parked by the curb. After awhile, he went outside himself, seeing that Damon was talking to the woman in it. She told Aran she was going to the store but wanted to know if Damon could come to their house after they got back.

"Sure."

Damon looked up at his father and smiled.

Aran gave her the phone number and she told him the directions to their home. She said they'd be gone less than an hour but would call as soon as they got back. He thanked her and, lowering her voice so the boys who were on the other side of the car couldn't hear, told him that Doug had been talking about Damon ever since he'd come home from the pool. "We're new here and I'm glad he's making friends."

Not long after Aran and Damon had returned to the house, the doorbell rang again. Once more Damon rushed to answer it. Aran heard Damon telling the boy he couldn't go swimming now because he had to go over to a friend's house in awhile.

"But – all right," the boy said, disappointed.

When he came back in the den, Damon looked depressed.

"What's wrong?" Aran asked.

"Nothing." Damon sat in the black lounger.

With difficulty Aran got the story out of him. Damon had promised the boy this morning he'd go swimming with him this afternoon but had forgotten about it when Doug had come over.

"I broke a promise."

"Can't you go swimming with him tomorrow? Or have him over this evening for badminton?"

"No. I broke a promise," he said shakily.

"It'll be all right."

"No, it won't. I've lost a friend."

"No, you haven't."

"Yes, I have. I don't know what to do."

"You just shouldn't be so popular."

Raging, Damon ran from the room, stormed up the stairs. Aran went to find him. Damon was standing by the window. He was fighting to keep from crying.

"Let's talk about it."

"No." Then Damon asked him what *he* would do.

"Let's go downstairs. Mary and Gaddi are still asleep."

During their discussion Aran told him he was glad he thought promises were important. He told him his situation was tough. "You promised two friends you'd go with them and you can't do both, at least at the same time."

"What would you do?"

"Come sit in my lap."

"No." Damon looked as if he thought he were unworthy of touching anyone.

"Okay. First, try to remember your appointments."

"I did but I forgot."

"That's right, but Steve'll understand."

"No, he won't. I'm not his friend any more."

"Sure you are."

"No, I'm not."

Finally Aran explained to him that since he'd already made arrangements with Doug to go to his house, he ought to do that, and that he could have Steve over in the evening. Damon said he didn't think he was going either place. Aran told him there wasn't any point in doing that, that he'd been in similar situations himself, and that people, if they were really friends, usually understood, "even though I know that right now that doesn't make you feel any better."

As it turned out, however, Doug hadn't called after two hours had passed, but near suppertime the doorbell rang. It was Doug, saying he'd been calling all afternoon, but the operator had said the phone had been disconnected. Looking betrayed, Damon glared at his father. Aran asked Doug what number he'd been calling. The boy's mother had gotten the last digit wrong. Slapping himself, Doug lunged for the phone and, placing the receiver to his ear, asked Aran if he could use it. "I've got to tell my mother."

"While you're talking to her," Aran said, "why don't you ask her if you can eat with us."

"Aww-right!" Doug yelped.

Aran winked at Damon. It warmed him to see his son beaming.

Mary came down while Doug was still on the phone and Damon, ignoring the fact, introduced his new friend.

"He's eating with us."

"Good," she said, smiling.

"It's about time for your meeting, isn't it?"

"Close to it," she told her husband.

"What're you going to do about supper?"

"If we don't eat there I'll pick up something on the way home.

Think you can manage?"

"Sure," he said, kissing her. "We're going to have ourselves a powwow."

"Gaddi's still asleep."

"I'll get her."

"Gaddi's my sister," Damon broke in. "She doesn't do anything except sleep and eat and make weird noises – both ends."

Having hung up, Doug said, "She couldn't be as bad as my sister. I've got two of them. The big one has bumps on her face and the little one picks her nose."

"Have fun," Mary said.

"You, too, Sweetheart."

They had the taco pie Mary had prepared earlier in the day. Doug said it was the best thing he'd ever eaten in his life and he wanted Mary to teach his mother how to make it. Aran was glad to hear that because he noticed Damon was eating heartily. When they'd finished, they all went into the back yard and played badminton; then tired of chasing after the shuttlecock sailing time and again over the fence into the next yard, they accepted Aran's suggestion that they go in front to throw the Frisbee. Gaddi wasn't any better at that than she was at badminton, but she didn't seem to get discouraged. In her hilarium, she kept congratulating herself, and if the boys laughed at her or criticized her, she laughed with them and insisted she'd get the hang of it before long: "I've improved a lot." Each time Damon or Doug threw or caught badly she'd laugh at them and tell them, "Keep trying, boys." Tickled, Aran turned away from them but instantly saw the red disc speeding toward his neck. Flinching, he caught it.

"Always watch," Gaddi told him. "You'll get your butt creamed."

He flicked it lightly at her. She caught it against her chest.

"See," she said. "I'm good."

"One hand," Damon told her.

"I don't have to."

"If you're going to do it right you do."

"I don't either, do I, Daddy?"

"Catch it any way you can."

"I'm good," she said, sailing it into the octagonal planter in the middle of the front yard. "Almost."

"Who was that for?" Damon asked, heckling her.

"You," she told him, "and you missed. You can't do anything.

I can almost catch it every time."

"Gaddi!" Aran called, stopping her from diving into the marigolds after it. Heedless of him, she ripped her way through the flowers and, stepping on periwinkles and anemones, slashed through other plants to snatch up the Frisbee. Damon looked disgusted. He shook his head at Doug who indicated he understood his grief. When Gaddi brought the disc to her father, he patted her on the head and said, "Nice doggy."

"Hear that, Damon?" she cried, sashaying away, "Daddy called you a doo-doo head."

Aran sailed it high and Damon went after it. The Frisbee settled above him then dropped, but Damon caught it.

"Do one like that for me," Doug said, and the next time Aran had a turn he did. Soon, though, the boys tried imitating his throw and Aran spent most of his time chasing it in the street.

"You three play for awhile," he told them.

"What're you going to do?"

"Play backstop."

"Me, Damon, me!" Gaddi cried, and each time she got it she'd throw it away from the boys and tell them they needed to be fast if they were going to play with her.

The shutters, Aran noticed, made the windows resemble smiling faces.

"I've gotta pee," Gaddi said and skipped into the house.

When she came back out, she hollered to Damon that their mother was on the phone.

"Aw," but he went in, yelling at the door to Doug that he'd be right back out. Reminding her father that her mother had just told her she could go home any time she wanted, Gaddi disappeared into the house herself.

After awhile Damon came back out and told Aran, "Mother wants to talk to you."

"Can I come in, too?" Doug asked.

"Sure."

The conversation on the phone was short. Mirma asked when he was going to bring the children home. He told her, "Everyone's having a fine time. The last of July."

"Gaddi said she wanted to come home at the end of June."

"She's having a good time, too. She's taking swimming lessons next week."

"Did she get my letter?"

"Right."

"That's funny – those awards she got: most popular girl, most beautiful girl in kindergarten, and first place for reading the most books."

"Yeah, she's a honey," Aran said.

On the other extension, Damon said he had a friend here.

"Good," his mother said.

"You want to talk to him? His name's Doug."

"No," she said, "that's all right."

"He's downstairs. I can get him."

"Your friend Jack has been asking about you. I think he's lonely because he doesn't have anybody to go fishing with."

"I'm going now," Damon said. "Bye." He hung up.

"Okay," Aran said, "we'll talk to you later."

"Is Gaddi still there?"

"She just went back outside."

"They sound busy."

"They are," Aran said.

"Give them a kiss for me."

Hanging up, Aran shook his head. There was something she hadn't said. It didn't make sense for her to ask him to the phone, unless she had expected him to shriek that the kids were driving him insane and he wanted them to go back where they belonged, fast. He decided, though, that Gaddi had said she wanted to come home before the two months were out, but that when Gaddi had left the phone abruptly, Mirma had had her plans kinked.

He told Mary about the call. "Big change from last summer, isn't it?"

"Certainly is," she said.

"I wonder how long it's going to take for her to break her part of the bargain."

"I think she's already planning to break it."

"If she does, she's going to get hell."

"I really don't think there's anything we'll be able to do about it," Mary said. "The decree calls for a month. And there's nothing to stop her if after that month's up she demands to have them back."

"I'll be damned if I'm flying them back early, or driving them back either."

"What if she insists?"

"Then she'll have to come get them. The decree doesn't say anything about how they're to get back."

"I'm just curious to see how she does what it's obvious she's getting ready to do."

"Right. What're you going to do this evening?"

"After we get the kids in bed, I think I'll read. Are you going to work?"

"Maybe, but I'm about ready to fall asleep now."

She touched his shoulder. "That would be nice, wouldn't it?"

"Voluptuous," he said, hearing Damon asking what they were talking about. "Nothing," he told his son.

"Yes, you are, too. What is it?"

"I know," Gaddi said. "Kissy-face."

"Are you?" Damon asked.

"You just mind your own business. This is private."

"That's all y'all ever do. Kiss and talk in private. I'm bored."

"Sometimes they shut the door," Gaddi said.

"Why don't you ever talk with us?" Damon asked.

"We're just having a conversation."

"In French? Like you always do when you don't want us to understand?"

"No, we're speaking English."

"What about?"

"Wallowing in the mountains and frying fish in caves."

"Easy," Mary said.

He wanted to rip off her clothes. She winked at him, told him she was going upstairs.

"I think I'll go with you."

"Later."

"Daddy," Gaddi whined, "I'm scared."

"I'll be there in a moment."

"Now!" she demanded.

"You don't ever do anything with us," Damon said. "All y'all do is talk."

"I'll be back down," Mary said.

"Good," he said sharply, seeing how drawn her cheeks had become.

She kissed him lightly.

"Now!" Gaddi said, sprawled across the black lounger and resembling a stunted jokester-odalisque. "Now!"

As Mary left, Aran glanced at the drainboard and sink. He was sorry he had already washed dishes.

3.

He taught from 9:30 to 12:40. Damon's swimming lessons began at eleven, and Gaddi's at twelve. Three mornings a week Mary played tennis at eight. Aran would rise shortly after six and make coffee and read the paper, feed the fish in the aquarium in the den, then fix breakfast. Mary kept asking him to sleep on through but, always awake before the alarm went off, he said he'd rather start the day with her than without her. On the mornings she played tennis, he got the kids fed and dressed, then dropped them off at the courts. On his way home after class, he picked his children up at the swimming pool where, before they left, they showed him each day what they had learned. Home, they'd have lunch on the patio. Naps followed. Afterwards, Damon would often walk to the pool or play with a friend in the house. Nights, they'd watch television together or play badminton or leave the house to play miniature golf. The days he had papers to grade, Aran skipped his nap. The times he'd try to write, Damon and Gaddi would come into his study to borrow pencils and paper. Loaded with bounty, they'd leave but return shortly, asking for more, ask him if a friend could come over, ask him to take them to the show or fishing, ask him to take them swimming again, ask him what Mary was reading in the bathroom, tell him about new flowers in the bed, different worms they'd found in the garden, show him the produce they'd gathered. Sometimes they'd drink from the glass of tea on his desk then ask him to come on downstairs and pour them something because, as they said, they were hot and thirsty and there wasn't anything to do here. "Let's mow the lawn."

Before the first week of lessons was past Mary had gotten a letter from an editor saying he was still interested in her proposal for a book covering the short story's development from ancient Egypt through the present, but until she sent him a list of all the particular items to be collected in the contents he couldn't offer her a contract. He said he needed page lengths and copyright dates. "This," he wrote, "will be an expensive project, but we need more definite information to make a cost analysis. I'll be looking forward to receiving the information by mid-summer."

"Sounds promising," Aran said.

"Well, at least he's still interested."

"Anything I can do to help, let me know."

"Thanks," she said, "I just don't know if I'm going to get everything done by late July. There's so much reading left to do."

"More than reading. That's the rough part."

"It sure is," she said wistfully.

He knew how much the book meant to her. She saw it as her chance to teach again. The two years before they'd been married she'd been teaching in a university as Visiting Assistant Professor, a title given Ph.D.'s in their first job. The title meant there was no possibility for tenure: three years and out. Last fall, though, after they'd been married in May, she'd been given four classes at the university where Aran had been teaching for ten years. It was a one-semester appointment; she was filling in for another teacher who'd gone on leave to complete his doctorate. Several members of the department, however, resented her being there, had tried to get her contract rescinded, even before she'd gotten on campus. Aran looked on them with contempt. Her degree and credentials were better than anyone else's in the department. Her publication list was longer than anyone else's but his. Two of the men most against her coming had even suggested to Aran in the months before that she ought to be hired, at least part-time, but during the spring they'd come to resent the chairman and dean and were trying, through her, to salve the pains of what Aran called their pissantedness. Her teaching, though, had gone well. During that semester, to increase salaries of full-time teachers, the administration started doing away with part-time appointments.

"If I can just get this book out, I might have a chance. All I'd like is a couple of classes."

Biting his lip, Aran remembered the Academic Vice President telling him one day, "It's not people like Mary we're out to can. Her record puts everybody else up there to shame. Plus, it's damned ridiculous for her to be stuck with freshman courses. She ought to be teaching seminars."

Several months later, in the spring, the man had told Aran that things didn't look good, "at this point," for Mary to be hired again. "We've initiated the policy against part-time people, and if you start making exceptions you don't have a policy."

Damon came in the bedroom and asked if he could get up from his nap.

"In a moment," Aran said.

"I'm not sleepy."

"You can get up in thirty minutes."

"I want to get up now."

"I said in thirty minutes. We're talking."

"What about?"

"Damon —"

"Can I go downstairs?"

Aran sighed.

"Honey," Mary said, "in thirty minutes I'm taking you and Gaddi to the library."

"That's a long time. I'm getting up now."

"Damnit," Aran said.

"I'm not sleepy."

"Just settle down for thirty minutes. Okay?"

"All right," he said belligerently and slammed the door behind him. Gaddi cried. Aran rose from the bed and left the room. He checked Gaddi who'd gone back to sleep, then went to Damon's room and, whispering in aggravation, told his son to keep quiet. "We're talking and Gaddi's asleep. Just let us work some things out. All right?"

"It's boring here."

Aran filled out the forms for library cards. Mary and the kids stayed in the children's department where she helped them pick out books. He later found that Damon had tried to get some Dr. Seuss, but Mary had told him he needed something more advanced. She guided him to the Hardy Boys, and he agreed to get one if he could also get a book on scuba diving.

Coming back downstairs, Aran found them talking between stacks.

"You're some mother," he said, touching her back.

"Look, Daddy, I've got the Hardy Boys. It's about Mexico."

"Did you get the cards?" Mary asked.

"Right. You two'll have to sign them, though."

That night Aran read the first two chapters to Damon, and the next night he read him two more chapters. Damon wanted him to go on, but Aran said it was bedtime and they'd read some more tomorrow. The next afternoon Damon asked if he could read during his nap.

"Sure."

In two days Damon had finished the book himself, during the church service. He leaned over and told Mary he was going to save his money and get all fifty volumes in the Hardy Boys series.

"It would be better," she said later, "to get your mother to get you a library card and check them out. That's what libraries are for. When I was a girl, my mother would take my brother and me to the library each week."

"You check out anything?"

"Sure. In the summers I'd probably read ten books a month."

"Gah! This is the first real book I've ever read."

"You finish those we got, then we can go to the library again and get more."

"I've already finished one of them. What about today?"

"You get the other one read and we will."

"It's boring."

"How much of it have you read?"

"The parts around the pictures, but there weren't very many."

"No. The way to do it is start at the first page and read straight through. You're old enough now that you don't need a lot of pictures."

"I'm going swimming."

"Not me," Gaddi said.

"Why?" Damon asked her.

"My teacher's mean. She yells at me."

"She's trying to help you learn," Mary told her.

"She's mean and I'm not going."

"She's just trying to help you," Damon told her. "There're almost twenty kids in the class and it's noisy. If she didn't yell you couldn't even hear her."

"So?"

"And besides," Damon said dutifully, "if you don't learn how to swim you'll drown."

"So? I wanta drown. I don't have to take swimming in Naredo."

"Laredo, Dum-dum. You can't even talk."

"Least I don't wet the bed."

"Well –"

"You do. You wet the bed. And his room always smells like a toilet."

"Honey," Mary said, "why don't you want to go swimming?"

"Because she sinks," Damon said.

"No, I don't. Just when I can't float on my back. And I'm not going any more 'less Daddy goes."

"Your father's working."

"Then I'm not going."

"Honey, you know my big brother couldn't float on his back either."

"Did he drown?"

"No."

"Then I'm not going."

"You won't get a certificate," Damon said.

"So?"

"I'll tell you what?" Mary said. "Let's both go watch Damon during his lesson and see how he does."

"Do I have to take mine?"

Before Mary could answer, Damon told his sister he used to be scared of the water, too. "But it's a lot more fun when you learn how to swim."

"I can swim. Just not on my back, and the teacher yells at me."

"Well," he said, "so does Ruda," their live-in maid in Laredo.

"She yells at you, too."

"I know," Damon said, then turning to Mary he told her, "You know what? She gets in my drawers and messes up my models on the dresser."

"I'll bet she's just trying to dust and put your clean clothes away."

"No way," he said. "She does it to be mean."

"Yeah," Gaddi said, "she messes up my room, too."

"You know her house doesn't even have a floor. It's dirt, and the roof blew off in a tornado."

"She doesn't even have a TV either," Gaddi said.

"She's poor," Damon said.

"That's all right," Mary said. "Poor people can be as nice as anyone else."

"Not her. It's her disposition what's poor."

Coffee cup in hand, Mary leaned back from the table. "Did you know," she said, "that my grandmother's house didn't even have a toilet in it?"

"Why?" Damon asked.

"They couldn't afford to put one in."

"Was she nice?"

"My daddy was, and that was the house he lived in until he went away to college."

Incredulous, Damon squinted at her. Then Mary told them her father had learned how to swim in the Mississippi River.

"Was it deep?" Gaddi asked.

"In some places. He used to swim across it. It was more than a mile wide."

"Gah!" Damon said.

"Without breathing?" Gaddi asked.

"No. He learned to breathe while he swam. And if he got tired, he'd float."

"On his back?"

"Sometimes," she told Gaddi, then Damon asked if he could swim in the Mississippi sometime. "It's pretty dirty now," Mary said, "but we'll see about it next time we go to Louisiana, if it's still summer." Putting her cup down, she said, "Why don't you get your suits on?" Damon said he already had his on and Gaddi, who was still in her yellow nightgown, said she didn't want to take lessons. Mary told her, "I know, but after all the other kids are finished with their lessons, you might want to go swimming with them – show them your somersault."

"Okay," she said, "but don't leave. It's too far to walk. Kiss," she said, throwing her arms around Mary.

When Aran arrived shortly before one-thirty to pick them up, Gaddi spent fifteen minutes showing him all she'd learned in her lesson that day, and Damon, who'd already dried off, said first he wanted to show his father how he could jump off the high board.

The heat was suffocating. Forehead prickly, Aran watched his son's descent. It was delicate in its lightness. The splash was small. Coming up, Damon waved. His eyes sang and Aran, full of love for him, waved back as Gaddi hugged his thigh and begged him to pick her up.

"You're dripping wet," he told her.

"I know," she said, giggling.

Going down the sidewalk to the car, Damon asked if the company had already come.

"I don't think so. It'll probably be tomorrow night before they're here."

"And you don't get to have anybody spend the night with you either," Gaddi told her brother.

"So? They're coming to see all of us."

"But mostly me," Gaddi said.

"That's just Annie," he said, "and she's my friend, too."

"They're all of them all our friends," Aran said.

"Maybe so, but they're not going to use my bed."

"We'll see."

"We get any mail?"

"I don't know. I haven't been home yet."

Passing through the gateway, Gaddi danced around and, walking backwards, hollered, "Bye, Teacher!"

"Just because you're nice doesn't mean you're going to pass," Damon said.

"I will so. She said I was the best one in her class."

"She did not."

"Didn't she, Daddy? See? I told you."

4.

The muffled ring of the phone as they stepped up on the front porch. When they walked in, Mary, leaning away from the stove, said, "It's for you."

"Me?" Damon asked.

"No, darling. Your daddy."

Aran took the receiver. The call was from the publisher of a collection of his poems. The volume had originally been scheduled to come out the previous spring, but the printing date had been pushed back to mid-summer. The man told him the layouts were done, the photographs for the body of the book had been taken, "So now all we need is a picture of you."

"When do you want me to drive down?" Aran asked.

"As soon as possible."

The children kept asking their father, "Who is it?" and Aran, waving them off, said, "You mean for me to come today, don't you?"

"I was hoping."

"Hold on." He told Mary what the call was about and asked her if anything was going on. She reminded him about the wedding they were to go to tonight. He told her he'd forgotten. "Hold on," he again told the phone. Out loud he figured how long the drive would take. "Eighty minutes. I can get there and back in time for this evening. Want to go?" She told him she'd better not, she had to wash her hair; she was to pour champagne at the reception. "Do you mind?" he asked.

Putting lunch on the table, she told him it was fine with her.

Looking at his children who had settled on the floor in the den, he calculated a moment longer; then placing the receiver to his ear, he said, "Sure. I can make it. I've got to be back, though, by seven for a wedding. Give me directions to your house." Writing them down, he said, "Got it. I need to wash my hair, but I'll be leaving here within thirty minutes. I'll be there by three-thirty."

After hanging up, he asked Damon and Gaddi if they wanted to go with him. Gaddi said she wanted to stay here to get pretty with Mary for the wedding. Damon wanted to know how long it would take. Aran told him.

"That's a long time. It's hot. I'd rather go swimming."

"You have to take a nap," Gaddi said.

"Okay," Aran said and stretched toward the refrigerator where Mary was pouring milk. He kissed the back of her head then swept into the den and kissed his two children, said on his way upstairs that he'd better skip lunch. "You all go ahead," he called back to them.

When he came downstairs, his hair was brushed but damp. Mary handed him a glass of milk mixed with raw honey and protein concentrate. He drank it and, putting the glass down on the drain-board, told her, "Do supper without me."

"Be careful," she said, pushing her fingers behind his belt buckle and kissing him. "You look gorgeous. I like the ankh," she said, fingering the emblem hanging on a thin gold chain around his neck.

"Take care," he told the children and kissed them goodbye. Damon said he might not take a nap and Gaddi said she'd be scared without him. He kissed them again and, stomach knotting, left.

On the highway, he put on an old tape of Ike and Tina Turner, turned the volume as loud as it would go without rattling the speakers. By the time he'd played Tchaikovsky's *B-minor Concerto* and Hank Williams' *Greatest Hits* he was fifteen miles from Denton. Blinking headlights, a truck swept past him; a pickup followed, its driver making rabbit ears with his fingers. Aran slowed down. Ahead was a group of cars, police light turning on the roof of one, Highway Patrolman standing on the road, his palm shoved toward Aran. Truncating the highway was a truck, its flatbed trailer jack-knifed. Hanging over the borrow ditch was half a tan Camaro. What was left of its front was a thin and jagged metal lip drooling into the steaming ditch. Screaming, an ambulance drove away and Aran was motioned on. At his left was a trailer park, a crowd of people standing on the shoulder. To his right three young men sat in the shade, a patrolman standing by them. A bloody fang, a piece of watermelon rind bucked out of what had once been a windshield. Wrenched, he swallowed back the acid, sour on the rawness of his tongue.

When he arrived in Denton, he found the house he was to go to. Accepting a beer, he toured the downstairs section whose walls were loaded with paintings, monoprints and silkscreens. Images muted, their colors faded into dun. In the corners of the spacious living room were pieces of antique tools: plowblades, a meat grinder, a milkchurn. Sculptures of nude female torsoes weighted the center of the room.

"Let's start in the backyard," he was told. "We doing all right on time?"

"Sure."

Outside, the man's son began photographing him. The heavy blockbenches, painted in the primary colors and spaced on a stone-slab floor at the top of the sloping yard, made the area resemble an amphitheatre. Shots were taken in the shade, in the sun, in places where shadows slashed across him. While Aran talked with the man and his wife, the boy roamed around him snapping pictures. A new roll, and more were taken, some of these in the house, as they talked about tennis and the trip Mary and Aran were taking later this summer to Mexico.

"Whereabouts?"

"San Miguel."

"De Allende?"

"Right. I'm giving a seminar at the Instituto."

Saying they'd been there, they gave him names of people they knew there, friends who'd show them around. Thanking them, Aran checked his watch, and the man said he wanted him to see what the photographer had done. "You got time?"

"I think so."

"We'll be back," the man told his wife, and he and Aran drove across town where they examined two strings of negatives hanging from the rod holding a shower curtain. Then they looked at the dummy-pages. "We'll be placing some of the books in art galleries."

Finishing his second beer, Aran said everything looked fine as far as he was concerned.

"I think you'll be pleased. We're excited about it."

They drove back to the man's house.

"Like another beer to take with you?"

"Better not."

"Next time we see you it'll be to sign the numbered copies."

During the drive home he played no music. The image of the crash was still with him. He felt disoriented, as if half of him were only now beginning the journey. When he walked in the house, the children called to him that they'd all been swimming while he was gone.

"You, too?" he asked his wife who was finishing dressing.

"Even me. How'd it go?"

"Fine," he said, going into the closet to get the suit he was going to wear to the wedding. "How were they?"

"All right," she said, "but my hair's not quite dry."

"Nothing like a rush, is there?" Clothes slung over his arm, he walked over to the dressing table where she was putting on make-up. Touching her hair then kissing the back of her neck, he said, "Feels dry to me."

"It is on the outside. I just hope it'll hold."

"Was your wedding like this?" Gaddi asked, wiggling in the pew.

"Silly," Mary whispered, "you were there. It was in your grandparents' home."

"Oh, I forgot. You're pretty," Gaddi said, touching Mary's face.

"You are, too."

"Shh," Aran said, his fingers to his lips.

"I want to sit by Daddy," Damon said, crossing in front of Mary and stumbling over Gaddi's feet.

"Don't, Damon," his sister said, "you're gonna mess us up."

Aran made a space for him and squeezed his leg as he sat beside him. Damon looked up at his father and smiled.

"Love you," Aran said.

"I love you, too."

When the bridesmaids began coming down the aisle, Gaddi said they looked like rainbows. "The third one's prettiest, the second one's kinda fat." Mary put her hand over Gaddi's to hush her but Gaddi said, "She is – looks like a poppahitomus," and laughed, but Damon told her to shut up and she said, "I don't have to. I think the one coming down now looks like a scarecrow. She doesn't even have bosoms."

"Shh," Aran said.

"She doesn't," Gaddi said. "Mine are big as hers, and Mary's are even bigger. Look."

"Honey," Mary said, "shh."

"Damon," Gaddi said, "we have to be quiet. Who's that?"

"It's the minister," Mary whispered.

"Why's he have a dress on?"

"It's not a dress," Damon said. "So shut up and behave."

"I *am* being *have*."

After the wedding, they walked across the street to the student union of the university for the reception. Entering the building, Aran asked Damon why he was walking funny, and Damon said he was trying to hide his shoes, "They don't look good. They're tennis shoes."

"You look just fine."

"No, I don't. I look ugly. Why didn't Mother pack me my good shoes?"

"I don't know," Aran said, "she should have. But you look just fine."

"My pants are too short, too."

"You're growing fast."

"Yeah, but I've got some in Laredo that fit."

"You should have brought them."

"I forgot about them when I packed."

"You mean you packed yourself?"

"Mostly."

Set on tables in the dining room were hors d'oeuvres: tuna and pimiento cheese finger sandwiches, black olives, cashews, and peppermint kisses. The four of them snacked and visited with the guests. After a time, Mary left them for her shift at pouring champagne. The children stayed with Aran, and before long Gaddi had picked out of the crowd a couple who'd been their neighbors before the children had moved to Laredo. The woman told her companions that Damon and Gaddi were "sort of like my own children – they used to spend a lot of time at our house while their mother was working. You're getting so big," she said, squeezing the children's shoulders. "How do you like Laredo?"

"Not much," Damon said. "The streets by our apartment aren't even paved."

"I bet you like it being here with your daddy, don't you?"

"Yeah."

"I don't," Gaddi squealed. "My mother said I could come home in a month."

"Oh, I bet you want to stay longer than that."

"No, I don't either. I'm going home a month from today or tomorrow."

"Well," the woman said, brushing Gaddi's hair off her forehead, "we sure are glad you're here."

"We're glad we're here, too," Damon said formally.

"You'll have to come see me. Will you do that?"

"Have you seen my mama?" Gaddi asked.

"You mean she's here?" the woman asked, looking startled at Aran.

"Yeah, she's over there in the turquoise dress pouring champagne. See how pretty she is?"

Smiling, Aran remembered last summer when they'd been in Louisiana. After church Mary had introduced them as "Aran's children, Damon and Gaddi," but before the couple had had time to compliment them, Damon had stepped close to Mary and told her, "We're some yours, too."

Toward the end of the reception, the children had gathered sacklets of bird seed and were scampering through the great room. Watching them, Aran felt Mary's arm go around him. "They're really cavorting, aren't they?" she said.

"They're good ones."

A friend standing with them asked if they'd be here all summer, and Aran explained the arrangement: till the end of the month for sure and possibly the next month, too.

"You think you're going to be able to get them?"

"Permanently? I doubt it."

"Why not? You've always done more than half the parenting."

"That doesn't make any difference. The woman gets the kids. Drunk, whore or addict – custody's almost always hers long as she doesn't act up too much in front of them."

"That's ridiculous."

"You're telling me. That's why I've always hoped the E.R.A. passes. Then we'd show up in court equal and no bullshit about the biological blessedness of mamahood."

"I agree," the man's wife said. "Is Mirma still hot on astrology?"

"I don't know. Last I heard," Aran said, "she was still interpreting her dreams by numbers."

"You're kidding."

"He's not either," her husband said.

"How about the Superwoman bit?"

"*Mas o menos*."

The woman, who had recently become a C.P.A., looked disgusted.

"One of her basic troubles," her husband said, "is that she doesn't have a sense of humor, especially about herself. We've known her a long time," he told Mary. "I used to think she was joking about all her crackpot ideas, but after the separation and a few conversations with her I realized she wasn't. She said some weird things."

As Aran saw Mary glancing at the children playing across the room, he heard the woman saying, "We're pulling for you." She put her arm through his. "It's a real home those kids need."

"I know."

"Maybe it's just a phase she's going through."

He laughed but, nodding, didn't reply. He was remembering another accusation: his suicide attempt. He had had cancer in his thyroid gland. That was nine years ago. Three years ago he'd found out from Mirma that he'd contracted it in order to reject her. It was a displaced suicide attempt, she'd said. She said she understood psychology and knew all about that kind of thing. He had a weak life-force. It also showed up in his refusal to fuck students.

"Phase hell!" the man said. "It's a lot more than help she needs. I just hope you get those kids. They need you and not just because she's a lunatic either."

"Honey! That's an awful thing to say."

"Not half as awful as what I'm keeping bottled up. And you needn't look at Aran either because it's nothing he's told me. Buddy," he said, clamping his big palm behind Aran's neck, "sometimes I wish you didn't have such a tendency to keep all the dirt to yourself. There's some of it a judge might want to hear."

"I've been keeping a record."

Kissing him, the woman said, "I'm glad," as Damon and Gaddi, running up to the group, handed Aran and Mary bags of bird seed.

"They're getting ready to leave," Gaddi said, excited.

"Just don't throw too hard," Damon said, settling against his father, "you'll knock'm out."

"Then they won't get to kiss," Gaddi said. "Kiss, Daddy, hold me."

He swung her up against his chest. She slopped a big kiss on his mouth then bit his nose.

"You little booger, quit!" He started to put her down, but she squirmed and wouldn't let him.

"See Mary?" Gaddi told the group. "How pretty she is? Daddy

looks like garbage."

"Well, you look like –"

"Damon!" Aran said, stopping him.

"She does. She smells like it, too."

Laughing, Aran told them, "I think part of the family's still back in the cave stage."

"I think you're in the cave stage," Gaddi said.

"They're going to put *you* in a cage," the woman said, poking Gaddi's ribs while Damon, grabbing Aran's leg, said his father was ticklish behind his thighs more than any other place, and Gaddi cried, "If you do, I'll get out just like Jesus and make scary faces," she said, trying to cross her eyes and swallow her lips.

"You all about ready to go?" Mary asked.

"We have to throw stuff."

"Honey, they've already gone. You little chatterboxes missed them."

"Aww," Gaddi said, crawling down off her father. "She was so pretty. She kissed me in the line."

"You all take care."

"You, too," Aran said.

"We'll call you," the woman said, "and have you all over for croquet and swimming."

"Tomorrow?" Damon asked.

"Soon," she said.

"Tomorrow," Gaddi told them, "we're having company and I get somebody to spend the night with me four nights in a row. Damon doesn't get anybody. He's going to be all by himself."

"Who cares? I get to sleep out in the tent."

"Monster'll eat you, too – drink all your yukky blood."

Stretching back to wave goodbye to their friends, Aran said, "See ya," then turning to his motor-mouthed issue, said, "Would you two house apes just hush?"

Laughing, the children tried to stamp his toes. They berated him with names and he ruffled their hair as Mary put her arm through his and the four of them poured through the door.

The breezy night air whisked around them. Stars shimmered, the glow from the horizon a gentle wash of paleness cradling their brightness.

5.

Elaine and Mary had gone through graduate school together in California, then Elaine had moved to Lubbock with her daughter and husband. A year later Mary had gotten a job teaching in the same university. The spring semester of Mary's first year there she'd met Aran, and Elaine and her husband separated two weeks before Mary introduced Aran to her. The three got along well and by the next winter Brendan, who was more than a decade older than them, joined them in their visits. He taught Philosophy. The next May the couples were married within two days of each other, and through the next year they made a number of visits to each other's home. In March, Elaine and Brendan had a baby they named Lucy, "For the light of the four of us," and Mary, who was not teaching that semester, had driven to Lubbock to take Elaine's classes during the two weeks she took off. On the trip back, during a conversation with Aran, Mary conceived the idea for the anthology.

"I've had to use at least twelve books each time I've taught Short Story," she said. "There's just nothing that's comprehensive." The ones Aran knew who'd taught the course ordinarily used a couple texts with enough yarns in them to mess around with for four months. "But that's not right," Mary said. "If you're going to teach it, you need to teach the full sweep. Elaine and I —"

"That's because you're not the riffraff."

"It's not. It's just the responsible thing to do. And to get all the material in, we've always had to use maybe a dozen volumes."

By the time they were home Mary had outlined the book's framework and had made a long list of writers and works she might include. It would begin with sections from the Egyptian *Book of the Dead* and the *Panchatantra*.

"Why not start with cave drawings?" Aran asked.

"Sure," she said, dancing with his irony, "a mess of skinny pictures would be good."

"Like a prehistoric prelude to the mess the world's in."

"Yes," she said, smiling. "Something both *modren* and *revelant*."

"I just hope it's not over the heads of the publishers."

"Surely not," she said. "I think most people teaching the

course would want something like it. Most anthologies operate on the assumption that the short story began in the post-Romantic nineteenth century. That's just not correct."

"Of course, it's not. But I doubt very many have tried to be what? thorough?"

"Sure they have."

"We'll see when you start getting editors' responses. Historical perspective and accuracy have a fine record for being underwhelming."

Within a month Mary sent out ten letters on the project. Six editors wrote declinations right away, two never replied, one came back negative "after much marketing consideration here," and the other one was full of enthusiasm, "though for the life of me," he wrote, "I don't understand why this hasn't been done before. Your prospective length, though, I'm afraid, is modest. Send a complete list of items with lengths and copyright dates. It may be too expensive, but let's keep hanging in there. Incidentally, you may want to drop things like *Aucassin and Nicolette*. If memory serves me right, things like that angle toward the dull."

Thanking him for his interest, Mary wrote back, saying she'd try to have the list by mid-summer, and adding at the end, "You must've had a bad teacher. Most of my students in World Lit. surveys and Short Story said that *Aucassin and Nicolette* was probably the most engaging piece in the course."

Within a week he'd replied, saying, "Just for the record, I can't toss my bad experience off on a prof. I read it years ago on my own. You may be right. I'll try it again. There's a copy, I think, still around the house. As far as translations go, try to get ones with as old a copyright date as possible. Your suggestion that you do some of the translating yourself sounds good. As I've said, the immediate obstacle is money."

Aran was more optimistic about the response than she was. By late May she was hard at work reading, but the children coming had made it impossible for her to do much more on the project. She thought, though, she said, that everyone's energies would settle in a few weeks and she could get back to work. "At least with the pressure I won't be tempted to read everything written. We'll still have August free." But in early June, Aran had gotten the call from San Miguel, asking him to come there in mid-July. He told the woman his children were with him, so he wouldn't be free until August. She said, "That's fine. We'll schedule you for two weeks beginning August first."

"Fantastic," Mary said. "I've never been to Mexico. I'll just have to work fast in July."

Aran hugged her. "You're not only the most beautiful woman I've ever seen, you're the most agreeable, too."

"I can be stubborn."

"That's what you and your mother keep saying, but you've never given me any grief."

"I hope you'll always be able to say that. I think you're pretty gorgeous yourself."

Elaine and Brendan, Annie and Lucy arrived at dusk. Wearing a halter-top, Elaine was nursing her baby and while Aran helped Brendan unload the car he heard Damon asking Mary, "If you and Daddy have a baby, are you going to nurse it?"

"We won't be having any babies, Sweetheart."

"I know, but if you did."

"I think so, if I were able to."

Scurrying like rabbits around the car and across the yard, Annie and Gaddi, who'd been with each other three times before, squealed and turned on the hose and let each other hold each other's dolls.

"Got it all?" Aran asked.

"Yeah," Brendan said. "Leave the red suitcase in the trunk. I'm taking it to Oklahoma City with me."

"How's your mother?"

"Fine. Doing better." She'd had a stroke in the spring. "The church is having a reunion there Sunday, so I'll be staying over with her for that. Ought to be fun, seeing all the old people, if you're into that kind of thing," he said, chuckling.

"How about a drink?" Aran asked everyone as they came back in the house.

"Sure."

"I'd love one," Elaine told him, hugging him and kissing Mary again. "You don't know how much we've looked forward to this."

"Screwdrivers or Scotch?"

"Either one," Brendan said. Flapping the front of his shirt, he blew down his chest to cool off.

While Aran poured drinks and took the herb curry dip and fresh cauliflower stalks from the refrigerator, the children buzzed in and out of rooms, Brendan began smoking, and Elaine remarked how beautiful the house looked. Mary told her they really hadn't done anything except paint the den: "That starburst wallpaper was driving us nuts."

"Isn't this whiskey barrel new?"

"No, we just moved it." A portable television set rested on it. "Aran did, though, sand down the bands around it."

Wandering into the living room, Elaine asked what they'd done to the piano: "It's more beautiful than before," and Mary told her they'd put another coat of tung oil on it. The piano was mahogany, a parlor grand more than sixty years old. "It's lovely," Elaine said, hugging her friend, and when Aran brought in the drinks, she hugged him again, too. Bursting into the room, Annie said, "There sure is a lot of kissy-goo going on here. That's all you ever do when you get together – that and talk talk talk."

"Honey," her mother said, "it's because we love each other."

"Yuk!"

Laughing with the rest of them, Aran remembered the Thanksgiving dinner they'd had here together with his parents and another couple. For five hours the men stayed at table discussing philosophy and the common misreadings of Plato. Brendan and the other man, who also taught Philosophy, had both come to see *The Republic* as an account of the mythic journey of the philosopher into the unconscious and his return into self-governing light. They did not see it as a prescription for an ideal society. Finally, though, Annie had come to stand by her mother. Aran remembered the perplexed look on the little girl's face. Able to stand confusion no longer, she asked, as if in pain, "Why do they keep talking about Play-Dough?"

During the visit Elaine often talked about how much she and Brendan needed time together, "just the two of us," and Mary suggested they let Annie stay the next week with them. "Gaddi and all of us would love it. We could bring her back Saturday, or meet each other half way."

"That sounds wonderful," Elaine said, "but I'm afraid it'll frazzle you two."

"What's another one?" Aran asked. "Besides, there aren't many girls in the neighborhood. And I'm sure we can make arrangements for Annie to join Gaddi's swimming class."

They agreed, and when Brendan got back from Oklahoma City, Elaine told him the plans. "We'll get lots of rest," she said, her eyes sparkling, then immediately told Mary, "You'll have to let us take Gaddi and Damon for a week later on. Okay?"

Receptive, Mary glanced at Aran who said, "That sounds like

a possibility," but he wasn't anxious for that to happen. He didn't get
to see his children enough as it was, he felt, and he didn't want his ex-
wife to get the impression he was trying to abandon them. For years
now she had raved about his not being able to relate to them, his not
really loving them, the ugly distance he kept between himself and
everybody else in the world. He didn't know where she'd gotten such
a notion. He'd been the one to take their son to Minnesota for surgery,
both times. He'd been the one who each day for a year had picked up
his son from kindergarten at noon and kept him the rest of the afternoon while Mirma drew pictures in the advertising department of a
store, a job she'd told him and everyone else he knew was the best
thing that had ever happened to her: "I was going crazy. Everyone
was trying to smother me and I didn't have anything left for myself."
He was the one who'd picked up Gaddi from nursery school; and after
the separation and divorce, something else she'd said was necessary to
what she called the fulfillment of her identity, "You smother me!"
she'd shrieked, "I want lovers!" she'd written herself in a note he'd
found, "and I've already found my magic helper, I want lovers – mil-
lions of them – I'm passionate! And Aran can't feel, he's autistic. I'm
going to do what Jung says – follow my libido and play with the kids!!!
It's the New Woman I've found – I'm mature and more adult than I've
ever felt in my life. And I'm not going to be pulled down by Aran's
moods, he's doomed to be unhappy." The poor devil, Aran thought,
she doesn't even know what Jung's notion of libido was; of course,
Jung didn't either, he thought. He also remembered that when she'd
told him she was moving to Laredo – a place she said was a bicultural
center – she'd said, "Whatever's good for me is good for my children."
She did, though, let him keep the kids with him in his apartment until
school was out. One night on the phone, however, she told him, "I
think I've sold my soul." Then he and the kids had moved Mary from
Lubbock, and a week later he and Mary were married. Mirma told
him that he wouldn't have to pay any more child support because she
was making so much money. Not trusting her motive, he told her he'd
keep paying and in several months they could re-examine the situation
and make an adjustment if it still seemed feasible. The children came
back in July, at Aran's insistence. When she balked, he told her, "The
decree says I get them a month in the summer. April and May aren't
summer." During that month she'd called them once and written them
once. The day Aran and Mary were to return them, he called Mirma
and told her they'd be there at 9 p.m. When they got to the apartment, there was a note saying she'd gone out to dinner, "Drop them

off at #F. I'll probably be back by 11." But they stayed until she returned.

In November he called her to ask about cutting child support payments. She accused him of trying to abandon his own children. He told her he wasn't and she knew it, but he'd noticed his last support check had been deposited in her savings account. She said she'd done that because the children might go to private school next year. "Listen," she'd snapped at him, "my children are the only thing standing between me and insan– between me and an unpleasant alternative."

"That doesn't sound very healthy," he'd said.

"I am! I'm the one healthy. You're always getting sick. And if you need more money, let Mary get a job!"

"That's not the point."

"It's hard getting a job. I got one."

"Big deal."

"It is a big deal. I'm happy and fulfilled. The kids and I are thriving. So bug off and leave us alone."

"Look," he'd told her, "I'm their father. They're my kids, too."

"They're not anyone's kids! They're their own people. They own themselves. You're so damn possessive."

"Shut up. You sound like a lunatic."

"Don't tell me –"

"I said shut up." Then after awhile he'd asked her if she'd pay half their transportation costs for the Christmas visit. Again she raved at him, told her all he thought about was money. He told her he knew many people who had just such an arrangement. She said the decree didn't call for her to pay half. He told her it didn't call for him to pay the whole amount either, that if she wanted to, he'd take her to court over the matter. She said she was calling his bluff, but before the conversation was over she agreed to cut the support payment in half in December when he'd have them two weeks.

The phone rang. It was Mirma, asking to speak to the kids. The conversation lasted no more than a few minutes. Damon said he had to go play with a friend down the street, and Gaddi, explaining that Annie was going to be with her a whole week, said she had to go, too, "We're doing the Frisbee."

Several times similar things had happened when he and Mary had called them, but he was afraid Mirma would panic and set about doing everything possible to get the kids back by July. He was right.

One night, late, he and Mary were talking about the situation. She told him that Elaine had said her own mother was a lot like Mirma, but that now it was her father she was close to. "She told me the kids would give me a lot of pain but that my pleasure would come from seeing them growing. It'll just take time."

"Sounds like a fortune cookie," Aran said. "But you are a lot better mother than what they've got most months of the year."

"I wonder. This summer's smoother than last, but it still outrages me to hear Gaddi give Mirma credit for what I've done. Like yesterday. I bought her two barrettes and fixed her hair so it swept back out of her eyes, and later that afternoon she came in and told me, 'Look at the pretty barrettes Mother bought me and how she's taught me to fix my hair.'"

"Maybe she was teasing or making a transference." He laughed. "Engaging in alchemy – transforming you into Mother."

"I don't think so. She even named the store where her mother bought the barrettes and she was with me when I bought them. In fact, it was the only thing we got."

"You're still doing beautifully."

"Sometimes I feel rotten."

"At least you're not stupid."

"Mirma's not stupid."

"She is. She doesn't have any ability to conceptualize matters – at least not with any clarity."

"I don't feel very clear."

"You don't sound hysterical either."

"I keep wondering," Mary said, "why she keeps harping on those awful illusions she has about you. She's the one wanted the divorce, you didn't. But she sounds obsessed with analyzing you and her and the relationship. Sometimes I think she's still in love with you."

"She doesn't sound like it to me. It's sure a pleasure, though, to be free of all that crap."

"I was telling Elaine that I thought Mirma must've had some illusion about you two being, somehow, mighty forces on opposite sides of town pulling together and away and then together again and away for years."

Laughing, Aran said, "Sounds like third-rate D.H. Lawrence, misinterpreted."

"It does, doesn't it?" Laughing together on the bed, they

kissed. "Elaine thinks I'm a threat to her, that Mirma's not so much interested in the children as she is in seeing you miserable."

"Maybe you are a threat. You're certainly smarter and better looking. Of course, she's probably upset because she was going to meet the big wide wonderful world. The only trouble is, the big wide wonderful world never showed up," he said brightly. "Especially when that lonely, doomed, autistic character me ends up in bed with the Queen of the Nile."

"You're a honey," she said, and curled into his arms.

Seeing that his wife was tired, he told her he'd read the girls their story tonight. Leaving the den, he squeezed her bare toes.

"That tickles."

"Indeed it does," he said, kissing her.

He rounded up the girls and Damon, but his son said he wanted his own story. Agreeing that was fine, he told the girls to get their baths and he'd read to them when they were finished. He read Damon the story of Rumpelstiltskin and, discussing with him the story's implications – fear of facing his own rottenness, fear of being found out, the split body at the end a sign of the earlier confusion, and the final exuberant descent into Earth where "in another country or situation he and all of us get another chance" – he massaged his son's back, smiling at Damon's indifference to all the hoorah he was associating with the piece. Damon told him it felt better when he rubbed directly on the skin, so running his hand up under his son's shirt, Aran rubbed him more. Thinking he was finished, he kissed him goodnight, but Damon said he wanted his tummy rubbed, too.

"You're a real voluptuary, you know that?"

"Don't use fingernails. That scratches."

Dutifully Aran trailed his fingertips over his son's abdomen then rubbed his scalp, his fingers going through the rich texture of Damon's wavy hair.

"Night."

"I love you," Damon said.

"I love you, too," and the two met and kissed each other goodnight.

Gaddi and Annie were shrieking with laughter and insulting the shape of each other's bottom. Trying to get them quiet, Aran sat on the bed, his back against the wall, and told them to hush or he wouldn't read the story. Legs crossed on the floor, they were silent for a moment then got tickled again, but when he rose they once more

turned silent and he agreed to read them "The Bad Little Boy" by
Hans Christian Andersen. Annie said she wanted Cinderella " 'cause
that's who Mary looks like."

"You think I look like the Handsome Prince?"

The girls held their breaths then burst into laughter.

"No," Gaddi squealed, "you look like doo-doo."

"Settle down," he told them, but both girls began mocking him,
again and again. Warning them, he started the story, but soon they
were giggling and he couldn't keep from laughing himself. Finally,
though, after starting and stopping and getting up and threatening to
leave and sitting back down and helpless with laughter himself and
warning them this was their last chance, he finished. They'd cackled
and wrestled through the entire tale. He told them he was going to
teach them a lesson about the importance of paying attention. They
thought that was even funnier and started pinching his toes. Making
them quit, he flipped back through the story and, sure they'd heard
none of it, began asking them questions about it. The girls became
sober. Then they stunned him, answering correctly every question he
asked. It amazed him to hear them bring up other details, a number
of which were minor. Bewildered, he got them in bed and kissed them
goodnight. They laughed at him, they laughed at each other, they
begged for water, and Gaddi shouted that Damon better go to the
bathroom or he'll pee all over himself.

"We'll all drown!" Annie screamed.

When he and Mary finally went to bed, they found the stairs
steep. Arms around each other, they plodded up them, Mary's head
against his chest. Aran found himself chuckling. He said, "I'm
deranged. I've got the giggles. They've infected me."

"I hope you don't try to work tonight," Mary said, yawning.
"You need some sleep."

"You, too," he said and, lowering his head, spread his palm
across the underglobe of her bottom and pushed her up the rest of the
steps. "I'm just helping you."

"Yes," she said, "you do that very well."

6.

The day before Annie left, a large envelope came in the mail. Inside it were two smaller, windowed envelopes addressed to the children. Gaddi ripped hers open and asked her father to read her the letter from her mother.

"It's from your grandfather."

"Which one?"

"Your mother's daddy."

"Oh. Read it."

Inside her envelope was another one with a twenty-dollar bill in it. He pulled it out for her and she said she was going to save it. Telling him not to read the letter yet, she went to find her purse. Money tucked away, she crawled up on his lap. Unfolding the sheet of paper, he saw the letter was a carbon copy. The heading said: *Hi! My dearest one.* A copy had obviously been made for each of the four grandchildren. The letter itself was sweet enough, Aran thought, until the middle where the man suggested ways they might spend the money: *You might want to use it on your next debate trip, on some space books, or fishing equipment, or a giant supply of popsicles or frisbees, just anything your special fancy takes a turn to.* All Aran could see missing was a line of instruction saying: *Circle the appropriate answer.*

"That was nice of Mother to send it, wasn't it?"

"It's from your grandfather, not your mother. Your mother just forwarded it."

"Right. I'm going to save my money."

When Damon got home from swimming, Gaddi yelled, "We got some mail from our grandpa."

Damon, hair stringy and damp, rushed the drainboard to get it, found the envelope, ripped it open and snatched the bill from it, yelped, "Neat! Twenty dollars!" and ran upstairs without glancing at the letter which, at that moment, with its envelope, fell off the counter. Aran rose to pick it up.

"Daddy!" Damon called. "Come on up here!"

"You come down here, Lazy-bones."

"Let me get dry clothes."

When he came back downstairs, Damon said he was going to

buy a new spinning reel with his money. "Can we go get it now?"

"You think about it longer."

"I want to get it now."

"How much do they cost?"

"I don't know."

"Why don't you check the Best catalog? It's on top of the wine rack."

Damon found six reels he'd like to have, but he couldn't make up his mind which one he wanted most, then some other items struck him, and before long he was again fussing at his father to take him to the store. Aran said he ought to wait a day or two, to think it over and make sure he got what he wanted, but Damon said he already knew: "One of these!" and he wanted it now.

"I'll swear," Aran said, "that money's going to burn a hole in your pocket."

"It's not in my pocket. It's in my hand!" he shouted, lifting his fist, and they argued about the trip to the store until Aran asked him how long his allowance usually lasted. Defiantly he said, "About a day."

"Which means thirteen out of fourteen days you're broke."

"So?"

"Learn to save your money. You may need it. When I was a boy," he said, only partly lying, "I'd end up lending money to the other members of the family when we'd go on vacation."

"Why?"

"Because they always spent theirs."

"They pay you back?"

"Sure."

"Not me. I'm gonna spend it now." They kept arguing until Damon told him that one month his mother had spent sixty dollars on models for him. "That's when she started giving me my allowance so I could buy my own."

"Sixty dollars in one month? On models?"

"Yep. Let's go to the store."

"No, Damon, and that's final. We'll think about it tomorrow or the next day."

"Then I'm going home early. I'm not going to stay here."

Without answering him, Aran left the room.

Mary had trouble believing the children had actually gotten a carbon copy of a letter, but Aran told her there was nothing unusual in that, that when Mirma's father wrote his three daughters he always sent carbons. "Sometimes he scrawls a name at the top, sometimes he doesn't. The three of them used to joke about never getting the original until they realized that none of them had ever gotten an original, that he must've thrown it away or filed it, to make sure he didn't show favoritism."

"Incidentally," Mary said, "Mirma called this morning."

"Why?"

"Guess."

"Did they talk to her?"

"No. They were at the pool."

"What did she sound like?"

"I think the proper word is *correct*."

As usual, Aran got up first. His joints felt as if they'd been bolted together. His sinuses were stuffed and his belly bloated. He made coffee then went outside to get the paper. Inhaling the freshness of the dew-sweet morning, he suddenly turned dizzy, wanted to pitch forward unconscious in the grass. He trudged back in, carefully shut the door behind him then heard Damon trouncing downstairs.

"Hi," his son said brightly. "We get to go to the store today?"

"We'll see. Mary and Gaddi are taking Annie to meet her mother."

"I have to go?"

"No," Aran said, collapsing back on the flowered sofa.

"I don't want to go with them. I want to go to the store. I've decided on the reel and tackle box."

"Good. I want to read the paper now."

"There's nothing to do here," Damon said, sitting across from his father in the yellow armchair. "It's boring."

"It's also six-fifteen."

"So? I'm getting my reel today."

"Settle down, Damon. I don't feel well."

"I don't either – not until I get my reel. It's my money."

"I realize that," he said, slapping open the paper. "Why don't you go pick a bowl of blackberries? We can have them for breakfast."

"I will if I get to get my reel."

"We'll talk about it later. Go pick the blackberries."

"Can I pick anything else?"

"Sure. Anything that's ready. Take the basket with you."

While he was gone, Gaddi came down and crawled up in her father's lap. She asked where her brother was.

"In the garden," he said, kissing her. "You want to go help him pick things?"

"Kiss," she said, then slid off him and left. Plumper than her brother, she reminded him this morning of a honey-glazed doughnut.

Scanning the paper, he found an item he liked: a story about a woman in Oklahoma who'd been growing opium poppies for forty years. The FBI and State Patrol had staked out her place for a week before leaping from behind the barn to arrest her. "Lands," she'd said, "I never seen such to-do about flowers. They thought I's pickin' seed pods. Had'm fooled. I's just pickin' beans. Some folks these days are just plain simple." The story went on to say the officers had pulled up enough poppies to fill thirteen plastic garbage bags. They burned them along with a gallon of seeds. No charges were filed, however; the police chief said, "Knowing the lady long as we had, we knew she was strictly just an innocent party in the thing."

"Can't believe they're all gone," the widow said. "Forty years with me, near a lifetime." The article said, though, that she admitted to hearing it was illegal to grow poppies, but "I never did pay that opium business no mind. I just couldn't see how one of God's beautiful flowers could do any harm."

Lifting his cup, Aran toasted the woman.

The children came in fussing about who got to go through the door first. Rising, Aran hushed them, told them there were others trying to sleep. He poured them some orange juice then asked how they'd like it if he made buttermilk biscuits for breakfast. "We can chop up the berries and put them in the dough."

Damon said he liked canned biscuits best, but Gaddi said, "Not me," and Aran told them, "We're having home-made biscuits this morning – the kind God meant us to eat," he said, patting their bottoms.

"God didn't say that," Damon told him.

"Did, too," Gaddi corrected him. "I had a dream and He told me He wanted Daddy's buttermilk biscuits to come home in my tummy 'cause I'd been so good."

"Unh-unh," Damon said.

"He did, too. God tickles my ears when He whispers."

"God doesn't talk to you."

"Sometimes he does. And sometimes He cries because you're so awful. He likes Daddy and me and Mary. He doesn't like you at all."

"Yes, He does," Damon said. "He loves everybody."

"Not you," she sang. "He told me. Just me and sometimes Daddy – but not very much."

"Well, I like you," Aran told his son.

"Well, I don't like you – not unless you take me to the store to get my reel."

Mixing the ingredients for the biscuits, he told them if they'd be careful he'd let them crush the blackberries.

"With our hands?" Damon asked.

"Sure, unless you'd rather use your feet," and he showed them how to do it, but told them to be careful not to stain their pajamas.

Soon after breakfast Mary packed Annie's clothes, and they left to meet Elaine and Brendan. While they were gone, Aran took Damon to the store to buy a reel and rod and tackle box.

"Can I get some jigs, too?"

"If you have enough money."

Damon piled his equipment on the counter and told the salesman, "I'm paying for it," then beaming, glanced around at his father who decided to buy himself a telescoping rod so they'd both have one. He also bought some hooks, weights and corks.

"Do I get to pay for those, too?" Damon asked.

"I'm getting these. We'll store them in your tackle box."

"I've got enough money. I'll pay for all of it."

"No," he said, squeezing his son's shoulder. "Save your change. You might need it."

"I hope we get to go fishing today."

"Perhaps this evening when it's cool."

"What about now?"

"The fish don't bite when it's hot."

"Sometimes they do."

Damon was napping when Mary and Gaddi drove into the garage.

"How was it?" Aran asked, opening the door for them.

"You should've seen them. Elaine kept gushing about how much rest they'd gotten and how important the time had been for them."

"How was Brendan?"

"He looked good, though he must've yawned eight times during the meal. He said be sure and tell you hello. How'd it go here?"

"Wonderful. We got the fishing equipment."

"I'm glad."

"We all might go out to the lake this evening."

"Me, too?" Gaddi asked.

"All of us."

"Where's Damon?"

"Taking a nap."

"Good," Gaddi said. "I don't have to take a nap. I slept in the car."

"I think I'm going to take a nap," Mary said.

"Are you taking one, Daddy?"

"Maybe."

"I hope not 'cause then I'll be alone."

"We'll all be here in the house."

"Okay, but you can't lock the door. I might get scared."

Squeezing his waist, Mary kissed him. "I'm going on up."

"So much for the voluptuous life," Aran said.

"What?" she asked, turning back around.

After supper, the wind was still blowing hard, but they drove to the lake anyway. At first Damon and Aran tried fishing off the dam, but their lines kept drifting back against the rocky shoreline below them. Trying out Damon's rig, Aran cast aslant the wind, but the line went limp when it arced and the jig barely cleared the rocks.

"It's a good one, isn't it?" Damon asked.

"A real good one, but we ought to try the other side. The wind's messing us up."

"What about Mary and Gaddi?" who'd walked down the dam to a dilapidated pier.

"They'll be back in a bit. We'll go then."

"Can I try mine again?"

"Sure," Aran said, finishing reeling the line in. Handing the rig to him, he watched his son's face as he prepared to make a cast. The line sailed out well. "That's a good one."

"Think I'll catch anything?"

"You might," he said, remembering the days they'd still lived together, when sometimes five or six times a week Damon would go crawfishing, using a hanger wrapped with pantyhose for a net to scoop up the crawdads in the ditch feeding along the edge of the school's playground near the house. One day Aran had boiled the tails for his son. They dipped them in melted butter and ate them, but after awhile Damon said he didn't like them very much: "I just like to catch'm and look at the colors on their pincers."

"You still go crawfishing?" Aran asked.

"Not much. Sometimes."

"Any luck?" Gaddi called as she and Mary, holding hands, approached them.

"Naw," Damon said, casting again. "Too windy."

"Too bad," Gaddi told him. "We saw a nail."

The spot they found on the other side of the lake was less windy but thick with reeds. Their hooks kept snagging, but the illusion of bites was delightful. He asked Gaddi if she'd like to cast, too. Damon tried showing her how, but she insisted, "Leave me alone, I can do it. Daddy, show me how." The first time she tried, the jig stayed on the tip of her rod. "You broke it," she told her brother. "You got gypped." Aran showed her how again. "Like this?" she asked, whipping the tip near his face.

"Right," he said, dodging.

"I don't want to," she said, dropping the rod in the water. "There's a snake out there."

"Where?" he asked as Damon scrambled down in the water for his rod and shouted at her for dropping his rig.

"There!" she said. "It's got feelers coming out of its eyes."

"Those are reeds," Damon said.

"I'm not talking to you! They're snakes. They're going to bite me," she cried, running to Mary.

"You're a little goofball," Mary told her.

"I gotta go to the bathroom. Bad!" As Mary took her behind the car, Gaddi cried out to them, "Don't look!"

"Nobody," Damon said, "wants to see your hiney anyway."

"Why not?" she sang. "It looks like a flower."

"It doesn't smell like one."

"Sometimes it does. You can look now. I don't really have to go."

"It's getting dark," Aran told Damon. "Why don't we go on in? We're running out of jigs."

"Can we come out here again?"

"Sure. Next time we'll find a better place."

"I found a catfish head in Laredo big as a basketball. Dead, though."

"Daddy," Gaddi said, running up to him, "can we play Putt-Putt on the way home?"

"We did that yesterday. It's getting time to get ready for bed."

The sun already below the horizon, the evening sky was brilliant: red bleeding into blue then waves of vermilion flowing through them. The hot gusting wind had died down to a breeze.

Putting his arm around Mary as the four of them walked between fanning clumps of prickly pear and over a hay-colored spread of buffalo grass to the car, Aran asked her how she was doing.

"All right," she said, distracted. "How about you?"

"Fine," he said, his chest muscles jerking. "You sure?"

"I'm just tired."

"Frazzled, too."

"I'll be all right."

"What's wrong?" Damon asked.

"Nothing," Aran said. "We're all just tired."

"Not me."

"The rest of us are."

"That's because you didn't take a nap. I'm beginning to like naps. They make you feel better."

The wind picked up again. Dust stung their faces.

"I'm sorry I'm out of sorts," Mary said.

"Don't worry about it," he snapped.

"You don't sound too good yourself."

"I'll be all right," he insisted.

"We'll see," she said.

7.

After church they went to eat Mexican food. Damon, however, ordered the shrimp platter. He didn't like spicy foods, but his sister, like his father, would eat almost anything. After clearing only half his plate, Damon said he was full. "Me, too," Aran said, pushing away the basket of tostados he'd been munching on. Leaning on his arms over the table, he felt fatigue-tingles prickling his skin: chest, back and arms; and the back of his neck felt knotted.

"Can we go swimming," Damon asked, "when we get home?"

"Maybe later," Mary said. "Your dad's about to drop."

Pulling a wad of bills from his shirt pocket, Damon said he'd pay for the meal, but Aran told him, "You keep your money."

"I want to pay. I've got enough."

"The treat's on me," Aran said, finding himself squinting though the light in the restaurant wasn't glaring. "Everybody ready?"

he asked, forcing himself up.

Damon begged to at least pay the tip. Scratching his son's back as they moved out of the booth, Aran agreed to let him.

"Is this enough?" he asked, laying down a dollar.

"That's perfect," Aran said, putting another one on top of it. Seeing the sudden look of disappointment on his son's face, he told him, "Just let me share. Okay?" Reluctantly Damon agreed.

Sunscorch blew against them as they stepped outside. The car's door handles burned their fingers. The inside of the car felt thick. Cumulus clouds pillowed the sky, but no rain was coming. It rarely did till late August.

The blue seatcovers hot, Gaddi said she couldn't breathe: "I'm drowning, get the air conditioner on."

"I'll get it," Damon said, making sure he beat his father to the knobs.

At first the fan only moved the hot hair around. Damon turned it higher while his father rolled down his window then adjusted the temperature control.

When they got home, Mary suggested they leave the car in the driveway: "We might have to go out again."

Damon rushed to the den to turn on the television set.

"Naptime," his father said.

"All *right*," Damon said. He was fuming. "We never get to do anything. I hate being here. You won't even let me go swimming."

"What do you mean? You go swimming every day – usually twice."

"Not today. Not right now."

"It's too hot."

"Not in the water."

"You can go after your nap."

"How long's that?"

Checking his watch, Aran said, "Three-thirty."

"Can I take Steve with me?"

"You can take whoever you want."

"I don't like taking naps."

"We all need a quiet time," Mary said.

"Not me," Aran and Damon said in unison, and Damon shot his father a glance saying he'd been betrayed. Aran winked at him. "All right," Damon agreed, "but just till three-thirty and maybe not that long."

Aran hit the bed first. Coming in after him, Mary shut the door.

"I guess at times like this," he said, "you wish you were back in France."

"Why do you say that?" she asked coolly. "I'm exactly where I want to be."

"Skip it."

"What're you trying to say?"

"Nothing. Just making a joke about being tired."

"Do you wish I were over there?"

"Not unless I were with you."

"So close your eyes," she said, "and go to sleep."

"I'm not sleepy."

"You're worse than your son."

Readjusting himself under the sheet, he watched her undress.

"At least over there you didn't have a couple urchins wearing you down."

"I didn't have a lot of clarity either."

"What about now?"

"I'm perfectly happy – just tired."

He lifted the sheet for her, and she crawled in bed beside him. She asked if he'd like to curl up spoons. "Sure," he said, disappointed. "Fine." He rolled over on his side, and she pressed against his back. Tiny shocks went up and down his skin. He mumbled he felt paralyzed. Finally giving in to an urge to twist, he lay on his back. His right arm was growing numb. He laid his hand between her legs. She squeezed his wrist and kissed him.

Not until the phone rang did he realize he'd gone to sleep. He lurched up to get it. Shifting her weight and moaning, Mary reached out for him, but he was already up, the receiver against his ear, his voice, distant even to himself, saying, "Hello?"

It was his parents calling.

"Did we wake you?" his mother asked.

"No," he lied.

"You feel all right?"

"Just sleepy."

She asked him how the two bambinos were and wondered if they could drive up tomorrow to take the kids for a day and night. "We could bring them back Tuesday afternoon."

"That's a lot of driving."

"We don't mind," his father said. "You might want to meet us half way."

Thinking of his father as a man always looking to strike a bargain, Aran said the kids would love it. Then his mother told him the circus was coming to Dallas in mid-July. They wanted to know if Damon and Gaddi would like for them to get tickets to it.

"They'll still be there, won't they?" his father said, the question more imperative than interrogatory.

"I think so. They're napping now but I'll ask them."

"No," his mother said, "don't wake them."

"I meant later. We'll let you know when you pick them up tomorrow."

Just as he was about to hang up, the door to the bedroom came slowly open. It was Damon wanting to know if he could get up.

"Wait," Aran told his parents and gave his son the receiver.

"Who is it?"

"You'll see."

While Damon talked to them, telling them all he'd been doing, Aran went to see if Gaddi were awake. She was but her eyes were puffy and she was sucking her lips. He told her who was on the phone. Without changing expression, she uncurled from her bed and wandered into the bedroom; then, as if floating, she turned back around and went downstairs.

When she came back up, she told her father that she and Damon were going to the circus tomorrow in Dallas. Acting as if he were struggling to maintain patience, Damon explained to her that the circus was several weeks away, that tomorrow was just a trip and a visit.

"Well," she said, "I might not be here. Mama may make me go home if that's what I want."

"You don't have to go back to bed," Aran told them. "Why don't you go downstairs and watch TV? It's still too early to go swimming."

Repeating details of the telephone conversation to each other, Damon and Gaddi left the room as Aran sat on the bed at Mary's feet.

"Never fails, does it?" he said. "We hit the sack in the afternoon and the phone rings. You get any sleep?"

"I think so."

"You look angry."

"I'm tired," she said, curling away from him.

The next morning, before anyone else got up, Damon packed his suitcase. Hearing him bouncing it down the stairs, Aran got up to see what he was doing.

"What time'll they be here?" Damon asked.

"About eleven."

"Can I go swimming first?"

"Better not."

"I don't really want to anyway. That's neat about the circus."

"Right."

"We saw one in Laredo, but it wasn't very big. Is this one – the one in two weeks?"

"The biggest in the world."

"Aw," he said, "really?"

"The biggest."

"You ever seen one?" Damon asked.

"Sure," Aran said, "but when I was a kid they had them in tents."

"Wow – they must've been tiny, with just little animals and stuff."

"No, no," Aran said, "the tents were huge – even bigger than football fields sometimes."

"Gah – I've never seen one that big. Are you and Mary going?"

"Maybe."

When Aran's parents came, Gaddi jumped up in her grandfather's arms and, splatting, smacked his ear while Damon hung onto his grandmother who told him this evening she'd take him to play tennis with her. "I bought a racket just your size."

"Is it steel?"

"No, it's wood, but the pro said that's the kind you should start on."

"I beat my daddy when we played last week."

"You didn't!" she said with an exaggerated air of amazement.

"Yes, I did but I don't think he tried very hard."

"I didn't beat anybody," Gaddi said, interrupting the conversation.

"You're too little," Damon told her.

"I am not. I just didn't try very hard. Me and Daddy do it just alike."

"You ought to learn to try hard everytime," her grandfather told her.

Giggling, she asked him to let her bite his nose. "I made Daddy's go bloody."

"You take care of your daddy," he told her, and Aran wished his father would lighten up.

"Wanta see my new fishing equipment?" Damon asked, pulling away to get his treasure from the closet.

"Of course," his grandfather said.

"Well," Aran's mother drily asked Mary, "don't *you* have anything to show us? Everybody else does. Don't you have anything to justify yourself?"

"Do bags under my eyes qualify?" Mary asked, laughing.

"Certainly not. I've had those for years. We expected something distinguished."

"How about coffee?" Mary asked; and, as they took chairs in the den, Aran, who was having the secretary monitor the tests he'd assigned, heated the coffee, and the children pummeled their grandparents with things they'd gotten and tales of what they'd been doing.

"Sounds like you two have had a good time," Aran's father said, adding with a gesture of weight in his voice, "here at home."

"We've got two homes," Gaddi said. "Here and Naredo. My mama's gonna let me come back in a month."

"You want to stay here longer than that," her grandfather told her.

"No, I don't either. I just want to stay a month from today. That's all I have to stay."

"Then you ought to check with your father. You very well may want to stay longer."

After they'd driven off, Mary asked Aran if he'd like another cup of coffee.

"That sounds good," then the phone rang. It was Mirma, asking to speak to the kids. Aran told her they'd just left to spend the night with their grandparents.

"What's the matter?" she asked. "You get tired of them?"

"No."

"Seems to me like every time I've called you've ditched them somewhere."

"I don't know how you get that idea. I'll be glad, though, to tell them you called."

"You do that, and I hope you two have fun there by yourselves."

"We usually do," he said, then she asked him when they'd be back, and he told her. She said she also wanted to check about when they were coming home. "I thought we'd already agreed on that," he said. "They're happy. We'll bring them back the twenty-fourth."

"Don't try to pull a fast one. We didn't agree on that date. The agreement was they could come home when they wanted."

"Well, apparently they want to stay the two months," Aran said.

"Apparently they don't. Every time I talk to them they say they want to come home as soon as possible."

"I doubt it," he said, "and I'd appreciate it if you'd quit trying to bribe them. We've already made plans, including the circus in Dallas a couple weeks from now."

"You're the one bribing them. The kids must be exhausted. Don't you ever let them get any rest? You're always clutching things – everything!"

"Come on. You've been trying to bribe them back – ever since they got here – with that penny-ante digital watch and all your mewling about how much you miss them."

"Well, I do miss them," she said. "They need love."

"They've got love."

"And I'm not trying to bribe them," she added. "In fact, Mother and Dad said I shouldn't have forwarded their letter with the twenty dollars in it, because it might look like we were trying to bribe them back and they didn't want that."

"Hell, I didn't object. I thought it was nice of you to forward their mail. Of course, it might've been nicer if the letter had been anything other than a carbon addressed to whoever it might concern. So just lay off. Let them enjoy their time here. They're happy."

"I know they're happy, but I think they need to be back with me. A friend told me it's disorienting for a child to be away from home longer than a month. He's a lawyer. They know these things."

"Your lawyer's an ignorant ass. They're not away from home, damnit. They're with their father. Do you understand that?"

"Don't talk to me like I'm ten years old."

"Then settle down and leave them alone. For your information, I've never heard Damon say anything good about Laredo. His friends will ask him what it's like down there and he always says, 'Not good.' And most of the time he doesn't even know I've heard him. So lay off."

"There's more to a place than a physical environment. They need to be back with their mother."

"They are," he said. "Close to eleven damn months out of the year."

"My friend told me studies have been made."

"Hell yes – lots of them. So what? There're all kinds of damn studies."

"And all of them show it's disorienting for a child to be away from home for longer than a month."

"Horseshit. They're not away from home. They're with their father. They've got two damn homes."

"They need love!" she cried. "They need me!"

"They've got you. Ten and a half months out of the year. So what's the problem?"

"I'm calling them back," she said, as if it were a threat.

"Good," he told her. "I think it's nice of you to keep in touch. Gaddi missed it when you didn't last year. I don't know whether Damon did or not. For some reason he scarcely mentioned you."

"I'm calling back!" she reminded him.

"Fine," he said.

"Goodbye!" she told him.

"Bye," he answered, but it was a long time before she hung up.

Gritting his teeth, he turned to Mary who said, "From now on it might be better if I answer the phone." He agreed and she asked him if he still wanted a cup of coffee. Wiping his mouth as if he were trying to dispel the conversation he'd just had, he nodded. She poured the coffee and brought his cup to him at the breakfast table. "What I wonder," she said, "is why all of a sudden this hostility. The divorce was over two years ago and it was her idea anyway. She makes almost as much as you do, yet she keeps sounding desperate about money, about the kids, no telling what else. Is she having trouble with her job?"

"I don't know."

"Maybe she thinks she's married to the kids and they're going to jilt her."

"I don't know," he said, "and I don't think she does either."

"Maybe Elaine was right. Maybe Mirma sees us as some kind of threat to herself."

"But why?"

"Because you and I have what you and she didn't."

"Yeah – but so what?"

"Maybe her vanity's been wounded."

"That sounds too obvious. I think it's something deeper."

"Like what?" Mary asked.

"Like the fact that a part of her's always thought of herself as homely and awkward."

Thoroughly amused, Mary laughed. "My dear, if she does,

that's just the female in her. We all think that from time to time."

"I know, but in some the notion's more justified than in others."

"Don't get too cocky," she warned him. "She may be wilier than we think. After all, she did just admit she's been seeing a lawyer."

"Socially I'd think."

"Maybe so, but pleasure's often business."

That afternoon they tried working: Mary on her book, Aran on the proofs which had come in the mail. Soon, though, she came in his study and told him, "I'm lying down for awhile." He thought her eyes looked fogged as she drifted back out of the room. The kids and all the chaos they meant seemed to be sticking her. They were having the same effect on him, too, and he knew that; but he also knew there was no way to wrench himself free from the confusion. That was why the appearance of his parents had added a burden. They were desperate for connection with their grandchildren. His mother would drive herself sick with activities during this brief period she had with them, and his father would do more of what he'd done the moments he was here: he'd hover around them and dispense wads of affirmative but cautionary advice. Even just thinking about it, Aran felt increasingly self-conscious, awkward, desperate himself and guilty for thinking of his parents' natural kindness as intrusive. But they weren't really the ones he was fighting; he knew he was fighting himself. The terms of the conflict, though, were obscure; and there was only one idea coming to him that seemed to make sense; the notion of quality time so many were trumpeting: nothing but bullshit.

Going through the proofs twice, he found only one error. He put them away and wandered in front of the shelves of his books. Often friends, they now seemed alien to him. He pulled a handkerchief from his hippocket and dusted them. He went then into Mary's study, which was also Gaddi's room; and the books there, less familiar to him than his own, pulled him toward them. He drew out Breton's *Selected Poems* and Apollinaire's *Calligrammes*, and went back to his desk. Browsing through them, as he often did, he found the cunning in their mythic sensibilities appealing. Playful and bright, even in pain, they seemed healthier than a lot of contemporary Americans whose interminably flat lines struck Aran as nothing but dreary, tone-deaf and dumb.

Thinking about all the notions of growth and change he'd heard Mirma and others spout, he was sorry capital punishment did-

n't apply to pop-psychologists who scrawled out self-help manuals.
But he also saw that his own contempt for such truck was distracting
him from the forces and figures he respected. Sliding his thumb across
the open volume in front of him, he listened to the soft flutter of pages
as the book closed itself.

He went into the bedroom and lay beside Mary. Cuddling with
him, she said, "I can't sleep, and I couldn't concentrate enough downstairs to do much work."

"Same here," he said, squeezing her, hearing her back pop.
"Feel better?"

"Not really," she told him.

"How about reading here in bed?"

"Is that what you're going to do?"

"No. I'm just going to lie here and fantasize us orgiastically
voluptuous."

"You mean that's a fantasy?"

"Only now and then," he said, "when the demons start biting."

Stroking his forehead, she kissed him.

"I love you," she whispered, their thighs now layering each
other.

8.

By the time the children came back, Mary had gone through
forty stories but still doubted she'd have enough time to examine carefully all she needed before they went to Mexico. He suggested she use
the library in the afternoons, or his office at school. "I'll take care of
supper and whatever house-chores come up."

"Library work comes later," she told him, adding, "Our time
here with the children is important." He said he'd still take care of the
evening meal, that that would at least give her another hour to work
if she wanted. So he explained to the children why they shouldn't go
into the bedroom when the door was closed.

"You gonna be in there, too?" Damon asked, a sharp edge in
his voice.

"No, I'll be down here with you or wherever we happen to
tramp to."

"But we won't ever get to see Mary," Gaddi whined.

"Sure you will. While I'm at school she'll be with you all morning. It's just a couple hours in the afternoon."

"Okay," Gaddi said. "Can I borrow some paper and one of your pens?"

"You going to draw?"

"No. I'm gonna make a book."

"You can't even write well," Damon said. "You always write backwards."

"I'll do it how I want to," she sassed him. "It's my book and you can't even read it. Only Mary and sometimes Daddy," she said, leaping to bite his nose.

Mirma didn't call again until the weekend, when she told the children she was in Houston visiting her parents for four days, and Aran heard Damon tell her he thought he was going to stay through July, but Gaddi said she wanted to come home: "Yesterday! Mary taught me a new song on the piano, wanta hear it?" she asked, dropping the receiver and rushing into the living room, where she banged out "Chop Sticks." Hurrying back to the phone, she shouted, "Wasn't that pretty?" Then after a long silence she whined, "I wanta come home. I miss you."

When he came back downstairs, Damon mumbled that he was walking to Doug's.

"You all right?" Aran asked him.

"Yeah," he said distantly.

For a long time Mary and Aran wondered about the call from Houston, about Mirma's telling the children she'd be there for four days. They couldn't decide if she were looking for a new job or had just taken several days off from work.

"Unless she's on vacation," Mary suggested, "I doubt she'd be able to take a couple days off."

"She could have. She used to take off at least one day a month."

"Why? I thought her job was salvation."

"She said she owed herself a reward. Same reason she used to weekend in Dallas now and then."

"By herself?"

"Yep."

"You mean when you were married?"

"I'd forgotten about it until just now."

"Was that when she was having the affair?"

"I don't know," he said. "In spirit it all amounts to the same thing anyway: running away from what she calls clutching and smothering."

"What would she do down there?"

"She said she slept a lot and was always grateful I never fussed about it. If she wanted to make the Hilton Inn Mecca, I didn't see much point in being difficult."

"Were you really that cool about it when she'd take those trips?"

Aran laughed. "At least on the surface and according to the Behaviorists, that's what counts."

"Vacation my eye."

The next Saturday morning Mirma called again, and after the conversation Gaddi came dancing to her father and saying that next week her mother was coming to get her. His insides wrenched.

"When next week?"

"She's driving up Friday or Saturday."

During the conversation he'd been drinking coffee and reading the paper in the living room. Damon had been on the extension in the den, and Aran heard his son say he was staying "until July twenty-fourth." He'd also heard how muted his son's voice was, especially the three times he'd told his mother, "I've got to go now," but each time, after a silence, he'd say, "What?" and the conversation would continue. Blood racing, Aran had gotten up to pour another cup of coffee. He noticed Damon glancing up at him, saying softly into the phone, "I don't think so. ... No. I think I'll stay. . . . He's here. . . . Yes. . . . I know, but the pool here's cleaner. . . . Fine. I gotta go now," but he didn't. "We're going camping today – all night," Aran, leaving the kitchen, heard him say.

After the conversation was over, the children came to the dining table while Mary and Aran finished getting the breakfast ready. Gaddi sang, "I get to go home!"

"So?" Damon said. "I'm staying."

"I'm glad," Aran said brusquely, his anger turning him inward. "It's good having you here."

"There's not much to do down there. It's just hot and dirty, and sometimes I can't even see my own feet in the swimming pool."

"I get to see Ruda," Gaddi said.

"So what?" Damon said. "She always messes up my stuff, even in the drawers."

"Maybe," Mary said, "she's just trying to dust."

"No way," Damon said, "she just messes up and breaks stuff. She doesn't even speak English."

"I don't care," Gaddi said, and counted to ten in Spanish. The phone rang. Mary told them she'd get it. In a moment Aran heard her say, "How about if I talk? ... Okay. I'll get him. It's for you," she said, nodding to Aran who had already risen from the table. The children asked who it was, and Mary told them, "An old friend."

"I'll get it upstairs." Answering it, he heard Mirma's muffled voice. "Wait a minute. Let me close the door. I can't hear you." Locking the door, he came back to the phone.

"I'm in San Antonio," she said, "and I'm driving up tomorrow to pick up the kids."

"Why?" he asked, shocked at hearing what he'd been expecting.

"They both told me they wanted to come home, and that's what the agreement was."

"They didn't tell you anything of the kind. I heard Damon's whole conversation, and he told you he was going to stay. And he just got through telling all of us – Gaddi included – that he was staying."

"I'm coming to get them," she repeated.

"The hell you are! The agreement was for them to stay here a month and then –"

"Yes," she said smugly, "and then another month if they wanted to, but they're ready to come home."

"That's not what Damon says."

"Gaddi is. She's been ready ever since she got there."

"Goddamn!" he said. "Don't you have enough sense to know you can't take everything a child says literally?"

"I understand that. And it's my responsibility to interpret what they say. Look, they've had a good time there, but now it's time for them to come back home."

"They *are* home!"

"I believe," she said matter of factly, "the court named me – I believe the term is managing conservator. I've got the decree right here."

"Good. And if you'll read it, you'll notice that it says when I have them in the summer that *I'm* to serve as managing conservator, if you want to be technical about it. I had that clause put in just for this kind of situation. So don't try getting back at me just because you didn't read the fine print. That means when they're with me they're home."

"No," she said. "It says right here that I'm managing conservator."

"Right. Then read the visitation part, which incidentally calls for me to have them a month in the summer in addition to 'reasonable visitation rights.' That's *in addition to*, not *instead of*."

"You've had your month. That's what the court allowed you. No more because everyone knows it's disorienting for a child to spend more than a month away from home. You want to try violating the decree? I'll take you on, Buster, if you want to go to court over it."

"Damnit, that time period's minimum, and when it was made I was seeing them three and four times a week. Besides, we agreed that they could stay here two months."

"I'm sorry. That was my mistake. I had no right to violate the decree. So now I'm going back and doing what's right."

"What do you mean what's right? You weren't thinking of the kids when you moved to that pit five hundred miles away."

"I had to move," she said. "I go where the money is."

"What've you fantasized yourself as now – a titan of industry?"

"I couldn't stay there. You gathered all your friends together and the whole town made me feel ostracized."

"Right. I mobilized 100,000 people and told them if they didn't throw stones at you and get down to serious gossiping that they'd be in big trouble."

"The point is, I'm getting them tomorrow. Has Gaddi gotten over her fever blister yet?"

"Yeah," he told her, "that was gone before the first week was up."

"Looks to me like every time the kids get with you they start falling apart and getting sick."

Pushing the pillow off the bed and remembering the times before they'd moved that he'd found out she'd left Damon at home by himself all day when he was sick, he asked her when the last time was she'd taken them to the dentist. Damon had always had trouble with his teeth: thirteen fillings by the time he was seven, root canal work Aran had paid for even after the divorce, the fluoride treatments he'd given him because Mirma wouldn't: she thought it was horrible for the dentist to prescribe for a child something that tasted so bad. "Hunh? When was the last time?"

She coughed. "He had a filling pop out the week before he came to see you this summer. We didn't have time to get it fixed. Why didn't you? He's been there a month."

"Because this is the first time I've heard about it. Besides, those are your responsibilities. That's part of what the child support payments are for."

"They are?" she asked cynically.

"You're damn right they are. I'd advise you to start exercising more responsibility. And you're not taking Damon back early. We made an agreement and you're going to stick by it. The kids need a father, and there's nothing down there for them during the day except a subliterate maid who doesn't even speak their language. So don't try to yank them away. Damon said he's staying, and he is."

"What're you going to do?" she asked. "Be like Solomon and split the two children apart? Is that your idea of responsibility? Splitting them in half?"

"You dumb bi–" but he caught himself, not wanting his cussing her out to be able to be used against him in a later court fight. "You don't even understand the point of that story."

"Sure I do. Big Jew patriarch was going to chop the kid in half."

"Better read it again," he said, thinking how much like her parents she had become. "Don't you understand? The kids need a father."

Then she railed at him, saying he was the one who had never had anything to do with them, who from the first of their marriage had abandoned her in an emotional vacuum, and screaming at him, she said, "You don't have any right to talk to me about responsibility. That's all I ever had with you, you never gave me any support – none at all! While you were dating all those other women you just abandoned me!"

"Hey, what're you talking about?" but he stopped himself from bringing up her own admission, made while she was insisting on the separation, that she had slept with somebody off and on for five months the year before. For some reason he'd felt neither surprised nor hurt by the information. All he'd said at the time was to ask her if adultery had given her a big kick, but she'd spewed at him that she didn't like the word: "It's so nasty and misleading." Six months later he'd found out that there had been someone else, too, but by that time he'd realized for months how peaceful it was to be shed of her. Amazed by her ability to forget things she'd said and done, he asked her again what she was talking about.

"Well, you felt unfaithful a bunch of times."

"I confess. Me and the reverend President James Earl himself: just lecherous as hell."

She didn't laugh. Her phrases tumbling, she told him she was picking up the kids, accused him again of abandoning her, "and always when I needed you, and I married you for life, because I thought that's what I needed and maybe then I did coming out of that emotional vacuum at home that I'd gotten used to, not knowing how I really needed to *fly* but I couldn't do it with you – you ran away on the anniversary of our divorce and got married – I'm the one who –"

He'd never thought of it that way, he thought, trying not to laugh out loud; but the time wasn't right for amusement. He kept arguing with her, trying to get her to understand that their own desires were beside the point, that the only thing important now was keeping the children in balance. "They need a father and you don't do it by long distance, goddamnit, two months out of the year's not excessive – no one here's even trying to wreck all the wonders you think you create for them," but she wouldn't relent and he wouldn't either, though he knew that, legally, at this point, there was probably nothing he could do to prevent her from snatching them away. It's not morality we're dealing with, he thought, hearing her blasting him, it's the law.

Finally, though, he decided to gamble. He asked her if she cared so much about the kids why she'd taken her vacation in June, when everyone was certain that they'd be with him.

"Do you know what a department store's like in August with all the back-to-school work?"

"Busy," he answered.

"That's right. I just couldn't take it any other time."

"What about July? When there was a chance they might be with you."

"It was just impossible this year."

"I'm sure," he said, knowing it was useless to ask why.

"And if you're worried about the kids being properly supervised – as if they need it – we're only talking about two hours in the day, when they're alone with the maid after school. And I think that finishes this conversation."

"Fine with me," he said. "You're paying. I just have one other thing to say."

"You're such a martyr. You're so desperate and clutching – so damn bitter and possessive. What is it?"

"The kids aren't in school in the summer."

"Well," she cried, "if you think you can make me out to be an unfit mother, you just try – I'll take you on in court with TV cameras and everything!'"

"All you're doing is trying to get back at me. You don't give a shit about the –"

"Damn right I am. You made me mad last year when you tried to cut child support and get me to pay half their fare there Christmas. You didn't have any right to even ask that. All you care about's money! And you even called me at the store and put me in an awkward position."

"I had a feeling how you'd react and I didn't want the kids in on it. I don't know what your arrangements are there. If there were a bunch of people around, all you had to say was 'I can't talk,' and we'd've made other plans. And with all the changes that have occurred, these matters can be reconsidered at any time. Besides, all I did was ask. You're the one blew up."

"You made me mad just like when you asked to have them for two months and threatened to go to court if I didn't agree. You intimidated me and I resented it. You've always intimidated me and you intimidate the kids, too. And now I'm getting back. No more adjustments to try to make you happy and help keep things smooth. I'm through covering for you. I don't know why I keep trying to help. You're mean! All you care about is yourself and your damn money. You're mean and intimidate everybody! I don't notice the kids holding back around me. They come at me vicious as anybody because we've got a *healthy* relationship."

"Sounds like it."

"I'm glad you admit it. I didn't think you had it in you. So. They've been there with you, and now I need to bring them back into me into me, you hear? I'm through. This conversation is over."

"That's what you said half an hour ago."

"I'll be there tomorrow," she said.

"Not early," he said. "We're going camping tonight."

"I'm sure they'll be miserable. I know what that's like – hot and dusty."

Having hung up, he got off the bed. Both pillows were on the floor, one of them half out of its slip. The sheets and crocheted afghan from Mary's grandmother looked tornadic.

Disoriented, he went downstairs. Mary met him at the foot. She said she'd been listening, said it was clear to her Mirma had been talking with a lawyer and "on his advice called to see if she could get you to agree to her coming. Do you think she taped the call?"

"I don't know," he said wearily. "Who cares? I didn't agree to anything."

She lifted her chin to kiss him.

Coming to the table where the children were, he told them he'd been talking to their mother. "She's coming to get you tomorrow."

"No!" Gaddi cried. "She said next week. I told her not until next week."

"She said she's in San Antonio now, and she's coming tomorrow at seven p.m."

"I'm not going," Damon said. "I'm not going."

"You don't have to," his father said.

"Good. And you're going to get awful lonely, Gaddi."

"Well?"

"I'll be back in a moment," Aran said. "You all stay down here with Mary."

"What're you gonna do?"

"I've got to make a couple of phone calls."

"Who to?"

"I'll be back down in a minute."

He went back upstairs and called four of his friends who were attorneys before he found one home. The information he got confirmed what he'd suspected: there was nothing he could do. The woman told him that even if the kids wanted to stay Mirma could take them home if she wanted to.

"Even with that verbal agreement about the two months?"

"What you're dealing with there is integrity. It doesn't hold much weight. It would just be your word against hers. What do the kids think?"

"The boy said he wants to stay here. The girl said she was ready to go home."

"Shoot, Aran, she was just trying to make her mother feel good. Just keep a record. And keep the kids happy as possible. Later on, if you still want, we can see about making some changes. Which court was the divorce in?" He told her and she said, "Good. If you get him in the right mood, he's the only one you can count on. The others still get choked up at the idea of mamahood."

As he was hanging up, Mary came in and he told her what he'd heard then asked her to send Damon up. "I want to have a talk with him."

"Good," she said, kissing him. "If the kids hadn't been involved, I'd've been more amused than I was to hear all those awful things she had to say about you."

"You find me intimidating?"

"No way. I find your pressure delightful."

Damon came up and, sitting at the foot of the bed, asked his father what he wanted. He looked as if he were afraid he'd be scolded for something. To soothe him, Aran smiled at him and told him he loved him.

"You, too. What's up."

"Doc," and briefly they laughed, then Aran told him, "I just wanted you to know that it means a lot to me, and to Mary, for you to be here with us."

"It means a lot to me, too. But I'm staying here."

"I know, but I want you to realize that whatever happens at any time, whatever you choose to do," he said, choking, "I'll support you and respect you. Not just about this situation, but any other situation that might come up."

"Like what?"

"Nothing in particular. I just think it's important for people who care about each other to remind each other now and then where they stand."

"I'm staying here. Mother can't make me go back."

"I don't think she'll try. I just thought it was time for us to have one of our talks we have from time to time."

"Good, and my friend Jack's not going to be back there until the thirteenth anyway. And the digital watch isn't that important. In fact, Mother'll probably bring it with her and I can wear it here. Gaddi's going to wish she'd stayed." He frowned. "Sometimes, though, I think I ought to go back."

"Why?"

"You know," he said, squinting down at the sheets he'd been crushing in his fists. "It's a problem like when I promised Doug I'd go to his house but forgot I'd promised Steve I'd go swimming with him." Nodding, Aran let him go on. "You see," he said, swallowing, "if I go home I hurt your feelings but if I stay here, I hurt Mother's feelings. And the circus, too. Sometimes I can't make up my mind."

"Just remember this," he said, squeezing his son's knee. "In this case, you shouldn't even bother about what she feels or what I feel. We both want you to do what's best. Whatever you do, I'll support it. Okay?"

"It's a hard decision."

"I know. But it's also about time for you and me to go get the stuff for the camping trip."

"I hope we catch some fish."

"You get your shoes on," he said, kissing the crown of his head.
"I'll meet you downstairs."

"You want me to get the packs?"

9.

"Your parents are going to be some disappointed," Mary said.
"You know how much they were counting on taking them to the circus.
They've even bought the tickets."

Aran just looked away and cursed, hoping they'd at least be
able to find a place to camp. It was the July Fourth weekend, he realized, but he and Mary quickly decided not to cancel the outing which,
because of tomorrow, already had a pall over it.

Driving up to the entrance of the state park, he saw the ranger
was not at his station. When they got to the next building, the park
director told them he'd been turning away people all morning, there
just weren't any campsites available. Finding that out, the children
started fussing, and Damon said he'd just as soon go back to Laredo
right now. But Aran bought a permit for their car, and they drove into
the park and at the concession stand got a fishing license. From the
parking lot they watched sailboats and motorboats skimming through
the white-capped water. People were sunbathing on the beach. A few
were fishing from the boat dock. Gaddi said she wanted to go swimming, but Mary reminded her, "You said you didn't want to – you said
'don't bring my suit.'" Damon asked if they could fish now, but his
father told them there was too much activity here for the fish to bite.

"We're not gonna get to go at all."

"We'll find another place."

"Where?"

"It's a big lake. There ought to be a lot of places."

They drove through the camping areas. A few sites were empty.

"Here's a place," Damon said.

"They're reserved," Aran told him.

"You can check."

"That's what I'm getting ready to do," he said, and Mary wrote
down the numbers of the empty campsites, but the ranger told them

all the places were taken.

As they drove around the lake, hot wind barreled through the windows. Aran drank a beer while the others sipped iced tea from their two-quart canteen. Below them was a meadow sliding into the lake, but a barbed wire fence stretched a barrier between the grass and the road. "Here!" Gaddi cried, but Damon explained that they'd get thrown in jail if they trespassed.

"Then Mother won't know where we are! She'll miss us!"

Ahead was a dirt road veining off the asphalt. Aran turned into it. Brush scratched the car's sides and bottom as they wound across it and off it to avoid the water-filled pits. Their car skirting a boulder-messed bluff, Gaddi rose toward the front seat squealing they were going to fall off and be killed. They kept on, the path narrowing. Ahead a ditch wallowed across it. The car slanted sideways as Aran guided them into the stalks of rust-crimson dock. Gaddi raved, "We're falling!" Aran said, "This is fun!" Damon said, "I wanta go fishing." Gaddi screamed, "We're all gonna die!" Mary kept watching the far away lake, its waves eating the tiny waterskiers pitching in it.

They bounced back onto the path. Ahead was a fence, its big gate closed. Past it was a dam, its chalky sides rough with rock. A stairway climbed the slant. Red and beige, two pickup trucks parked at its sides resembled huge crocuses broken off their stems. Aran stopped and Mary got out to try to open the gate, but the latch was stuck. Grabbing the steel bars, she shook it then kicked it, jerked the latch free. To their left, a police car approached on the main road. It stopped but drove on after Aran had driven through and Mary had shut the gate. For a time they considered fishing here, but Gaddi cried she was afraid of the snakes in the rocks they'd have to pass on their steep climb down. Agitating her, Damon told about the time "before you and Mother got divorced" that he'd almost been bitten by a rattlesnake sleeping by some deer antlers he'd found for his collection.

"We'll find another place," Aran said, asking for another beer.

Back on the access road, they rode the curves and dips. No place they found seemed right. Either houses were thick around them or the reeds too high. They stopped at several spots but found out the property there was private. Damon began fussing that this wasn't any fun at all, that they weren't ever going to get to go fishing. He wanted to go right now: "This isn't fair! I had my mind counting on it."

Mary, trying to distract them, told stories about the times she'd gone fishing with her father in the Louisiana swamps "all up and down the bayous, and one day I counted 234 snakes."

"Poisonous?" Damon asked, hope in his voice.

"A lot of them," but Gaddi cried she didn't want to get bitten. After driving for more than an hour, they turned around, having decided to try an open place they'd passed, a place Mary reminded Aran he'd said looked as good as any they'd find, but he couldn't remember it, and she told him, "I can't imagine what your mind's on."

"Right."

"What're y'all talking about?" Damon asked.

"A place for all of us," Mary said.

"There isn't any place," Damon said. "We're not ever gonna get to go fishing."

"We are, too," Aran said. "It's just taking longer than we thought. Sometimes you have to change plans."

"Not me. It's not fair."

"Sometimes that's the way things are."

"If I don't get to go fishing, I'm going back home. Now!"

They found the place again, but Aran scarcely remembered having seen it. Sides globing, the area sloped down into the water. The wind had gotten rougher. Waves spat at the beach. Their car going over the hump at road's edge, and sharply down, Gaddi screamed they'd all drown. Soon, though, they'd gotten the fishing equipment from the trunk, and Damon, suddenly serene, was casting into the wind. Several times he said he wasn't sure if he were getting bites or hitting snags, but he thought this was a good place and asked his father if he'd like to try his rig. They exchanged rods, and Aran enjoyed the singing of the line sailing out. Gaddi, who had stayed with Mary near the car, brought them a sack of cherries.

"These are really good," Damon said. "Aren't you glad I suggested we get them?"

"Sure am," he said, then asked Gaddi if she wanted to fish for awhile.

She tried it for a time then said she was going back to Mary "where the food is."

Before long, both Aran and Damon were certain they'd had a few bites. Damon waved back at the car where Mary and Gaddi were then asked his father, "If we catch something, can we eat it for supper?"

"Sure. We don't have to leave until dark."

A boat, medallion on its hull, came fast around the point and into the cove toward them. Four men were in it. Aran saw they were wearing uniforms. He and Damon kept fishing, and when the boat got near them, one of the men jumped out onto the bank, told Aran he wanted to see his fishing license.

"It's back at the car. I'll get it."

After examining it, the ranger asked them what kind of luck they were having.

"Some bites," Aran said. "Listen, there's no chance in us pitching a tent and camping here all night, is there?"

"Don't know any regulation against it. Fine with me."

After setting up the tent with Mary – Gaddi helped with the stakes – Aran fueled the stove and lantern then blew the two air mattresses full.

Toward dusk they were cooking: "If that's what you want to call it," he told Mary, having discovered that he'd bought smoked sausages instead of wieners, that they'd also forgotten the ketchup and mustard. The meal was much simpler than the ones he and Mary had cooked last summer 10,000 feet up in northern New Mexico.

"Two finicky kids," Mary said, "do change the menu."

Watching the sausage cook, they reminisced about the trip, the meals they'd taken hours to prepare, the hot coffee in the cold morning, the stars packed overhead, making love on top of a mountain in a pine forest whose floor was soft and thick, and the Milky Way as clearly shaped as white ribbon.

Neither child complained about having to do without ketchup and mustard, though Gaddi said she wished they'd brought chili.

Fireworks began exploding over the wave-loud lake. Sitting on the car's fender, they watched the sparks spraying and flashing and worming through the darkness. Lights from cars passing on the road behind them blew at them like waves of wind, and horns honked. The tentflaps whipped. Grasshoppers rattled, and when they'd all gone to bed the sounds inside the tent were even louder than those outside. Tussling for comfort, the children's bodies were noisy on the mattresses. Aran was lying between them on the floor of the tent, and Mary, beaten by the flapping sides, stretched next to Gaddi. Soon, though, the children were asleep, but neither Mary nor Aran could get comfortable. Mary tried curling on her side. Aran's feet and one of his shoulders were on the air mattresses, but the rest of his body jammed into the crack between them. Carlights sprayed at them, horns honked, and firecrackers burst, one of them just outside the tent as Aran was finally getting numb with sleep.

After awhile he sat up, saw Mary was still. Then he lay back down but soon realized he'd probably be awake all night. Merciless with storm, the wind and waves raved, the mattresses scraped loud. Going out in the night often calmed him, so he found his boots, unzipped the tent and left it, but there was no peace outside. He opened a beer and sat on the car. He laughed at himself for thinking that the vastness of stars in the spread of the night might soothe him. The light was too high for more than a few stars to show themselves, and the wind, mindless in its anarchic force, battered him. By this time tomorrow, he thought, the children would be gone. It wouldn't be right to put pressure on Damon. He doubted that his son, at this point at least, would demand much more than the flash of a surface. "If he goes home and regrets it," Aran said to himself, thinking the carelessness of nature had no right to have all the voice, "maybe he'll learn something it's getting time for him to know. What's that? Go to hell."

Crushing the can, he placed it behind the back rear tire so it wouldn't blow away, and went back in the tent to keep what he considered was a pointless vigil.

In the morning they ate Granola bars and drank milk for breakfast. Damon fished and Gaddi explored the beach while Mary and Aran broke camp and put their things back in the car.

"Get any sleep?" she asked, washing her face with water from the drinking can.

"No. Hope I didn't scare you when I came back in the tent last night."

"I didn't hear you."

"Good."

As she put on lipstick, she glanced at him.

"What is it?" he asked.

"I feel like we're getting ready to go to a funeral."

On the drive back, Damon said, "I still haven't made up my mind," then out loud made a list of items drawing him to each place. He said the fishing was better in Laredo, but the pool was better here. He counted his friends in both places. He weighed the circus against how much his mother would miss him, "but then you'll miss me, too. Here there's a piano, but there there's a – I don't know what to do. I can't make up my mind."

"Do what you want," Aran told him. The longer the measuring went on, the more hostile he felt until an image came to him of Mirma in a one-car wreck, every bit of her blown like jigsaw puzzle pieces across a countryside far from the place they were driving now. "It's easy," he managed to tell Mary without the children understanding him, "why the rednecks go after each other with shotguns."

"Yes."

What he saw as aftermath, however, was jail: irrevocable removal from the three here with him he loved.

"It's hard," Damon said. "I still can't make up my mind."

"Keep thinking," Mary said with restraint, "about what's important."

"I have!" Damon shouted. "If I go, I hurt —"

"When do we have to come back?" Gaddi asked.

"Not until Christmas," Mary wearily told her.

"I don't wanta come Christmas!" and Aran saw an image of the girl's mother grinning: pursed lips covering big teeth, her arms crossed stingily, and in victory, before her. Gaddi whined, "I wanta come *before* Christmas!"

When they got home they showered and bathed. Mary put the dirty clothes in the washer. Aran said, "Let's eat out."

They went to a restaurant. During the meal Damon made his father promise that next time they came he'd let him pay the whole bill. Gaddi said, "I have thirty-one dollars."

"What's wrong with my father?" Damon asked.

"He's thinking."

"What about?"

"A lot of things," Aran said.

"About us having to leave?"

"That's part of it."

"I wish we didn't. It's kinda boring there. Least we don't have to take naps. I can't eat all my shrimp. You want it?"

"Thank you," Aran said. "Just leave it."

Gaddi asked when her mother was coming. Mary told her, "She said she'd be here at seven."

"Is that a long time?"

Crossing an intersection, Aran saw Mirma stopped at the traffic light. In French he told Mary. She asked if she'd seen them. He said he didn't think so. He told her she'd looked foul.

"*Comme toujours.*"

"What're y'all talking about?" Damon asked.

"The importance of keeping agreements."

"Oh," Gaddi said. "Mother took Spanish lessons."

"Can she speak it?" Mary asked.

"She quit," Damon told her. "She said it was hard."

"Bright, too," Aran mumbled.

"What?"

"I said when we go to Mexico we'll take you out to eat the night we pass through."

"Where?"

"You all pick a place," Mary said. "There'll be plenty of time to think about it."

While the clothes were drying, the phone rang. Mary said she'd get it. The party hung up. They packed the suitcases. Mary went to bed. Aran played checkers with Damon in his room. Gaddi praised and criticized their moves. Aran kept looking out the window. Damon asked him why he kept doing that. He told them he'd seen their mother. They said it wasn't time for her to come. He told them she hadn't gotten here yet. Angry, Damon spewed, "I might not go with her. She said not till seven."

"She told me next week," Gaddi said. "What's she doing?"

Watching Damon jump him, Aran said, "I don't have any idea."

"She said seven. She better not be lying."

A car engine's sound. Rising, Aran saw she was here, parking at the curb. Gaddi saw her, too, and squealed, "My mama's here!" The children rushed downstairs to meet her. Aran stayed to put up the checkers. Through the window he saw them running outside to the car, a ten-year-old Chrysler she'd paid cash for without ever driving it or even starting it, she'd once told him, explaining what a lucky deal she'd gotten on it. Lifting the two suitcases, he lugged them downstairs after telling Mary who'd arrived.

Damon ran back in the house first. He showed his father his new digital watch, then Gaddi came in and showed him her new turquoise and silver bracelet, "It's pretty and just like Mary's."

Shoulders rounded, Mirma entered. Her hair was mussed, frizzy at the edges. Polite, she asked Aran how he was.

"Fine," he said, fingering the pocket of his denim vest, a gift from his brother who'd knocked a man unconscious in a barfight last year, a fact Aran had been conscious of when he'd selected the garment from the others in the closet.

"It's hot," Mirma said brightly. "And that wind is really something."

"Has been," Aran said, putting his arm around Damon who'd come to stand by him.

"Wanta see the garden?"

"Of course," Mirma told him, and Gaddi shrieked that there was a badminton set, too: "I'm getting good!"

"It sounds as if you two have had a real time," she said, dragged by them toward the back door. She glanced back at Aran and, smiling, told him, "I can really tell. They've had a wonderful time."

"Right."

Running ahead of her in the back yard, Damon showed his mother all the vegetables, named the beans and tomatoes and beets, dug under big leaves to show her zucchini and summer squash, whirled to point out the chili peppers: "They're not ready yet. What're these called?"

"Hungarian wax peppers," Aran said, having come on out with them.

"This is some garden," she told him. "Must take a lot of work."

"Some."

"What're these?" she asked, stepping under the peach tree into another section. "And peaches, too."

"Broccoli and cauliflower," Aran told her.

"My! I've never known anybody to really grow those."

"Those're blackeyes," Damon said.

"Where?"

"On the other side of the broccoli," Aran told her.

"And there's an apple tree, too!" Gaddi sang, "way over there," she said, pointing to the far corner of the yard.

They wandered back out across the lawn through a stand of golden lugustra, and Damon and Gaddi ran to show her where the two kinds of lettuce were, and the carrots and asparagus.

"Do you all really eat all this?"

"I don't like most of it," Damon said, "but I get to be in charge of picking it."

"I do, too," Gaddi insisted. "And we get to take naps here."

"I guess that's all right," Mirma said, "if you can still sleep at night."

"See those?" Damon said.

"What?" Mirma asked, taking his hand.

Jerking free, Damon said, "Off the patio. What're they called?"

"Yellow jasmine," his father told him.

"Right. They look like they're hanging in air. See? They're on a – what's it called?"

"A trellis."

"I don't see it," Mirma said.

"You're not supposed to. My father made it out of fishing line. It makes an illusion – like the leaves are just hanging up in air."

"Gee."

"Just another version of the old shell game," Aran said, wandering back toward the house.

He found Mary in the kitchen, but before they said anything to each other the three had come back inside, Damon asking Mary if he could show his mother what he knew on the piano.

"Sure."

"It's nice here," Mirma said, walking past them.

Rolling her eyes, Mary whispered, "Did you notice her lips? They've almost disappeared."

"Maybe she ate'm."

Damon played "The Sting" with one finger then a section from "*Für Elise*" which, he told his mother, "Beethoven wrote. He's deaf."

"I get to play, too," Gaddi said, and fought with Damon until he let her have her turn.

Standing by the oven, Aran told Mary he wished she'd go in there and whip through Chopin's "Revolutionary Etude." She declined, saying it would seem like sacrilege to play for her after what she'd said and done. "I don't like that insipid sweetness she affects. It's dishonest and corrupt. Music means too much to me to play whore with it."

Damon showed his mother a collection of Scott Joplin pieces. Flipping through it, she said, "This looks hard – like classical music and stuff. Do you really play this?"

"No, but Mary does," and he asked her to play something. "Show my mom how good you are."

"No. This is your time."

Picking at Gaddi's lip, where the fever blister wasn't, Mirma said, "I can tell they've had a wonderful time. I really appreciate that."

Damon said, "Let's go upstairs. I wanta show you the shelf I made," and Gaddi said she had some things to show, too. They left the room, Gaddi asking her mother why she hadn't even noticed "my pretty hair. Mary fixed it with barrettes and Daddy cut my bangs off my eyes."

When they came back down, Damon was complaining that his watchband was too loose, but when his mother said they could take it to be shortened he said he liked it loose and shook it around his wrist, up and down his arm.

"Whatever way you like it," Mirma said, picking up a suitcase. "We'd better get back on the road. It's a long trip ahead of us."

All five of them walked to the car. Mirma unlocked the trunk. Aran put the two suitcases in alongside a huge one which was already there. The children ran back inside to check if they'd left anything.

Coming back out, Damon said he was leaving his models here; and Gaddi, throwing her arms around her father and Mary, said she wanted her jumprope to stay, too.

They got in the car, and Aran leaned inside to kiss them again. He noticed Mirma sucking in her thin lips, her eyes narrowing. He thought she looked agitated that they were all wasting such time. Telling his children he loved them, he kissed them again and slammed the door shut, checked it to make sure the latch had caught. But the door popped open, Gaddi crawling over her brother, saying, "Mary! I wanta kiss you!"

"Have a good trip," she told the children and hugged both of them. "We love you."

"I love you, too," Damon said stiffly.

When the car sped away, Aran and Mary, their arms going around each other, waved at the children, who kept waving back at them, until the car disappeared left around the next corner.

"I'll be damned," Aran said. "She made a wrong turn."

Mary laughed. "She's good at that."

The hot wind stung, and leafy limbs of a sycamore wimpled over that part of the street where he'd last seen the car. It was empty now save for the biting after-image of his children's presence.

He and Mary would return to the house. They would strip beds and clean rooms. They would put back in closets toys and the remains of unfinished projects. The house would be quiet. In a few days they would telephone the children who, by then, would be involved with another environment. But even if they said they missed being there with them, even if the kids said they were counting the months until the next visit, their presence would only be an idea, an illusion without texture, a ghost of a circus; and Aran, even as a child, had never enjoyed circuses and carnivals. Everyone tramping through them seemed lost and seedy, as if their hair were matted with stickiness from cotton candy, and their hands were smudged, their faces glossy with old sweat, and their eyes filmy because their bowels were churning. But that, too, was illusion, as much as his fantasy of storming into court and repairing what was broken: the dismemberment of his children from his flesh.

They all loved each other, but the spectacle of their being together as family was transient. An image came to him of an acrobat falling. There was no net to catch him. His twisting body floated through the fall until he turned a neat flip and his hands met the grip of another set of hands belonging to someone swinging upside down on a trapeze. They swung back and forth. Weightless, he rose and embraced her.

"That was close," he heard himself say.

"The closer the better," she said, smiling, and squeezed the back of his leg. He bit her neck. "Goodness," she said, "the lawn needs mowing and the weeds are a fright."

Blowing the tickle of her hair off his nose, he told her, "They don't even exist."

"They do, too," she said, pinching the inside of his thigh. He spread his fingers across the back of her waist, her spine pressing into his palm. She kissed him, and as he guided her back toward the house, she asked him how he planned to spend the rest of his day.

Four Letters

Brother Bill to His Cousin

Dear Geoffrey Wayne,

Because the girl down the road is nubile. Is remembers what was will be and in the lambent and furious suspension of odors wafting like the old Confederate's dreams I lose myself in wisteria this time of year when in concomitant bloom azaleas come out of the ancient tilled earth like bursts of blood frozen benignly by the avatar of some old god. I am sitting on the white verandah and becoming what I smell as what I drink becomes what I was. Although this world is not mine it is not yet unmine either, but a puny portion of the possible and glorious grief that was when we first began to talk the old and senseless necessary talk of youth. It was then in the mortmain drive of summer that the dragons we feared padded out of their lairs, primitive denizens hidden in terrific insubstantiality in that maelstromlike time whose lichenedgray boulders and overgrowth of time's detritus and floodbrought flotsam offered them sanctuary. The corn did not come in this year so this is not a happy time.

Yet all of us, my brothers who though they do not know it are in bondage to the land we have been fool enough for generations to think we hold in trust, my brothers and all of us here, the workers and those others, the peaceful adrift in idiot serenity beneath the roiled and dogged stars' mindless whorl, we all of us here hope youll be able to spend July with us. The world is a catfish and so is mother but she doesnt know it yet, having soared in her bovine femaleness to a realm beyond mind or even need for mind. Everyone here says they do for her but that is a mere notion she has fostered on us (her men) who,

except me, do not know they are but meager and temporary exten-
sions of her boundless fecundity annealed and tempered by the night's
courageous negritude. Everyone here says hi and awaits your reply.

W (Bill) F, Esq.

Papa Writes Pound

Querido Ez,

We just left Ronda where the girls do that thing that is better
than death, and you do not have to ask them. But now I'm not there
and the window of my compartment on this train will not close. The
dust blows in and powders my face. I'm commencing to look like a
minstrel. They take you lightly when you look like that. They throw
you in the ring and make you dance and you have no dignity. Then the
look in your eyes gets the fear and your cojones shrivel. They go to the
size of a turkey's and do not hang long and true. They warned me
about that, the waiters who speak well and don't rot your head.

The girls I knew in Ronda drink with you and do that thing I
said, and you should try it, too. It will help both your backhand and
your serve. It will make you so you will be the one to jump over the
net, and no one's dust will ever dare powder your face. You will eat
buffalo then, and barbecue, and never have to touch that which the
butterflies eat, those who keep breaking their wrists when they talk.
You will never have to have a Croque M'sieur again. You will eat meat
that dies well. You will also go back in the ring, but not to dance, never
to dance. Only those with bad nerves dance and mince their feet fast
and pray to St. Vitus, though he is only a nothing now. But you are
not. You have a forehand full of balls that glow in the dark. Come
back to Spain. Go into the ring and kill that bull that wants to do that
thing to you which the girls in Ronda do better.

Adios,
Big Ern

Heidegger to Mama from College

O Mutter:

The journeyness of this period forlorns me, and the being-not-there with you melancholies me. I am not just telling you these things, I am speaking these things, languaging them. The speaking speaks with you in this. The forlorning is not just homesickness, the pain of awayness, but something deeper, more fundamental than that. The depth itself speaks: an evocation of the insufficiency of my meness in the being-here in this cold and cheap rented room. My hair is also thinning and I've only been here a week.

Soon, however, the place and I will have brothered each other. I will will that if I have to. But the knowledge of the absence of the presence of the with-youness stirs sadness loose in me. Brothering, I know now, is not as deep as mothering, or in my case soning, the that-within-which my facticity occurs. Although this rootless rude world nothings everything in acknowledging the nothingnessing that is everywhere now, something of you still somethings me, even at this distance; and I think it always has, even before I read Nietzsche. That which has been without has become that which is within, but the melancholialization of my portion of world has brought me face to foot with erasure, the autumnal speech of decline, and I'm not even anywhere near twenty. The world is cold and damp, but that's because the world is still Bavaria. Realizing that, I suddenly feel better.

As you already know, having always participated in the othernessing of others, what Papa sternly and erroneously called gossip, I have been downcast of heart these last days. Knowing no one and having been aliened by the first-seeing of this place, I have felt adrift. Maybe I've been reading too much Hölderlin. But I have to. Goethe is too facilely expansive. Someday, though, school will be done, and when it is I will home myself to you. I can't wait to have cookies and blood sausage with you, and a lot of May wine and coffee. I can't wait for us to talk again, and for you to laugh and pat my (ever shinier) head and make me think you think I'm wicked when I try to understand why the guilt that guilts me gilds me.

Liebe dich lots,
Martin

Hammer's Home

Pop

You're the one named me Mickey. You're the one got me involved in all this. You get a moniker like Mickey you get on edge. I do and always have. Now I'm in the city and it's worse.

I may be crude but I'm not slow, despite what some sissies around here think. I've been here two months now and a lot's gone down, including two guys who stepped out of line. One was a broad. You would've been proud. They hit the floor fast. Part of the reason was you. You're the one named me Mickey. Not even Mike or Michael, just Mickey. I had to drop them. Out here you don't take a chance. The two guys, they looked at me wrong, and the broad had some serious knockers on her too, but I plugged her dead between the jugs. She's strong, though, still alive and well on the mend. And if she straightens out her act, that look in her eyes, I might take her out.

Last week I got my license, so I'm now a Private I. That means Investigator. I work for myself. I had some trouble, though, after the test, the last one. Some smart-mouth on the force I knew came up, stuck out his ham and said congrats. As I thanked him I noticed his eyes looked weird. Something in him wasn't right. Then he went too far. He called me a dick. He said, "Now you're a real dick." That's when I dropped him: knee to the grines then a rabbit punch on his way down. I'm glad I didn't have my gun. If I had I'd have drilled him, twice between the eyes plus a belly shot to make him remember. But my gun was back in the room with my comb. My permit hadn't come in yet, and out here you don't take unregistered guns to final exams.

I found out later I'd done a bad thing. He'd called me a dick but he didn't mean dick. That's slang here for what I do. It means detective. So I said I was sorry. I bought him a drink and he took it. I'm learning fast. You have to. You have to learn the difference between being a dick and being a dick.

I'm also changing my name to Mike. It's really the same as Mickey, yet it's not. Like a lot of things: the same and yet not. I realized that when I was talking to this foreign guy I met. A squirrely little bad-eyed guy from Buenos Aires, Argentina. I met him in a bar, a tough place called Mom's. Said he writes detective stories, the little foreign blind guy. Name's Borges. Said I ought to write some myself. I told him I might when I got more experience. He said forget about experience. He said I could steal what I needed from books. He said he always had and planned to keep on. He said he made up a lot of stuff, too. He said you have to when you've been a grown man for years and your mother still calls you Georgie, and that's not Jorge either, and you can't even go to bars unless you leave the country or even the hemisphere. I knew what he meant. I told him about me and Mickey and Mike. He said good, said I had what you need. I liked him right off. He said what he meant. He even said Eva Peron was a whore. I don't know for sure who she is, so I'll have to look her up, and if she's not too much of a mess I might take her out.

Hugs & fists,
 Son Mick(ey)

Patterns of Illusion

There's just something about her," Aran said, "that bothers me."

"Why?" Mary asked. "She's attractive enough. Is that it?"

"No, it's something else," he told her. "The look about her: big doe eyes but they somehow seem vacant or mean even. I can't figure it out."

"You don't even know her," Mary said. "At least I don't think you do," she added, looking at him askance. Quickly, though, she turned her attention away. She asked the two children, her stepchildren, if they'd like another lemonade or Seven-Up.

Aran watched them shake their heads that they were doing all right. They had just gotten into San Miguel an hour before, put their bags in the apartment the Instituto had assigned them, and come immediately across campus to the hotel for lunch.

Suddenly Aran's daughter Gaddi was laughing. She was nodding toward a little boy running naked around the pool outside. Periodically he'd stop and stomp the shadows of giants' hands that the banana leaves cast on the cement. Aran glanced back at his own children. Although he and Mary would be here for close to two months, the children would leave after two weeks to go back home to their mother. Squeezing Mary's knee, he once more heard his son Damon announce to the table what he had said three times already: that though he was just ten he was going to get to take Spanish in a college.

"You'll probably flunk, too," Gaddi said. "Go ahead, Daddy. Ask me some words," she said to draw attention away from her brother. "I'm taking sculpture," she told everyone. "I'm going to make monuments to make the highways pretty."

"No, you're not," Damon said.

"I am, too. Ask Mary."

"Is she?"

"Let's all settle down," Mary told them, looking worn from two

days of driving with them. "We'll get all our schedules straight tomorrow."

"See?" Gaddi said. "I'm taking sculpture and Damon's flunking Spanish. He's dumb," she said, "real dumb."

"Shut up," Damon told her.

"No way," she answered. "And your food looks like something
we ran over on the highway."

"Gaddi," Aran said, "now hush."

"It does," she said. "Look at it. Something ran over it and
squeezed all its guts out."

"Settle down," Mary told her, but Gaddi was already reaching
across the table for Damon's plate, and demanding:

"Let me have some!"

Squeezing her leg to hush her, Aran was struck once more by
the presence of the woman who had aggravated him last year when
they were here, and now she was sitting with a couple several tables
over. He felt foolish. He had no idea what the source of his anger was
– or was it even anger? He didn't even know the woman's name; he
had only seen her several times last summer. She was tall, statuesque,
her clothes were elegant and her cheekbones high, her skin was
smooth and olively tanned, and the silver of her hair was as striking
as the large pieces of jewelry she wore. She looked like the spirit of a
place, but which one? Maybe that wasn't it. Maybe the trouble was he
couldn't attach her to any place, or to anyone; but if that were true,
he noticed, she gave off no look of misery because of it.

During the last year when anyone had asked him what San
Miguel was like, Aran had always answered, "Shangri-la," and each
time he had used the cliché he had felt as if a membranous element
were peeling inside him. The sensation was with him again. This year's
apartment was much plainer than the one they had been given last
year, with its 35-foot high living room ceiling domed in exposed brick;
bathroom fixtures, upstairs and down, golden; two patios overlooking
a tropical garden, and the leaves of the aloe vera bordering it as large
as broadsword blades. Even the roof had been brilliant with a spread
of bougainvillea. Although homely in its appointments, this year's
apartment was large – two bedrooms joined by a patio and living
room; there were terra cotta tile floors throughout, and a plague of
huge termites swarmed on the vigas. "It's the season," the school's
vice president insouciantly told him.

He glanced again at the woman. He couldn't get rid of the botherment she brought him.

He and Mary had first noticed her last year at an afternoon program given by a painter who had quickly managed with his palette knife to turn a promising sketch of the parochia into mid-level motel schlock. Aran had noticed the woman narrowing her eyes at the lecturer. Her attitude of earnestness at such sober drivel had made him want to stick his foot out and trip her when she moved closer to the canvas or backed away from it as she purred about the "delicately eclectic" things the painter was doing with light. All about her seemed studied. She fit her white jeans well; the two top buttons of her blouse were stylishly unclasped; and her silver necklace, its pendant a large crescent, dipped at her cleavage, not so much, it seemed, to emphasize the swelling of her breasts as to say: *This is the casualness affected by those of us who are wealthy with taste.*

"Her features are perfect," Mary had said.

Glancing at them, the woman tossed her head to indicate how interesting all this was, whatever this was. Aran's stomach, that afternoon and for days later, felt full of ants and frogs, and each time he saw her he found himself doing battle with himself. He was confident, however, that the stomach disorder had nothing, or little, to do with the woman. It had a lot to do with noxious bacteria: *Amino acid ergo sum.* Psychology, after all, his anger said, was often little more than clever fiction.

"Don't worry about her," Mary said. "She's not important."

But to him she was. She herself was what she called eclectic, and the term was nothing more than a euphemism for mishmash.

"Perhaps you find her attractive," he imagined Mary saying, but he knew that that was not the problem. The force of her presence called to mind something else, some factor that made him feel diminished; and unreasonable though it was, he found himself spewing at her in his daydreams. He fantasized himself striking her. He also felt the same about the wise-cracking painter with the ruinous palette knife, so maybe, he thought for awhile, *it's only the corruption in my belly making me feel this way.* Then she had come to his reading.

Sitting on the front row, she had seemed to be the fulfillment of the surfaces being developed by others there before him. The glitter, being cultivated by them, was already fully developed in her; and the grandness of her presence said she knew it, but the lines flaring from the corners of her eyes indicated that something within her was hungry, desperate even for a kind of certification that only the makers could provide. Still, like many others he had seen here, she was too genteel to look greedy. Hell, he thought, maybe she's just more interested in her illusions than mine, and that's always, he laughed to himself, ample enough reason to kill someone.

Flipping pages, he had found his next poem, one about the nausea that came when he missed his children. Then his fingers and voice found another, this one full of outrage at their mother for taking them from him; but when he came to the ending, he found himself surprised. He had closed with something other than an outburst of bitterness, with something other than a cry against injustice. The poem ended with a reference to his own loss of redemption. Instantly the woman got up and left. He thought he had somehow stung her, and himself with her, until he noticed that her eyes looked as blank as marbles.

The malachite setting was round and far too large for the man's finger, but the man was desperate, Aran and Mary discovered early in the evening. After his wife had died, the man had taken early retirement, for the second time, he said, from his job as managing editor of a Chicago newspaper. He was going to travel until, as he said, "I drop, and I might do a novel on the way – get serious scribbling myself," he told Mary then quickly asked, as he patted her leg, "You really happy with your husband?"

"More than happy," Mary told him, and Aran stayed silent.

Caressing now the mouth of his glass with his lips, the man said, "You're pretty. I'd like to kiss you. May I? A kiss because you're pretty?"

Giving the man little reaction, Mary leaned against Aran. Looking from one to the other, the man affected a courtly air and asked Aran, "Do I have your permission? There's nothing to fear."

"I realize that," Aran said.

"Then may I?"

"What's the point?"

"She's so pretty."

"How about another drink?" Aran asked. "A bit of sublimation might be good for you."

"I don't think," the man told Mary, "he's letting you get very far."

"I hope not," she said.

"You might come to resent that," he told her. "Most women do."

"Maybe so."

"Then a friendly kiss? It won't hurt anything."

"I don't think," Aran said, "the issue we're dealing with is her pain."

"Certainly not. Maybe yours, though. After all, we men do have a weakness: being smart enough to know we know far less than we need to know. So how about it if I give her – probably – just one kiss?"

"No," Aran said.

"Very well," the man said and turned away, his eyes as superciliously self-possessed as the woman who bothered Aran.

The party soon moved from the house where they were having cocktails to a restaurant off the *jardín*. The man leaned over to speak to the hostess who, though she nodded distractedly, pointed to the table and told Mary that the seating arrangement called for her to sit here, next to the man. Aran's place would be at the far end of the table.

Mary caught his arm as Aran turned away to leave. She reached up and kissed him. "After awhile," she said, "come ask me to dance."

"Sure," Aran said, trying not to sound pissed.

The meal began with Aztec soup. The entrée was broiled chicken. The wine, red and white both, came in carafes to hide the screwtop bottles, Aran mused. The vegetable was broccoli smothered in a white cheese of the region and steamed onion. From around the table, and beamed down upon it by waiters and others slipping by, came the animated singing of flirting, eyes dancing at necklines and laps, hands spasming to pat wrists as if something serious had just been emphasized. Then sudden gestures of sobriety fell when it came time to whisper while waving at someone else across the room or down the table where a new pair of bobbing eyebrows munched the atmosphere. Alien to the gaming, Aran finally caught Mary's eye. Rising, he said he was coming to get her, and moments later, when he asked her to dance, the man from Chicago who wanted to kiss her and who had said he was dizzy for her stood up and told Aran that he had just been planning to ask her himself:

"You wouldn't mind, would you?"

"Not at all," Aran said. "Say what you want. It's just that she and I are having this dance."

"Certainly," the man said. "I just need to be faster."

"A lot faster," Aran said. "Next time, though, I'll let you lead."

Smiling, the man nodded to acknowledge his rival's temporary victory, then Mary kissed him on the forehead.

Putting his arms around both of them, the man said, "After you finish, come on back here and get me. Ask me down to your end of the table," he told Aran. "The people here are worse than the wine."

When they came back to the table after two dances, the hostess was inviting the group next door for a drink at the opening of a disco-bar. Feeling absurdly responsible, Aran tried to find their new friend, but the man was gone.

"We don't like our room," Gaddi said, their first night in the apartment. "The dressers are built like coffins."

"Yeah," Damon said, "why don't you give us your room? Our room smells creepy."

"Something's going to bite us when we're asleep," Gaddi said. "I'm not going in there, not unless you're in there with us."

"Look," Aran said, trying to be patient, "we've opened the windows. It'll air out. It's just been closed up for awhile. And besides, you've even got your own patio. We don't."

"Sure," Gaddi said, "where something can climb up the wall and get us. You won't be able to hear it either."

"They don't care," Damon said. "They probably hope a thing'll get us."

"That's ridiculous," Mary said.

"Then give us your room," Damon told her.

"Right," Gaddi said. "Girls with girls and boys with boys."

"I've already told you," Aran said, "you've got your own room. If anybody comes in, they have to come through our part first. Nothing's going to get you. Besides, the door has two locks on it, and we'll always lock the screen."

"That won't do any good," Damon said. "The locks are made in Mexico. They don't work right."

Although frustrated, Aran couldn't keep from laughing as he told them it was late, way past time for them to be in bed, "And I'm taking you in there now – both of you."

"If we have to go to bed," Damon said, "you and Mary do, too."

"Fine," Aran said, rounding them up in his arms and pushing them toward the door, pinching their bottoms and woollying their hair to distract them.

"I'm not going first," Gaddi squealed. "Something'll kill us!"

"Right," Aran said, leading them across the patio, "maybe me." Opening the door to their room and caught up in the mayhem of his children, he howled like a ghost to tease them, but instantly knew he had made a mistake. They were crazy with anarchy again.

After finally getting them dressed for bed, he gave them massages, but they stiffened under his hands. Damon insisted he was sitting up all night: "I'm working on my stamps," and Gaddi told her father he'd probably never see her again because something would kill her during the night and stuff her in the dresser. She screamed.

"At least I'll know where you are," Aran said, bending down to kiss her, but she bit his nose and, throwing her arms around him, told him she wasn't ever letting him go, he was going to sleep with her forever.

"We're gonna smooch, too," she giggled. Laughing, he pinched her foot under the cover. "I want my hiney scratched," she told him. "There's a flower in it."

"Night, little booger," he told her, then kissing her again told her he loved her.

"What about me?" Damon asked.

"I've already kissed you good night."

"You didn't say you loved me."

"I did, too."

"You didn't mean it very much."

"Sure I did."

"Prove it."

"Sweet dreams," he told them. "I'll see you in the morning."

"We'll probably be dead," Gaddi said, then Damon told his father:

"Make Gaddi quit. All she does is cut the cheese all night. I'm tired of her farting."

"I'm never gonna stop," Gaddi said, "it feels so good." Damon started laughing but quit when Gaddi said, "Every time he wets the bed, it sounds like rain, and I get cold."

He tried talking them into taking siestas, but they had no interest in such, and when he explained that siestas were an old Mexican custom, Damon said, "So what? We're American."

In spite of their protests, the children would often fall asleep at night in restaurants, with Gaddi even dropping off before they got served. Both Aran and Mary repeatedly told them why they were so tired: "The rhythm here's different from what you're used to, and the altitude's high. So tomorrow we'll all take a siesta."

"Not me," Damon said.

Curled up in Mary's lap, Gaddi jerked, but her eyes stayed closed.

Walking home, they crossed the crowded *jardín*, and Gaddi, who had become lively again, skipped, like the cool gusting breeze, around the people who were standing and talking, walking in couples, sitting on benches. A block and a half later, though, she said she was tired and wanted her father to carry her home.

"Would you like a ride, too," he asked Mary who jammed her thumb up under his arm then puckered her lips for him to lean over and kiss her.

"Maybe later," she said.

"What're you talking about?" Damon asked.

"Making love," Gaddi sang. "They're gonna smooch and I'm gonna watch. Now carry me," she demanded.

"I'll carry her," Damon said. "Piggyback. I do it all the time."

"She's too heavy," Aran said, squeezing the back of his son's neck.

"I'm warning you," Gaddi said, pulling her brother's arm from around her father's waist. With hip-flicks she pushed herself between them. "Carry me!" she ordered, and grabbing her father's arm, told Damon, "Get lost. Me and Daddy are tired."

"My God, she's brilliant!" the big-girthed, red-bearded painter said at the reception after his talk. "I've got her in two classes and she does twice the work of anyone in there."

It took Aran, who had just come into the gathering at the snack table, awhile to realize that the woman being praised was the one who had been irritating him. Glancing across the room, he saw her; she was talking with Mary. Ignoring the conversation he was standing now in the middle of, he watched the two women. Instantly turning toward him, the woman waved as if, of course, she knew him. A big hand clapped him on the back.

"Keep looking," the painter said. "She's worth it. Gave me sixteen yards of Belgian canvas this week. Said she didn't think her painting was good enough to justify flying it home."

Aran laughed hollowly, then sipping his beer, noticed the large wooden tribal mask on the wall, its red and white teeth painted bone. Glancing away, he saw the calm image of Mary, alone now, then heard another woman saying his name. Turning to meet her, he saw the smartly dressed woman who had been bothering him. She was coming directly toward him.

Announcing her name, she extended her hand and said, "I've been talking to Mary. I was at your reading last year."

"I remember," he said.

"Got to go now," she said, "another engagement but maybe sometime while you're here, we can all get together."

"Sure."

"Take care," she said rapidly, "loved seeing you again," and Aran, noticing how rapidly his attitude toward her had changed, began wondering if he were so impressionable he was characterless.

The spread of crackers and cheeses, raw vegetables, tostados and chips was now meager. Shapes of buzzing people floated around him. The children, he imagined, were sleeping in peace or having nightmares; they often did, especially Damon. Aran felt adrift. Missing his children confused him.

"Are you all right?" Mary asked.

"Sure," he replied, bewildered to realize that sometime before he had sunk himself into a rawhide-backed chair.

Mary was sitting beside him, whispering. Others in the room were talking. As Mary touched his thigh, Aran heard a man saying, "An inclination to hallucinate, you know, might be at the source."

"I don't know," the painter said, stroking his beard upward until it rose from his chin with the roundness, stiffness and size of an earthenware plate. "What do you think?" he asked Aran.

"I don't know." He didn't even know what the conversation was about. He was thinking of his children, of the blocks of time spreading without them, of the nausea that came when he missed them, of the fact that their time here together was ending. He wouldn't see them again till Christmas, and maybe not even then.

"Indeed!" Leonard cried, his face radiant, and Aran realized he had missed another part of the conversation. The man thumbed his glasses back up the bridge of his nose and began telling about his boyhood hero: "I was just eleven. We were living in Framingham and he was the champion pole-vaulter at Harvard. Hell!" he said, laughing, "he probably couldn't even go fourteen feet, but I thought he was God."

"No!" the hostess shrieked, "no!" she cried, her white caftan billowing. "Don't start it! Not again!"

Ignoring her in his enthusiasm, Leonard said, "My real hero, though, was a guy in my own prep school. I was fourteen and he was around sixteen, but something like six-four," he said, "and he walked with a slump," Leonard added, rounding his shoulders and strolling around the room as he told them, "He was the most heroic figure I'd ever seen – played end – and for two years I walked in a slump myself just like him. It made me feel tall."

"Magnificent!" the painter roared as Leonard pantomimed jostling a pole to show them how he had tried to combine the football star's slump with the pole-vaulter's lope.

"That ended up disaster," Leonard said.

"Good way to get a rupture, too," the painter said.

"That's why I switched to doing dashes."

"He set a record, too," his wife said.

"How long did it last?" Mary asked, her palms pressed together in friendly mimicry of rapture.

"It's still standing," Leonard's wife said, squeezing him high on the back of his leg. As he glanced down at her, his glasses fell off on the rug.

Retrieving them then sticking one of the earpieces in his mouth, he said, "Listen, dear, the boys who run the dash in my time now can't even make the team."

"Lord!" the agitated hostess raved. "This is disgusting – worse than last week when you spent half the evening describing Notre Dame playing NYU."

"SMU," Leonard corrected her.

"The first time?" Aran asked, and when they told him yes, he said, "I was there. We were living in Dallas. It was a cloudy, misty day."

"Damnit!" the hostess said, "you stay out of this."

"Kyle Rote," he said reflectively.

"Who the hell's Kyle Rote?"

"Three touchdowns," the painter said, with Aran adding:

"And Doak Walker on the sidelines, tackled out of bounds against a wheelchair during the Rice game, and tears coming down his cheeks during the coin-flip because all his life, he told the papers, his big dream had been to play Notre Dame."

"Who the hell's Doak Walker?" the hostess asked.

"Maybe the best football player ever," the painter said, winking at Aran to celebrate their new friendship.

"I was a freshman that year," the host said, speaking for the first time. "I was there. Remember Johnny Champion?" he asked, smiling as he wiped the back of his tonsure down. "Little stocky guy – five-six and having to block Leon Hart at six-six – diving between his ankles to trip him."

The hostess, with whom he'd been living for six months now, slapped air at him.

"Settle down," he told her, then turning to the others, he said, "And for all the first half, little David gave Goliath the fits."

"No!" the hostess cried. "Hush! You talked about this same thing last week."

"I know," Leonard said, spreading his fingers over the ends of the armrests on his chair, "but we left a good part of it out."

Sitting on the floor, the hostess wrapped her arms around her knees and pouted. She looked to the other women for aid, but they offered none; and when Aran said Notre Dame had been a forty-five point favorite, she butted in, saying, "You're making this up. You weren't even born then."

"The greatest thing, though," Aran told them, "was the head-line in the newspaper: *Ponies Stomp Irish: 20-27!*"

"That doesn't," the hostess said archly, "even make sense. They lost."

"Not if you were there," the host said. "It was wonderful – back even before I met my first wife."

"You leave her out of this," the hostess told him.

"Listen," Leonard said, attempting to include the hostess in their play, "didn't you have heroes?"

Peremptorily she announced, "I don't believe in heroes. I did-n't back then and I certainly don't now."

"I mean when you were a kid."

"Never!" she swore.

"I don't believe it," he said.

"Maybe one," she relented, "when I was twelve, maybe ten: Katherine Mansfield."

"Hell!" the host said, "when I was five I was partial to Marcel Proust myself."

The guests laughed, but the hostess found nothing funny in the uncalled for effort at lightness.

After he came back from market the next day with the chil-dren, he and Mary decided it was time for a nap, for all of them. They had stayed out late and gotten up early. Defiantly Damon told them he was going to play.

"Sure," Aran said, "no problem."

"I don't ever need naps," Damon insisted, determined to get the fight he obviously thought he was due.

"You're probably right," Aran said. "A lot of us, though, aren't quite so strong."

"I mean I'm going outside," Damon told him. "That's where I'm going to play."

"Sounds good to me," his father told him, and Damon and his sister hurried out the door.

Several hours later, shortly after Aran and Mary had risen for coffee, Damon came running into the apartment chattering about what he and his sister and one of their friends had just seen: a man and a woman up on the roof of the art building, photographers below them taking pictures of them. Aran glanced out the window; patches of rainclouds looked like bruises on a clear blue sky.

"And they were naked!" Damon said, "naked! You could even see their hineys and front things, too," he added, "hers and his, too."

"Where's Gaddi?" Mary asked.

"She and her friend," Damon said, trying to stop panting, "they're still out there looking."

In memory Aran could hear his daughter's throaty laughter. "Look!" he remembered her squealing one morning during a summer visit two years ago when she and Damon were helping him fix breakfast. On an impulse she had yanked up his bathrobe, and with it his nightshirt. "Ay!" she had shrieked, trying to defy her surprise, "his thing's got a ring around it!"

Now, though, he was thinking about the woman he had met on his way back from market: the woman who'd been talking to Mary last night and had then come over to introduce herself to him. But she hadn't even really stopped; she'd sashayed away almost the moment she'd announced herself to him.

Awhile ago, passing on the sidewalk, they'd met again. The imagery of her still vivid, her blouse was turquoise, her well-fitting pants the color of bone. Bracelets torqued her wrists and an opal moon-crescent rocked at the nadir of her lavalier. Her hair as silver as a polished ceremonial shield, she had asked him why he had the bunch of orange flowers.

"For squash blossom soup," he had answered.

"You mean you just use the flowers, and not the zucchini itself?"

"Sure," he'd said, "along with a leek and some other items. I'll give you the recipe."

"I'd love it," she'd said, reaching out to touch his arm, then flipping the gesture into a wave, she'd said she had to rush on; and she did, though a ghostly remnant of her remained oddly antic with him. A trick of memory making him repeatedly watch her rush off, she'd suddenly be before him again. Always, though, she'd hurry away.

Burning his eyes, the onion he was dicing was making his nostrils weep. Imagining he and the woman were again on the street, he tried sniffing his head clear. Were the two of them going in the same direction? And if they were, had she noticed? Backhanding the onion bits into the hot oiled skillet to sauté them just enough to mellow their tart fragrance, he found himself wishing he'd been on the roof with his children when they'd seen the naked people. He enjoyed the bursts of anarchy they brought him, but soon they'd be leaving, disappearing from him; and they and the portions of the world they'd all passed through would turn into little bursts of memory, shapes that were vivid but dimensionless.

Acknowledgments

Acknowledgment is made to the following publications where these
stories first appeared, sometimes in forms slightly different from those
here:

> *Blue Mesa Review:* "The Scapegoat"
> *Descant:* "The Way the World Is"
> *Mississippi Review:* "The Embodiment of the Times"
> *New Texas 91:* "Turning the Deer Free"
> *New Texas 95:* "Four Letters"
> *Partisan Review:* "A Gift from the Scorched Moon"
> *Redbook:* "Wild Onion Leaves"
> *Southwest Review:* "The Leaning Tower of Babel,"
>   "Mesquite," and "No Accounting Shall Be Asked"
> *Southwestern American Literature:* "Woman of the Region"
> *Texas Short Fiction:* "Waiting for Rain"
> *Texas Short Stories:* "Patterns of Illusion"
> *Texas Short Stories 2:* "The Last Campout"
> *Vanderbilt Review:* "A Bit of a Bitch"
> *Wichita Falls Magazine:* "Night and the Blood
>   Washed Away"

About the Author

James Hoggard recently completed his first stint as the poet laureate of Texas. He is also a past president of the Texas Institute of Letters. Currently, he is the Perkins-Prothro Distinguished Professor of English at Midwestern State University in Wichita Falls, Texas.

Hoggard's work in multiple genres is routinely called "brilliant." He is a poet, short story writer, novelist, playwright, essayist and translator. The author of more than fifteen books and seven produced plays, he has won numerous awards for his writing and no end of critical praise. His novel, *Trotter Ross* (Wings, 1999), was called "far and away, the finest novel about masculine coming of age in current American literature" by Leonard Randolph, former director of the NEA literature program. Hoggard is the recipient of the Hart Crane and Alice Crane Williams Memorial Award for poetry, the Texas Institute of Letters prize for short fiction, the Soeurette Diehl Fraser Award for translation, the Stanley Walker Award for Journalism, a National Endowment for the Arts fellowship, and other honors. His work has been published internationally in the U.S., India, England, Canada, the Czech Republic, Cuba and elsewhere.

About the Cover Artist

David Horton is currently an associate professor of art at Nicholls State University in Thibodeaux, Louisiana. Born in New York, he grew up in Louisiana, Texas, and Arizona. Over the years he has studied and maintained studios in Paris, Provence, Spain, and around the United States. His work has been shown in numerous important shows, including the Grand Palais in Paris. Horton says of his art, "The combination of myths and symbols integrated into Mediteranean society has resulted in the magical realist attitude of my paintings of the past ten years. Combining ancient meanings for symbols with new icons, I try to make my images into new fables, both mysterious and literal at the same time."

Colophon

Two thousand copies of the first edition of *Patterns of Illusion*, by James Hoggard, have been printed on 70 pound non-acidic paper. Titles have been set in Caslon Openface Type. Text and interior titles were set in a contemporary version of Classic Bodoni, originally designed by the 18th century Italian typographer and punchcutter, Giambattista Bodoni, press director for the Duke of Parma.

This book was entirely designed and produced by
Bryce Milligan, publisher, Wings Press.

Wings Press was founded in 1975 by J. Whitebird and Joseph F. Lomax as "an informal association of artists and cultural mythologists dedicated to the preservation of the literature of the nation of Texas." The publisher/editor since 1995, Bryce Milligan is honored to carry on and expand that mission to include the finest in American writing.

Other recent and forthcoming
literature from Wings Press

Way of Whiteness by Wendy Barker (2000)

Hook & Bloodline by Chip Dameron (2000)

Splintered Silences by Greta de León (2000)

Incognito: Journey of a Secret Jew by María Espinosa (Fall 2002)

Peace in the Corazón by Victoria García-Zapata (1999)

Street of Seven Angels by John Howard Griffin (Spring 2003)

Cande, te estoy llamando by Celeste Guzmán (1999)

Winter Poems from Eagle Pond by Donald Hall (1999)

Initiations in the Abyss by Jim Harter (Fall 2002)

Strong Box Heart by Sheila Sánchez Hatch (2000)

Patterns of Illusion by James Hoggard (Fall 2002)

This Side of Skin by Deborah Parédez (Fall 2002)

Fishlight: A Dream of Childhood by Cecile Pineda (Fall 2001)

The Love Queen of the Amazon by Cecile Pineda (Fall 2001)

Bardo99 by Cecile Pineda (Fall 2002)

Smolt by Nicole Pollentier (1999)

Garabato Poems by Virgil Suárez (1999)

Sonnets to Human Beings by Carmen Tafolla (1999)

Sonnets and Salsa by Carmen Tafolla (Fall 2001))

The Laughter of Doves by Frances Marie Treviño (Fall 2001)

Finding Peaches in the Desert by Pam Uschuk (2000)

One Legged Dancer by Pam Uschuk (Fall 2002)

Vida by Alma Luz Villanueva (Spring 2002)